ALL THE LOST GIRLS

A PSYCHOLOGICAL THRILLER

BILINDA P. SHEEHAN

For Mom
I guess your obsession with Forensic Files
finally paid off.

ALL
THE
LOST
GIRLS

1

18th October 1996

THE MUSIC HUMMED AROUND ME, filling me up. The pressure of the relentless beat built beneath my skin until I was sure it would explode out through the top of my head. The thought made my stomach heave and I clumsily slapped my hand over my mouth in an attempt to stop the acrid sugar-sweet vomit from belching out past lips that were still sticky from the cheap lip gloss I'd applied earlier.

Just the effort of keeping that last blue alcopop I'd split with Lauren in the bathroom of the community hall from escaping my stomach sent the room spinning. The hall became a blur. The too bright, pulsing lights—red, blue, green, and yellow—swirled through the crowd. I closed my eyes and the lights swam sickeningly on the inside of my eyelids. I opened my eyes.

The teenagers surrounding me pressed together, blurring together until watching them made my head hurt.

If I could just get out of here without upchucking everything, I would never drink another blue drink again as long as I lived. I made a silent prayer, appealing to Padre Pio just for good measure. He was the Saint my granny always swore by and she was seldom wrong about these things.

I slid along the back wall, groping along with my fingers, ignoring the sticky surface as best I could. A cold hand wrapped around my upper arm roughly, fingers digging into my soft flesh as I was jerked to a halt. A sweaty body pressed mine. Dizziness washed over me as I looked up, barely recognising one of the lads I'd fawned over earlier with Lauren. One of the lads from the boys' school down the road from the all-girls Catholic secondary school I attended.

What was his name again? Tom? Or was it Thomas?

I tried to smile but it was probably more of a grimace as I fought against the bile churning in my guts. Not that he noticed. His brown eyes were fever bright as he leaned in close. His breath, warm and smelling of salt and vinegar crisps, washed over the side of my face as he spoke. Only the movement of his lips told me he was saying anything at all; I couldn't hear him over the thump of the music. I shook my head and shrugged. Was that the proper reaction? I ha no idea; my brain was swimming in a liquor bath.

He pressed his mouth to my ear, his moist breath making my brown hair stick to the side of my face as he shouted, "Will you snog my friend?"

His freckled face loomed in front of me as he pulled away, smiling expectantly. The overpowering scent of Lynx deodorant washed over me, swallowing my senses whole.

I clamped my hand over my mouth, trying to keep the inevitable from happening.

Stinging bile poured up the back of my throat as Thomas—or was it Tom—grabbed my hand insistently and tugged it away from my mouth.

"Will ya?" He shouted again, somewhat frustrated. At least that's how my panicked brain translated his expression.

My mouth formed an 'O' of dismay and the wide grin disappeared from his face as I half hiccupped, half vomited down the front of his black shirt.

"Jesus Christ!" he bellowed, shoving me away from him and against the wall.

Crack.

My head snapped back, slamming into the partition that separated the bathrooms from the hall. There was a moment where the world went black, the disco I'd begged my parents to let me go to disappearing into the fog of my alcohol fuelled brain.

When everything returned, I was slumped on the floor, huddled against the wall. The sparkly silver dress I'd so proudly bought with my pocket money was damp down the front of the chest panel, further proof that I clearly couldn't hold my drink. Tears blurred my already impaired vision as I struggled to my feet, humiliation driving me on.

Was everyone staring at me?

Oh, God, what would they say in school?

Pain throbbed in the back of my head where I'd hit the wall.

Please, God, just let me get outside without vomiting again. I swear I'll never drink again! I mean it. I swear.

Hail Mary, full of grace...

Gone was the warm glow I'd felt after the first few mouthfuls of the drink we'd hastily gulped down while waiting for the doors to open. The first one had been fine. It was the third one that was causing all the problems. Lauren's older brother had hooked her up with the drink. It was easy for him now that he was eighteen.

Stumbling toward the main exit, I slipped past the hawk-eyed gaze of the female chaperone manning the door. The cool autumn night was a balm to my sweaty skin and I drank down mouthfuls of the crisp air, sucking them in as fast as my heaving lungs would allow, the churning of my stomach finally slowing down.

"Alice McCarthy, just what do you think you're doing running around in that state?" The stern tone of the chaperone I'd darted past just seconds before rang in my ears and my heart sank.

I turned to face her, my movements awkward as the ground beneath my feet rolled precariously. Was it me or was the world really spinning?

"I'm sorry, I..." I couldn't remember her name. She was the mother of one of the girls in the year above me in St Brigid's but my brain refused to work and my tongue was stuck to the roof of my mouth as my throat went dry.

"You're a disgrace. You McCarthy's, you're all the same. You and your sister have your mother's heart broke. If you were my daughter I'd..."

I blocked out her tirade, my hands balling into fists by my sides as she prattled on. They were all the same; judgmental and holier than thou, like they'd never done anything wrong in their lives.

"Alice!" The familiar voice of my sister washed over me, bringing with it relief, and I turned to see her moving towards me from the other side of the car park.

"And you." The woman standing behind me turned on Clara as she reached the bottom of the steps. "You've some nerve showing your face here. It's disgusting!" She clucked her tongue against the roof of her mouth in disapproval.

Clara's expression was defiant but even in my half drunken state I could see the flinching around her eyes the way she dug her fingernails into the palms of her hands. She was trying desperately not to cry.

Anger swelled inside my chest and I turned to face the chaperone once more.

"Piss off you old cow!" I said, my emotions causing my blood to boil. Just who the hell did she think she was? "She's only pregnant. It's not like she's killed someone."

"Just wait until your mother hears about the things you've been doing," the chaperone said, her anger washing over me as she screwed her shrewish face up in disgust. She reached for my arm, dragging me closer. Rage spread up my throat, hot and bitter...and I realised a second too late that it wasn't anger but more bile.

I let out a belated screech as the vomit splashed down onto her shoes.

"Alice, we're leaving now," Clara said, taking me firmly by the hand and dragging me down off the top step. I stumbled after her, my feet tangling with one another as I half tripped, half skipped over the gravel-covered car park.

I said nothing as my sister dragged me away, suddenly not trusting myself to open my mouth.

Clara dragged me toward the road, out of the well-lit car park that surrounded the community hall. We reached the road. The white lines in the centre of the tarmac wavered in front of my eyes.

"Wait, I'm going to be—" I cut off as I broke free of her grip and darted toward the grass verge that ran alongside the crumbling mossy-covered stone wall.

The dry heaving brought more tears stinging to my eyes and I scrubbed the back of my hand across my face. Glancing dismally down at the black mascara and the expensive sparkly eye shadow I'd nicked from Clara's room—and that was now smeared across my hand—only brought a fresh bout of tears.

My parents were going to kill me.

Ever since we'd found out Clara was pregnant everything had changed. Mam cried a lot and Dad never seemed to come out of his foul mood. They weren't really angry with her; I'd heard Mam telling Dad she felt frightened and uncertain about the future.

"What's going to happen to her, Michael?"

"You done yet?" Clara asked, keeping her distance from me.

"I thought people drank to have a good time," I lamented as I straightened up and held my stomach gingerly.

Clara's hands were on her hips as she glared at me, her sandy hair piled on her head in a messy imitation of a bun. The hem of her jeans was dark, the rain from the road soaking up into them. I noticed the rip in the denim shirt she wore. It hadn't been there when we'd left earlier. When I met her gaze, I could tell she'd been crying.

"Where's Liam?" I asked, glancing around as though half expecting her boyfriend to come bouncing out of a nearby farmer's gateway.

"We had a fight," Clara said, her tone informing me that she had no interest whatsoever in pursuing the conversation further.

As far as I was concerned, her tone meant I should ask more questions, like any good younger sister would.

"About what?"

"Nothing, it doesn't matter..." she trailed off and glanced back toward the community centre. "You know Mam is going to kill you for giving cheek like that to Mrs O' Grady, right?"

"Yeah I know, but the silly cow deserved it. Who the hell does she think she is?" My stomach contorted painfully.

"Close your eyes and take a few deep breaths," Clara said. "It'll help the sickness pass."

I did as she suggested and within a couple of seconds the bile that had been once more creeping up the back of my throat had dissipated.

"Thanks," I said sheepishly.

Clara grinned at me. "Next time you decide to get drunk like that, you should tell Mam and Dad you're staying at Lauren's. That way, they won't have to see you stumbling into the house like an extra from the Exorcist."

"They're never going to let me out again are they?"

Clara shook her head and her grin widened. "They might. When you're fifty."

I threw a dirty look her direction before the urge to vomit washed over me once more.

"Oh God, I—," I didn't finish the sentence as I buckled over and the ground rushed up to meet me.

"It'll pass," Clara said, rubbing my back comfortingly.

"It won't and then Mam is going to murder me," I said, dreading what would happen as soon as we made it home. If I was lucky, Mrs O' Grady hadn't rung her yet. No, I'd never be that lucky. She'd probably already been on the phone, telling Mam what a complete disgrace her two daughters were.

Headlights lit up the road, two blazing yellow orbs that turned the trees surrounding us into little more than a tunnel. The rumble of the engine broke up the silence of the night air, quieting the squeak of the passing bats that dipped and swooped overhead.

"I think it's Dad," Clara said, sounding unsure.

"Great," I grumbled more to myself than anyone else as I tried to scrub the worst of the make-up smears from my face.

The thought of sitting in a too-warm car while getting a lecture from my father only twisted my stomach further. Bile poured up my throat once more, bringing with it the painfully sweet tang of the alcopop. My stomach clenched painfully but there was nothing left inside to get rid of. Dry heaving caused the world to run in colourful streamers and the darkness crept closer. Sucking a deep breath in through my nose I prayed for the nausea to pass. Now was really not the time to pass out.

"Alice." Clara's voice was odd. "It's not dad." She dug her fingers into my arm with enough force that I knew I'd have bruises there in the morning. She pushed me back onto the grass verge, standing protectively between me and the van.

It drew to a halt, the white peeling paint on the side panel luminous in the darkness. I tried to focus on it but my brain was made of mush and I couldn't think past the pain in my stomach. From where I stood, the driver was nothing more than a silhouette behind the wheel, the headlights creating a barrier I couldn't see past.

"We're fine, thanks," Clara said, her voice high and thread. Hearing the odd tone as she spoke was enough to let me focus a little more.

The driver mumbled, the male voice barely registering over the hum of the engine and the echo from the radio playing the kind of music dad liked to turn up, blasting it out of the car speakers as he zipped around town.

The van rumbled away and Clara stood over me. "I'm going to kill him in the morning," she said.

"Kill who?"

"Liam..."

"Was that him? Couldn't we have gotten a lift with him?"

"It wasn't him." Clara's voice was tight.

"What was the fight about anyway?" I straightened up and swiped my hand backwards over my mouth, my head swimming at the sudden movement.

"I don't remember," she said softly. "He's just so bloody infuriating."

A giggle erupted from my mouth and Clara glared down at me.

"What are you laughing at?"

"You two," I said. "You're always at each others throats. How you managed to make a baby is beyond me."

Colour spread up into her face and she looked away quickly, following the red glow of the headlights as they receded down the road.

"If it wasn't Liam in the van, then who was it?" I asked.

"Just some bloke," she said. Even in my drunken state, I knew she'd said it too quickly to be true. Whoever had been in the van, she'd known them. Not that it was strange; in this place, everybody knew everyone else's business. As far as I was concerned it was creepy. I didn't want everyone knowing what I did every second of the day. Not that what I wanted actually meant anything in this place.

Clara glanced back down the road, in the direction the van had disappeared. Something in her face told me she was contemplating confiding in me.

"You can tell me, you know," I said hopefully.

She opened her mouth and I fought the urge to hop up and down impatiently. Of course, the fact that I was bursting for the bathroom didn't help either.

"It's nothing," she said suddenly and decisively. If

the grim determination on her face was anything to go by, I wouldn't get anything else out of her.

"Well, I need to go the loo," I said, glancing into the bushes that lined the side of the road.

"What, out here?" she said, wrinkling her nose in disgust.

"I have to. I'm not going to make it home and I'm enough of a mess as it is."

"Fine, but make it quick," she said, rubbing her arms vigorously, "I don't want to stand out here half the night waiting for you."

I wasted no time crashing into the bushes, the branches from the trees catching in my hair as I scrambled forward. My foot slipped and I grabbed a tree limb to steady myself, the sap sticky against my fingers as I slid down the sloped embankment that lined the roadway. The grass was wet underfoot, making it even harder to stay upright, but I made it far enough into the tree line to feel sure that I couldn't be seen.

"Hurry up!" Clara called from the road as I crouched in the weeds.

In the distance, I could hear the sound of an engine rumbling toward us once more. It sounded suspiciously familiar but I blocked it out as something scuttled over my foot.

"Jesus Christ," I yelped.

"That creep is coming back again," Clara said.

"Who is?" The van was too close and the noise from the engine drowned out my question. The headlights swept over the trees, momentarily blinding me as I pulled up my knickers and tights.

"I said we're fine," Clara said to the driver, her voice carrying shrilly through the trees and I picked up my pace struggling to flatten my dress back into place as I stumbled back toward the road.

"Where's the other one?" The male voice was rough.

"What are you doing?"

"Get in the fucking van!"

"Alice!" Clara's terror slammed into me, causing my chest to constrict painfully as I fell face first into the hollow of the embankment. Muddy rainwater rushed up my nose as I splashed to my feet, digging my fingers into the mud as I scrambled back up onto the road. Clara's frightened screams echoed in my head. The red brake lights gave everything an eerie glow and the back of my neck tingled with terror.

A work-roughened hand tangled in my hair, the nails scraping my scalp with enough force to bring tears to my eyes. He snapped my head back with a jerk that sent stars dancing in my vision.

"Got ya." He was closer, so much closer than I'd expected, his sour moist breath fanning over my cheek. My stomach twisted into a knot. His grip tightened as he dragged me backward toward the van, his breath quickening with the effort as I writhed and kicked. I fought to twist in his grip. If I could just get a look at him, I could kick him in the balls like they did in the movies. But his grip never wavered.

Clara was suddenly there, in front of me, the terror in her blue eyes unmistakable.

"Get off her!" I watched her mouth form the words but I couldn't be sure I heard them leave her mouth. There was a blur of movement and the hold on me disappeared. Our attacker doubled over with a grunt of pain.

I paused, sucking in a deep breath as I met Clara's frightened gaze.

"Run," she urged, her panic lending me a strength I hadn't known I was capable of. Wrapping my hand through hers I started toward the trees once more, dragging her after me.

My lungs screamed as we ran. My legs were pumping up and down but it was like running through molasses.

Clara's hand slipped from mine and I glanced back, watching as she slid down the embankment after me. Terror boiled in my veins as I sucked air in through my nose rapidly, too fast, and the world started to tilt dangerously.

"Go, go," she said, scrambling after me.

I ran.

I fled until my legs gave out and the ground rushed up to meet me, my head smacking off the soft dirt. Even then I continued to move, crawling on my hands and knees, Clara's voice echoing in my head, urging me to keep moving. If I stopped he would get me. Get us...

The ground gave way and I tumbled forward, my scream choked off as I hit the icy water of the river with a dull splash. The darkness claimed me, sucking me under, my arms and legs kicking uselessly. Opening my mouth, I tried to scream but instead swallowed a mouthful of foul tasting river water.

The cold seeped into my bones, making me feel heavy.

I wouldn't drown. I couldn't. Clara would get help.

She wouldn't let me down...

2

Present Day

I AWOKE WITH A START, the taste of muddy water coating my tongue as I fought upwards through a river of blankets and pillows. The shrilling of the alarm on my phone grew muffled as I buried it in a cocoon of duvet and sheets.

Pain crushed the inside of my skull, feeling like fingernails scratching against my scalp.

Panic held me in its grip making me fight for every breath. I ran my hands over my tangled hair. It was a gesture of reassurance, one I'd been doing ever since that night. I huffed out a sigh and flopped back against the pillow.

Nothing.

The empty room was ominous in the gloom of the

autumnal morning light that filtered flatly through the gaps in the curtains. Ominous or not, I was alone here. There was no one waiting for me, no one crouched in a darkened corner.

Alone.

My breathing slowed but the frantic beat of my heart still hammered in my ears.

Clara...

How long had it been since I'd dreamed of her? Guilt gnawed at me. I hadn't forgotten her. Wouldn't forget her, no matter what. Yet there was no denying the fact that years had passed since I'd last dreamed of her like that.

The sound of the alarm on the phone changed, the shrill tone morphing into a Take-That song.

"Shit—" I dug through the covers, emerging victorious a moment later, phone clutched in my hands.

"Yeah— Hello?" I pressed the phone to my ear but silence greeted me instead of a human voice.

Pulling the phone away from my face, I stared at the screen.

1 Missed Call.

The message blinked brightly on the screen. The colourful display glowed, hurting my eyes. The phone buzzed violently, enough to make me jump.

"Take a chill pill, Alice," I chided myself as a small envelope flashed on the screen.

1 New Message

Opening the message, I scanned it quickly, a knot forming in the pit of my stomach as I read Gerald's name.

Need you in the office. Now.

I stared at the time on the phone. 05:33am. If he was calling me in at this hour, then something had happened. In my line of work, that wasn't good.

After everything that had happened with Clara that night, I'd studied to be a social worker, my desperation to make a difference, to help those who couldn't help themselves, the driving force that got me through school.

The reality of my job wasn't at all what I'd hoped it would be.

You did your best and usually, that wasn't good enough. The system was broken; a sinking ship of epic proportions. Lack of funds, training, and staff left us grasping at straws, fighting desperately to keep the ones we could reach afloat. It was never enough. No matter how hard you tried, no matter how hard you fought, someone always slipped through the cracks. And when they did...

I stuffed my fist into my mouth and screamed around it before dropping my phone back onto the covers.

All I wanted was to climb back beneath the duvet. It was a pathetic and cowardly reaction to the text but I still felt it. The childish part of me, hidden beneath the scars of my past, promised that if I stayed in bed everything would be fine. Whatever terrible reason Gerald had for calling me would just go away if I closed my eyes and hid.

Sucking in a breath, I let the roiling in my stomach settle before I swung my legs from the bed.

Icy air swirled around my calves, the fine hairs on the backs of my arms standing to attention as my skin broke out in goose flesh.

Grabbing a black hair elastic from the bedside locker, I proceeded to scrape my hair back from my face and secured it in a high ponytail. Getting dressed took a little more work as it involved sorting through the heaps of clothes that were spread haphazardly around the room.

One of these days I was going to clean up. I wouldn't just dump my newly laundered clothes on the chair in the corner, allowing them to mingle with the pile of not yet washed items; a pile which seemed to grow by the minute as if the clothes themselves were somehow managing to procreate. Perhaps they were. I'd read of stranger things happening in the tabloids.

Grabbing my black faux leather handbag from the top of my chest of drawers, I narrowly avoided looking at my own reflection. It wasn't going to be a pretty picture and depressing myself further just didn't feel like a proper use of my time.

Barely ten minutes passed and I was already out the door, locking it carefully behind me before I dropped my keychain in to the black hole I called my bag. The phone buzzed once more, the noise registering only briefly from somewhere in the depths of the tote. I already knew it would be Gerald. Reading his increasingly agitated texts was pointless and would only waste more time.

Ignoring the buzz of the phone, I set off down the ice-slicked path. Trying desperately to stay on my feet, I half shuffled, half slid down the pavement that ran alongside the road.

It was quiet at this time of the morning, the city only just beginning to come alive. It was hard to believe that an hour from now, the roads would be congested bumper to bumper with cars and trucks. A van rumbled toward me, the yellow lights momentarily blinding me as it grew closer and the fear I'd pushed aside after my nightmare resurfaced once more.

"Don't do this to yourself, Alice." My breath fogged, forming tiny clouds in front of my face as I spoke the words aloud. It was stupid always having to talk myself down off the ledge. Usually I wasn't this bad but the anniversary was coming up and with it came the dreams about that night crashing down around my ears.

The phone's ringtone blared through my thoughts and I fished in my bag, pulling the device out before it had a chance to stop. Even talking to Gerald right now, listening to whatever crisis he had for me would be better than what I was currently doing to myself.

"I'm almost at the station," I said answering the phone without bothering with a greeting.

"Alice, it's Mam." Her voice caused my heart to stall out in my chest.

"Oh, right, sorry..." I cleared my throat awkwardly. "I'm just on my way into work and I—"

"I was just ringing to ask if you were coming home for the Mass?"

Ice slid down my spine. She knew I hated it, hated standing there in the church while a priest who'd never even met Clara spoke about her as though they'd been personally acquainted. To make matters worse, it wasn't an anniversary mass like the one we had for Gran on the anniversary of her death every year. No, Clara's Mass was all about praying for her safe return, as though after all these years saying a few prayers in a church would somehow allow to walk back in the door in her torn jeans and denim shirt as though nothing had happened.

If that were true, she'd have come home years ago.

"You know it's important to present a united front and—"

"Mam, you know I can't," I said. "I've got work. There's a big case at the minute and..."

"Alice McCarthy, you listen to me." My mother's tone was fierce. "Clara is your sister and she needs you right now. She..."

"Mam, I've got to go," I said, cutting her off mid-sentence. "I'll think about it all right?"

I wanted to get off the phone. Listening to her talk about Clara as though she were still alive hurt too much. I knew it was part of her coping mechanism, that she needed to do it, but I couldn't handle it. Never could. I'd grieved Clara on my own and everyone else behaved as though she was still out there, living her best life somehow.

"Alice," she said, her voice softening. "I just..."

"I know, Mam," I said, cutting her off. It was always the same thing. She loved Clara, she loved me, and she just wanted us to be a family again. In her mind, this was the best way to do it. "I've got to go." I ended the call before she could say another word. I attempted to let the tension hunching my shoulders go.

The phone buzzed again and I answered the call without looking at the screen.

"I said I'd think about it, Mam," I said automatically.

"Alice, I've been trying to call but your phone keeps going to voicemail." Gerald's voice was tense.

"Shit, I'm sorry, Gerald." I spoke rapidly. "I'm on my way into the office now."

"Alice, I—" He was hesitant and the breath I'd been about to exhale caught in the back of my throat.

"What is it?"

"It's the Stockwell case," he said and the blood in my veins turned to ice.

"Zoe..." Simply saying her name aloud was enough

to conjure an image in my mind of a bright, blue-eyed girl of seven.

"They think her father's taken her." Gerald was still talking but I barely heard him over the rushing in my ears.

"What do you mean they think he has? For Christ's sake, Gerald, she's seven and it's practically the middle of the night. Either they know he's taken her or—" Bile rushed up my throat, cutting my words off as acid burned the back of my tongue and my eyes watered.

This isn't the same as Clara.

"The police have some questions. Do you think you could swing by the mother's place and check in with them there?"

"How did he know where to look for them?" It was an accusation rather than a question.

"They're still unsure of the details..." There was an edge to Gerald's voice that hadn't been there a moment before.

"Bullshit."

He sighed, the sound whistling down the phone and into my ear.

"Look, you haven't been working with Rachel and Zoe," I said. "You haven't listened to her talk about Dan. She's scared of him."

"If you can't handle this," he said. "I can send someone else down there, maybe Jennifer could take it over for you."

"Don't you dare," I spluttered.

"Alice, contrary to popular opinion round here, I actually want this all to work out. But if your head isn't in the game then—"

I hung up and stared down at the black screen. I didn't really think he would replace me. At least I was fairly certain he wouldn't. But I didn't appreciate the threat either. He didn't get it. He was too long out of the field, sitting in his ivory tower of an office, passing down judgments over the rest of us from on high.

The mobile phone buzzed in my hand once more and Gerald's name blinked on the screen. Shoving it back into my handbag, I squinted against the oncoming headlights of the approaching taxi, the illuminated golden sign on top declaring to the world that it was available. It was a luxury I really couldn't afford but what choice did I have? Every second that ticked by with Zoe missing was a moment too long.

Raising my hand, I flagged the cab down and slid into the backseat quickly, giving the driver the address I needed to get to before I sank back against the worn leather seats.

"Going to be a miserable one," the driver said amicably as I pulled a notepad from inside my bag.

"Yeah." I nodded absently, flicking through the pages, scanning the notes I'd made on my last visit to Rachel and Zoe.

"Where you from then?" he asked, catching my eye in the rearview mirror.

"What?"

"Your accent. It's not Mancunian, not even English," he said with a chuckle.

"Ireland," I said and dropped my attention back to the notepad.

"Lovely over there, I bet," he said. "I've always wanted to go to Dublin."

I smiled awkwardly.

"I'll let you get back to your work," he said, turning his attention back to the road and the traffic that was slowly beginning to appear.

I stared down at the page of notes blankly, my mind refusing to read the words as my brain churned over the recent events.

Everything had been so normal. They'd been settling into a routine and Zoe was finally catching up at school.

"Dan keeps apologising." The words jumped out at me from the page. I hadn't added anything else to the note but I could remember Rachel's face as she'd told me. The way her fingers had knotted into the hem of her blue sweater.

At the time I'd dismissed it as just another of his ploys, nothing more than a tactic to make her believe his sob story all over again.

Had I missed something important?

Dan was a manipulator, a narcissist, and a liar but he wasn't the type to harm Zoe. Or himself, for that matter. Was he?

"Dan keeps apologising." I read the words again, this

time hearing Rachel's voice in my head as she said it. There had been something in her eyes. Was it fear?

Had I misread him? Misread the situation?

Shit. My fingers drummed nervously against the papers as I stared out the window. Should I have told Gerald about Rachel's concerns?

3

THE YELLOW TAPE flutters in the breeze, the noise bringing with it memories of other things.

What is it about the discovery of a body that creates such a solemn atmosphere? With the flick of a switch, bang. Somebody's day is in tatters.

Not that it wasn't before.

But people have a peculiar way of pretending everything's just dandy.

They fight tooth and nail to hold onto that pretense.

I've never been much for pretending. The real deal is much more enticing; a kind of drug that draws me back time and again.

Standing along the edge of the police tape, I watch them move back and forth in their white coveralls, searching for the tiniest of clues.

Something.

Anything.

Hoping that when they find what they're scouring the ground for, it'll scream to the high heavens and point them straight to the wrongdoer.

Desperate if you ask me.

Not that anyone does.

They bring the body out in a white plastic sheet. Smaller than I remember it going in, not that it was very big then either.

They don't know the game's begun and it gives me a little thrill to know I'm standing on the edge of a precipice. Only a matter of time before they find the other one.

But it's this little white rabbit that will send Alice tumbling down the rabbit hole. And then, finally, she'll be home.

4

TWO POLICE CARS sat on the driveway of Zoe's house as I made my way up the path toward the front door. As the sound of the taxi's engine rumbled off into the distance, my gaze snagged on the familiar pink bicycle that lay on its side under the living room window.

Zoe loved that bike.

Without thinking, I crossed the small square of grass that made up the lawn and picked it up, setting it against the wall, mindful not to knock the ribbons on the handlebars askew.

"Can I help you?" A female officer appeared in Rachel's doorway, her brown eyes heavy with suspicion when she saw my hands on the handlebars of Zoe's bike.

"Sorry," I said, fumbling for my identification badge inside my shirt. I winced as the lanyard snagged on my hair, tugging loose several strands straight from the roots. "I'm Alice McCarthy, the family social worker assigned to the case."

She scanned the badge and nodded curtly. "Got a call from your boss. We've been waiting for you," she said, stepping back into the hall allowing me to follow her inside. "My name is Officer Shaw, we need to ask you a couple of questions and—"

"Have you tracked Dan down yet? I mean, Mr Clayton?" I cut her off, unable to keep the eagerness from my voice.

"We're following all lines of enquiry," she said, effectively dismissing my question as she directed me toward the kitchen.

"Ms Clayton hasn't yet been able to tell us the arrangements she has in place with her partner."

"She doesn't have one," I said. "The court awarded her full custody of Zoe. Dan has supervised visitation but he hasn't turned up for any of the appointments."

I noted the slight tightening around the mouth of the woman standing in front of me. Clearly Rachel hadn't told them anything at all.

"I don't know why you keep asking me all these questions. Why aren't you out there looking for he?" Rachel's voice rose in hysteria, breaking through the awkward silence. I slipped past Officer Shaw and into the kitchen where Rachel stood. Her back was to the kitchen sink, head buried in her hands as she sobbed. "I don't understand why you aren't looking for her."

"I'm sure they're doing everything they can." I crossed the room toward her. She looked up at me and tears spilled over her lashes from bloodshot blue eyes. She looked like she hadn't slept for days. What the hell was going on here? Rachel's gaze softened, recognition helping to quell some of the frantic panic I'd seen lurking in them just moments before.

I faltered.

Her eyes were identical to Zoe's. Why hadn't I noticed that before?

It was an idle thought, gone as quickly as it had arrived and I let it go. I couldn't get hung up on little things like that right now. Not when every moment counted. Seven year olds didn't just go missing in the middle of the night for no good reason.

I focused on the situation directly in front of me. It was all I could do. All I was good for.

"I keep telling them Dan wouldn't take her, not like this..." It was an odd thing to say and I caught Officer Shaw sharing a look with the other policeman in the room.

"We still need his contact details, Ms Clayton," the unknown police officer said, notebook gripped in his long fingers. "Perhaps you could help with that?" He turned his attention over to me, his brown eyes sliding over me in assessment.

"Sure," I said, slapping my case file down on the counter. "I've got his current address in here." I pulled a slip of paper free and handed it over to the uniformed officer, who took it with a nod.

"I'm going to go out to the car," he said, "and call this in. Officer Shaw will stay here with you two."

She nodded and followed him to the door, giving me a moment of privacy with Rachel.

"What happened?"

"I don't know," she said. "I was asleep and—"

"Rachel," I said, the warning in my voice drawing the attention of Officer Shaw. I lowered my voice before continuing. "We've spoken about this before. Don't lie to me, not about something like this."

It wasn't that Rachel was really a liar; it was just where her ex was concerned she had a terrible habit of omitting certain things in order to protect him. When questioned about it, she'd said she felt as though she was being disloyal to him, as though by telling us about the abuse she'd suffered at his hands she was the one in the wrong.

She sighed and turned her back to the room. Her knuckles blanched as she gripped the edge of the sink.

"Dan hasn't been attending the supervised visits because I've been letting him see Zoe here."

Her words hit me like a slap in the face.

"You've been letting him come here to see her? After everything I said? After everything you told me he did?"

"He's changed," she pleaded, meeting my gaze

head on. "He was clean and everything and I can't just cut him out of Zoe's life. She loves him."

"So tell me what happened this time," I said. "Why is it different this time?"

"I let him take her for the weekend." Her voice was small. "He said he wanted to take her to the fair that's opened up on the outskirts of town."

"And when was she due to come home?"

"He brought her back last night," she said, without the slightest hint of deception in her voice. "I put her to bed around nine and..." Her words choked off. "He just kept apologising, said he hadn't meant to hurt us. That he knew now what he'd done wrong and he was going to fix it." She closed her eyes, her shoulders tense, and I knew there was something else she wasn't telling me.

"What happened then, Rachel?"

"He kissed me but I pushed him away. I told him it was a mistake. We were in a good place and I didn't want to ruin it. I tried to tell him that but..." Her tears spilled over her lashes and tracked down her pale cheeks. "He was so angry, Alice, I've never seen him so angry."

"And?"

"And nothing. He just left..."

"I went to bed. I checked Zoe first, of course, and she was out like a light. I fell asleep. Then I thought I heard a noise. When I got up, she was gone—" Her voice broke over the words and I could see the haunted look in her eyes.

"I'm going to ask you something very important now, Rachel," I said as gently as I could. "Does Dan have a set of keys for the house?"

Her lower lip trembled and she nodded, tears dripping down from her lashes onto her cheeks. "I gave him one last week because he was going to pick her up after school and bring her back here while I was at work."

I nodded and plastered as reassuring a smile as I could muster onto my face. "I'm going to tell the police officers this," I said. "You just wait here."

As I turned away from her, she grabbed my arm suddenly, her fingernails leaving half-moon imprints in my skin. "I just want her back, Alice. I didn't mean for any of this to happen. I just want her back."

Extricating myself from her grip was easier than I'd expected. I left her at the sink and crossed the kitchen, exiting into the narrow hall, the walls of which were littered with Zoe's artwork. Drawings of houses and horses, which she adored, seemed to be the predominant theme running through the images. Dotted throughout were figures.

Judging by the yellow marker she'd used to colour the hair of the tallest women I guessed them to be portraits of Rachel. Sometimes she appeared alone; other times she stood next to a tall dark haired man. Zoe had used a wide slash of red to indicate their smiles in all of the pictures save one.

The last picture on the wall was of the same tall

man that had appeared throughout the images. But this time there was no smile. Instead, his face was dotted with blue tears that seemed to stream from his eyes.

And people thought kids didn't pick up on the situations going on around them. They were versatile and that often made the adults in charge somewhat complacent about what they allowed the kids to see or hear. The picture on the wall was by no means definitive proof of Dan's state of mind but it seemed odd for Zoe to create an image in which her father was crying.

"Something I can help you with?" Officer Shaw appeared in the doorway and I jumped, so engrossed in the images I hadn't even heard her approach.

"Rachel has just informed me that her ex-partner Dan has been seeing Zoe regularly."

"I thought you said he hadn't come to any of the supervised visitations?"

"He hadn't. Rachel's been letting him come round unsupervised and she's just told me he had a set of keys."

Officer Shaw's expression was implacable, her gaze steady as I explained to her everything Rachel had told me. When I finished she just nodded, her lips a thin line as she reached for the radio near her shoulder.

"DCI Radcliff and DS Carter are on their way over," she said. "They'll be here soon. If you'll give me a few moments here I'll be in to take a more formal statement from Ms Clayton. Also, we're going to have to take any electronics she has, such as mobile phones, tablets, and computers."

I stared at her in surprise. "You don't think Rachel is a suspect, do you?"

"We're taking all necessary precautions at the moment," she said. "Zoe is a high risk missing person and as such we need to ensure we don't miss anything."

It wasn't an answer but I could tell from the look on her face that I wasn't about to get anything more out of her.

"We'll keep you informed of any progress until the F.L.Os get here and then they'll take over." She turned away from me and I knew I'd been dismissed.

I retreated down the hall, back toward the kitchen and paused, straining to hear the hushed conversation between the two police officers but I couldn't make out anything over the sound of the driving rain on the kitchen window.

When had it started to rain?

I thought about Zoe outside in this weather. She was asthmatic and the last thing she needed was to get soaked to the skin.

Moving back into the kitchen, I paused inside the door and froze. The back door was wide open and there was no sign of Rachel.

My heart dropped into my stomach.

I darted to the back door. The small garden out

back with the bright yellow Wendy-house was deserted.

Instinctively I knew what Rachel had done. She'd taken matters into her own hands and gone to get her daughter back.

5

"OFFICER SHAW," I shouted as I hurried down the hallway toward the front door. She poked her head around the door in answer to my shout, her expression grim.

"I said we would keep you apprised of—" She cut off, catching the concern on my face. "What is it?"

"Rachel," I said. "Ms Clayton. She's gone. The back door is open and she's nowhere to be seen. I think she's gone after them."

"Would she have a different address to the one you've given us?" Officer Shaw asked, pushing past me so she could move down the hall. "Another car has done a drive by of Mr Clayton's address but they said the premises are empty."

Officer Shaw's partner headed toward the panda car parked out front. "I'm going to do a drive around, see if I can pick up her tail. She can't have gotten very far on foot."

"I'll head out through the back," Officer Shaw said, moving down the hall. "Maybe I can catch up to her that way."

"What should I do?" I slid my hand up and down the strap of my bag, a nervous habit that was slowly seeing the faux leather wear away. I followed her down the hall and hesitated in the kitchen doorway.

"Wait here in case she comes back." She thrust a small white card at me. "That's got my mobile number on it, so if she comes back, contact me."

I stroked the thin card stock and nodded.

The stern faced police officer exited through the back door. I watched from my vantage point at the kitchen sink as she headed for the gate that sat at the furthest point of the handkerchief-sized piece of lawn.

The silence in the house became deafening.

Rachel's mobile phone sat on the edge of the table and I stared at it. It wouldn't be right to look at it.

What if she's in trouble?

The little voice in the back of my head spoke with authority. It was true after all. What if she was in trouble? If Dan had sent her a message telling her to meet him somewhere, would she go? Of course she would and she would do it without a second thought for what might happen.

I scooped the phone up and pressed the home key.

The screen brightened for a moment, showing me a picture of Rachel, Dan, and Zoe, together and smiling. Then it was gone and the screen demanded I enter a pin code to unlock the phone.

I tried Zoe's birthday but the phone buzzed it's irritation and punished me for the incorrect answer by telling me I had just two more attempts or the sim card would lock.

Setting the phone down, I couldn't get the image of their smiling faces from my mind. My mind superimposed Zoe's drawing of the tear-stained Dan over the grinning man from the photograph. I wasn't supposed to jump to conclusions but in the pit of my stomach I knew that something was terribly wrong. We'd missed something. The feeling of dread in my gut made me snatch the phone again.

I clicked the home button and was once more treated to the smiling photograph of the three together once more.

Was that what he planned? For them all to be happy together again?

"Hello?" Gerald's voice echoed from the hall, making me jump. The mobile phone slipped from my grasp but I caught it before the fragile glass screen connected with the edge of the granite counter top.

"In here," I said, setting the device down on the counter unsteadily, my hands shaking violently enough that I tucked them into the pockets of my winter coat out of sight.

Gerald poked his head around the door, raising his eyebrows in surprise as he found me alone. His brown hair was a little tousled, as though he'd just rolled straight out of bed and hadn't bothered to comb it. The collar of his shirt was open. The only thing keeping it together was his tie, which I noted was the same one he'd been wearing the day before. Only now, it was crumpled and sat askew around his throat.

"Where is everyone?" He scanned the room as though he might find Rachel and the other police officers hiding in the corner, waiting to pop out at him as if they were at a surprise party.

"Rachel's done a bunk," I said. "Officer Shaw's gone out back to look." I jerked my thumb in the direction of the still open back door, where rain pattered onto the linoleum floor. "The other officer is driving around the area to see if he can see her."

"Where would she go?" Gerald asked, scrubbing his hand over the stubble on his jawline.

"She's gone to see Dan, I presume," I said. "She's been letting him see Zoe outside of the supervised visitation. He even has a key to this place."

"Fuck." Gerald swore emphatically and shoved his hand up through his hair. "Why would she do it?"

I shrugged. "She loves him and doesn't want Zoe to have the same childhood she had."

"She told you this?"

"Not in so many words," I said. I caught the look of chagrin that contorted his expression and added hastily. "I know I'm not supposed to read between the lines but I've read her file and she hints around it. Like really hints around it."

"You know we're only supposed to work within the bounds of the information presented to us," he said. "If you've got a suspicion of something, you should come to me and we can examine it a little more closely."

"There was nothing to tell," I said, suddenly feeling defensive. "She told me this morning that she's been letting him see Zoe."

Gerald smiled sympathetically. "I know it's easy to get attached," he said, "but you have to maintain a professional distance."

I opened my mouth to argue further with him but the static of Officer Shaw's radio cut over me. She appeared in the doorway a moment later, her gaze going from my face to Gerald's, the question implicit in her gaze.

"I'm Gerald Banbury," he told her smoothly, holding out his badge for her to see. "We spoke on the phone this morning."

"Of course," she answered brusquely.

"You didn't find her?" I couldn't stop the question from exploding out of me.

"Nothing. The alley at the back here leads into the woods and—"

I tuned out her words and stared out the window. A nagging suspicion that had lodged in the back of my mind fought to surface. There was a play area in those woods. I remembered Zoe swinging back and forth on the swings, legs dangling in the air while I met Rachel there for one of our visits. It was the same place from the photograph on Rachel's phone, when all three of them had been together and happy.

"The woods," I said suddenly, cutting across Officer Shaw abruptly. "There's a play area for the estate kids. It was erected at the same time they built the houses here."

I scooped up the phone and presented it to the Officer Shaw, who stared at it like I'd just presented her with a time bomb. "Click the home button," I said. "The photograph of the three of them together, was taken in that play area."

"And you think that's where they are now?" Officer Shaw asked, studying the phone.

"I can't be sure," I said, "but you said it yourself, she can't have gone far and she was standing right here staring out the window before she left. The phone was right next to her. If she got a text from Dan, she could have walked straight out the door and to the play area. It's just a short walk from here."

Officer Shaw picked up her radio and spoke rapidly into it before turning toward the door. "Can you show me where this play area is?"

I nodded and dumped my bag on the floor next to the sink before following her to the door.

"Should I come too?" Gerald asked, sounding more

than a little reluctant as he caught sight of the rain slanting in through the doorway.

Officer Shaw shook her head. "No, if this is the path she took, the less people we've got wandering around out there the better."

It took me a second to realise the sub-text behind what she was saying. The path was potentially a gold mine of evidence; they needed to keep the pool of people they would have to check against as small as possible.

I stepped out into the downpour and pulled my hood up against the onslaught. Not that it was much good; it didn't seem to matter in which direction I tried to turn my face, the rain still flung itself under the hood and slapped me in the face.

"Strange place to put a playground," Officer Shaw said. "In the middle of the woods, I mean."

"Yeah," I said. "Although it's really a copse rather than a wood. When they first built these houses, the trees were probably immature but they've grown up a lot since then. Ash always grows fast."

She gave me a sideways glance and I smiled. "I grew up in the country. My father was an arborist."

"Was?" There was mild interest in her eyes.

"Retired," I said.

She nodded and her pace seemed to quicken.

"Mine was a DCI," she said. "Mom always worried he'd get injured on the job when really he should have been worrying about his cholesterol."

"I'm sorry," I said.

"He's not dead." She grinned at me. "Just had to retire early. Lots of doctor's appointments, three stents in his heart, and high blood pressure all made him a candidate for early retirement. He's still kicking but the way he complains, I sometimes think he'd prefer it if the heart attack had taken him out instead of forcing him to retire."

I paused as we reached the edge of the pathway. It wound up into the trees and I understood why, in the early dawn light, Officer Shaw had called it a wood. From this vantage point it certainly looked like one.

"I've got a torch," she said, fishing it off her belt. The beam lit up the area directly in front of us and I followed her into the trees.

"The path should take us straight to the—"

I cut off as the sound of a woman's voice drifted to us on the breeze. It sounded like Rachel. I couldn't make out what she was saying but her voice was definitely strained, as though she were on the verge of hysterics.

Officer Shaw started to jog forward as she spoke rapidly, in hushed tones, into the radio on her shoulder.

We reached the edge of the playground and I could see Zoe, wrapped in her favourite Frozen duvet sitting inside the large bucket swing. The canopy of foliage overhead was keeping her relatively dry.

Near where we stood, still hidden by the trees, I could see Rachel with her back to us.

Dan stood between the mother and daughter and as my eyes fell on the anthracite coloured handgun in his left hand my heart skittered to a halt. He raised the gun and pointed it at Rachel. Her knees buckled and she dropped onto the soft-play tarmac, sobbing.

6

"I HAVE eyes on the girl and the suspect." Officer Shaw rattled off the coordinates of the playground into her radio.

Dan had lowered the gun and was pacing back and forth in front of Rachel who was still sobbing on the ground.

"Stay here," Officer Shaw whispered to me, her face an impenetrable mask as she inched toward the gap in the trees.

Where the hell did she think I was going to go? There was no way I was going to go out there, not while he was waving a gun around the place. He'd take one look at me and probably blow my head off.

"Daddy!" Zoe's voice cut over the sound of Rachel's sobbing and my chest constricted painfully as Dan wheeled around to face her. At least he hadn't pointed the gun at her. Yet. Just what was he planning on doing?

I remembered the painting Zoe had made of her father. The childishly drawn blue drops that fell from Dan's eyes. Did he plan on using the gun? Pointing it at Rachel would suggest that he had certainly thought about it. It was also entirely possible that he was depressed and intended on escaping the life he now found himself living without his daughter or his wife, by committing suicide.

There was another, much more disturbing, possibility and just thinking about it was enough to cause my skin to break out in a cold sweat.

I hadn't pegged him as a family annihilator but I remembered a study I'd read that talked about substance abusers who were also jealous and overly possessive of their partners. It was a lethal cocktail.

As I watched him try to soothe his upset daughter, I realised Dan ticked all of those boxes. In his own way, he loved his family but his love bordered on obsession and that made it so much unhealthier. I glanced at Rachel as she pushed up onto her feet. Looking at him now, there was nothing of the man she'd once described him as being when she'd fallen in love with him.

Every time she pulled away from him, every time I thought she'd managed to extricate herself from, his hold had sucked her back in as though he were capable of exerting a force of gravity over those who fell into his orbit.

Dan started to cross the playground toward his daughter, his grip on the gun wavering. My heart began to gallop in my ribcage. I couldn't just stand here and watch him hurt his child.

"Mr Clayton," Officer Shaw called from the relatively safe cover of the trees.

He wheeled around, raising the gun and pointing it wildly in the direction he thought her voice had come from.

"I'm going to step out now, just so we can talk," she said, moving out from behind the trees. "I need you to put the gun down so we can talk properly."

"I need you to fuck off so I can talk to my wife," he said, his voice bordering on hysteria.

Ducking low to keep myself out of sight, I started to move around the edge of the play area through the trees. Zoe knew me and if I could get her attention, I might be able to persuade her to come to me. At least then she would be safe. My heart hammered in my chest, the noise echoing in my ears in time to the patter of rain against leaves on the trees. They'd mostly all fallen and the wind that was starting to rise would finish off those that remained, clinging to the branches.

I crept through the undergrowth, painfully aware of every branch that groaned, every twig that snapped underfoot and the rustle of foliage and debris that littered the ground.

"Mr Clayton, I'm not trying to stop you from talking to your wife, I just want to facilitate a safe discussion between the two of you, is all." Officer Shaw's voice was calm, her tone placating. How could she do it? My palms were sweating and my heart was beating so hard I was sure that at any moment, Dan would hear it.

"Stop fucking talking to me," he said his voice pitched higher and I glanced through the trees. The gun dangled from his fingers, almost forgotten as he beat his fist against the side of his head. "I need to think and you're not letting me think."

"Mr Clayton," Officer Shaw said. "Can I call you Dan? My name is Tamsin. I just want to help."

She was standing between Dan and me, her feet inching forwards with every second that ticked by. Clearly she'd had the same idea as I'd had and she was moving toward Zoe.

Dan started to pace, each circle bringing him closer to Zoe who sat on the swing, her eyes wide with terror, thumb jammed in her mouth.

"Just let me get Zoe and then we can all sit down and—"

"No!" he screamed, the sudden ferocity in his voice made Zoe shriek, her face blanching as her tears came once more, hot and heavy.

"Please, Dan," Rachel pleaded, "don't hurt her. Just let me hold her. I swear, I'm sorry. I just—"

"Shut up the lot of you!" He cried again, beating his hands against his head once more.

I edged closer to the tree line and tried to catch Zoe's eye but she was too upset, too distraught, to even register my presence. I was close enough to her now that if Officer Shaw could keep Dan's attention for long enough, I could grab her but I knew any sort of sudden disturbance right now could set him off so I didn't dare attempt it.

Adrenaline sang in my veins and the urge to move, to do something—anything—to diffuse the situation was a constant mantra in my head.

Rachel rushed forward, her eyes focused only on Zoe, but Officer Shaw caught her arm, dragging her back as Dan once more raised the gun and pointed it first at his wife and then at the police officer.

Sirens split the air and I felt a momentary shot of relief spike through me. Our backup had arrived. Surely Dan would see the situation was pointless and would give up the gun. Everything and everyone would be fine.

"Daddy," Zoe moaned through her tears.

He turned to his daughter and crossed the space between them before crouching next to her.

"It's all right, baby. Daddy's right here."

She started to cry harder as he bumped the gun against her arm and I could feel my heart climb into my mouth. Zoe struggled against his grip, fighting to get away from him, to move away from the cold metal.

Dan's expression twisted. The tenderness I'd seen just moments before vanished as he looked down at his struggling daughter with disgust.

He pushed himself onto his feet once more, turning his attention on Rachel. "You've done this to her. You've turned her against me," he said, using the gun to emphasise each of his words.

"Mr Clayton," Officer Shaw said. "Please put the gun down."

The sirens grew louder and I could see the faint pulse of red and blue lights bouncing off the trees surrounding me.

"I said get back," he said.

"Just let me reach Zoe..."

"I said GET THE FUCK BACK—"

Crack!

Silence flooded in to fill the void. It took my brain a moment to realise what had happened. My mind moved as though it had legs that were stuck in molasses. Officer Shaw turned from Dan, her eyes wide with surprise as her knees buckled, and she collapsed to the ground. I'd always thought that if I were faced with a traumatic event that everything would feel so much clearer, the adrenaline making the world sharper somehow. As I crouched in the bushes, I was catapulted back to that night with Clara. The feel of her fingers as they'd slipped from mine was as real now as it had been then. Officer Shaw's eyes found mine and in them I could see a plea, a silent cry for help.

Sound returned to my ears with a deafening roar. Zoe and Rachel's screams mingled to create a cacophony of noise.

My gaze flickered from the face of Officer Shaw, who now lay on the ground, her legs bent back behind her body at an unnatural angle. I took in the scene in what felt like tiny snapshots of information. As though my mind understood that if I tried to focus on everything all at once, I would fall apart.

I wanted to go to her, to check to see if she was breathing, but my gaze was drawn up to Dan. He was moaning like a wounded animal. Low guttural choking sounds came from deep within his throat.

Listening to him made me think of home. Ireland.

I remembered one Summer time when I was standing on the back porch, hearing the sound of a cow gasping for air. Low guttural choking noises crawled out of its throat as the animal lay dying. It had broken through a fence into the clover pasture and gorged itself on the lush plants. It lay on its side, stomach swollen into a high mound.

"I didn't mean to..." Dan's words cut through my ruminations. Shock. I was in shock, that was what was wrong with me. I recognised it as the same emotion I'd experienced when I'd managed to pull myself from the river and realised Clara was nowhere to be found.

Curling into a ball on the bank of the river, I'd started to sob, teeth chattering, mind reliving the moment when her hand had slipped out of mine.

But I couldn't curl into a ball now. Zoe depended on me.

Only a few seconds seemed to have passed but the sirens were louder now. The sound of voices shouting, searching, drawing closer, broke through Dan's panicked babbling.

Zoe had slipped off the side of the swing and was making her way toward the trees, moving in my direction on unsteady legs. Her hair quickly became plastered to her face as the rain pelted down from above. The pale pink pyjama set she wore rapidly turned a dark rose colour under the unrelenting weather. Yet the grinning panda on the front of her long sleeve bed shirt was undeterred by the downpour and still proclaimed how much he loved to sleep.

Beckoning her forward, I moved as close to the edge of the tree line as I could, careful to keep myself out of sight of Dan. If he saw me...

Zoe's left foot hit a small stone and she stumbled, dropping the doll that had been in her grip. My heart tried to crawl out of my chest as it hit the ground with a dull thud. For a moment I was certain Dan hadn't heard anything but as Zoe bent down to retrieve her lost companion, he swung around and stared at his daughter. His face displayed a myriad of emotions, completely unreadable because of their brief duration. They flashed across his face in the blink of an eye.

Time slowed to a crawl as he raised his arm. The gun trembled in his grip. Rachel's scream ripped through the night air.

"Sorry, baby, it'll be better soon," Dan said.

My legs were moving, my body in motion before my mind fully caught up. Zoe's blue eyes were wide with terror as she faced her father, shock and fear sealing anything she might have said to him behind her lips. My fingers brushed the edges of her soft pink pyjamas.

Crack!

7

"You sure you have to leave, Siobhan?" Paul asked, wrapping his arms around my waist as he tried to tug me back into bed.

Giggling, I pulled away and finished tucking my blouse into my navy slacks.

"You know I'm sure. The fact that they're letting me in on this is a big deal for me."

He pouted, his sandy hair tousled from the pillows and I reached over to brush my fingers against his cheeks.

"I'll be back at the weekend," I said. "Maybe sooner if they decide they don't want my help."

Paul grabbed my fingers and tugged them to his mouth. "And what am I going to do in this bed all on my lonesome?"

"Sleep," I said with a grin.

My phone started to vibrate and I tugged my hand back, straightening up before I read the message.

"Shit," I swore. I was going to be late.

"Something the matter?"

"Just Brady. You know what he's like."

Paul smiled, his eyes crinkling at the corners. "He's an asshole but he's a good guy." His smile faded. "He's not going with you is he?"

"No." I shook my head. "I've got to send my reports in to him. And he keeps sending me new memos on the case."

He sat up on the bed. "You know you can talk to me about it."

I smiled. "I know but if I don't go now, I'm going to miss my train and I really don't think being late for my first day is such a great impression to give."

"I guess not..."

I leaned over the bed and pressed my lips to his, a quick kiss that quickly deepened as he tried to tug me back onto the bed alongside him.

"I've got to go," I said, pushing him away.

"You're going to leave me wanting?" Under normal circumstances I would have given in and climbed back into bed with him. But my job was too important to me.

It was easier for him; his position with the NBCI was already secure. I was the new girl and the last big case I'd worked had hardly turned out in my favour. Evidence had gone missing—mislabelled apparently

—although I found that hard to believe. And the suspect we'd had in mind had walked away scot free thanks to the DPP deciding there was insufficient evidence to go ahead with a prosecution.

A year later, they'd finally agreed to take the training wheels off by sending me down the country to take over the murder enquiry that had just opened up. It was important and I wasn't going to screw up a second time.

This time, I had something to prove.

"I'll see you soon," I told Paul.

With a sigh he let me go and for a moment I could have sworn that what I saw reflected in his eyes was resentment. It was gone in an instant and I dismissed the thought, pushing it aside in favour of the other thoughts filling up my head.

A LITTLE OVER two hours later, I was sitting inside the Garda Sergeant's car as he drove me through the winding back roads of Tipperary. We'd left what had looked like the only decent road outside of Cahir and were now winding our way upwards.

I stared out the window at the mountains that surrounded us like giants standing in judgment of those who lived in their shadow.

"Much further?" I asked.

I turned to stare at the man next to me. His light brown hair was greying around the temples and, from the looks of things, beginning to thin. His mouth was set in a grim line and had been like that from the moment I'd told him I wanted to go straight to the site where the body had been discovered.

"Another bit," he said, his eyes never leaving the road.

Great. I'd already managed to piss off the locals.

"Look, I know you're not thrilled about me being here," I started to speak but trailed off as he took a hairpin corner without slowing down. My hand found the handle that sat near the roof of the car and I held onto it until my fingers began to cramp.

"Doesn't bother me in the slightest," he said, never once losing his tight-lipped expression.

Turning my head, I rolled my eyes and returned my gaze to the world beyond the window.

The clouds hung low over the mountains, giving an oppressive atmosphere to the area.

"Which mountains are they?" I asked.

"The Galtee's," he said as though that explained everything.

He swung the car into what looked like a car park and hit the brake. Across the lot, I could see the fluttering Garda tape that announced to everyone who saw it that this area was strictly off limits.

"Up through there," he said, jabbing a finger in the direction of a path that wound up into the trees.

"Are you coming?"

"Why would I? Haven't I been up there enough

over the last twenty-four hours? You're the one who won't take our word for it."

With a sigh, I bit my tongue. I had expected them to be awkward, to chafe against my presence, but I wasn't expecting outright obstinacy.

I pushed on the car door, the wind sucking it out of my hand so that it flew open. The sergeant said nothing as I climbed out and started over the car park toward the path and the police tape. Reaching down into my pocket, I swore softly. I'd left my notepad and pen in the car along with the rest of the files.

Good job, Siobhan. You're off to a cracking start here.

Ducking beneath the tape, I followed the path into the trees for about a hundred yards. It was easy enough to spot the burial site; the forensics had cordoned off the area with metal posts and more tape. The tent was gone now, along with the body. And where it had lain there was a gaping wound in the earth. Fresh dirt exposed to the elements had turned to mud under the rainfall of the last twenty-four hours.

I turned around and stared at my surroundings. It was close enough to the car park. An easy dump site, really. Just a short walk to the tree line. Something niggled at the back of my mind as I studied my surroundings.

"Solved it yet?" An unfamiliar male voice cut through my thoughts and I jumped. As I whirled around, my foot slipped on the path and I felt myself tip towards the open hole in the ground.

A strong arm wrapped around my bicep, halting my forward progress toward total humiliation.

"Sorry, I thought you were examining the scene and not the natural beauty of the area." The man standing before me gave me a small smile, a bare curling of the corners of his mouth. His red hair was cut short, clearly to keep the natural curl in his hair from getting out of hand. His blue eyes were striking in their icy colouring, emphasised further by the smattering of freckles across his nose and cheeks.

He looked like he belonged in an advertisement for Irish Tourism, not half way up the side of a mountain next to a killer's dumpsite.

"Who are you?" I could tell he was Gardaí but he'd deliberately crept up on me so I wasn't going to be nice to him.

"Jee-zus," he said, placing a strange emphasis on the word. "Take a joke would you?"

Narrowing my gaze, I folded my arms over my chest and waited.

"Fine. I'm Ronan McGuire," he said. "Garda detective hereabouts. And you're Detective Siobhan Geraghty, right?"

"Does everyone know who I am?"

"Mostly," he said. "We don't get many of your sort down here. There's the local lads like me but you're a bit more special, what with you coming all the way down from Dublin to hold the hands of us country bumpkins."

"Well, thanks for the welcome wagon," I said, moving back down the track to the car park.

"If you're looking for the sergeant, he's already left."

His words halted me in my tracks. "What do you mean already left?"

"Something about wasting his time..."

"My stuff is in his car."

"Nah, it's in mine now," he said. "He chucked it all in my boot before he high-tailed it out of here back to the station."

"So I'm supposed to get a lift back with you then?"

"Suppose so," he said. "Unless you fancy hiking back down." He scrubbed his chin as he took in the view. "Bit of a stretch though."

Irritation sharpened my tongue and it took every ounce of resolve I had to stop me from turning on him. Banter was one thing but whatever he was doing was something else entirely.

"What do you make of it then?" he asked, falling into step next to me.

"This wasn't where it was originally buried," I said, picking my way over the loose stones that were spread haphazardly over the pathway.

"What makes you think that?"

"Shallow grave out here in the wilds and no wildlife disturbs it in the twenty-two years it was here for? Fat chance."

From the corner of my eye I watched him absorb

what I'd said. "Suppose you're right," he said. "Why move it now? Why not leave it, wherever it was?"

"Because they wanted it to be found."

"Now that sounds like a leap," he said, chuckling. "Who murders someone, buries their body, and then after a while digs it back up only to plant it out here so it'll be found?" He pulled a set of keys from his pocket and depressed the lock. His cherry red Ford across the car park beeped cheerfully and the lights flashed in response. "That makes no sense at all."

"I never said it had to make sense, just that it's my theory."

He shrugged and tugged open the driver's door. From where I stood, I could see my handbag and travel bag on the backseat. They'd been tossed inside so carelessly that some of the contents from my purse had spilled across the seat.

"Well your theory sounds like it's got plenty of holes in it."

"Have you got a better one?"

He fell silent and slipped into the car as I rummaged in the backseat and replaced my belongings in the bag. When I finally climbed into the front seat, I turned to face him.

"Well, have you?"

"No," he said. "I don't have a better one." There was a bitter note in his voice, as though he were a naughty child who'd been caught him out in a terrible lie.

"How many murder enquires have you worked?" I asked.

"One," he said, "but it got passed over to your lot from Limerick because of a drugs connection."

It was my turn to fall silent as he put the car in gear and spun the car round out of the car space. The motion jolted me against the door and I swallowed back the rush of nausea. What was it about this area that made everyone drive as if they were taking part in an off road rally?

"How many murders have *you* worked?" he asked.

"Twelve," I said. "This is the first one where I'm working independently."

"Off the ol' teat then," he said. I shot him an incredulous look and he had the good grace to colour, his face flushing a rather becoming strawberry that clashed brilliantly with his hair.

"I heard there's another girl missing," I said, changing the subject abruptly.

His expression instantly changed, growing almost guarded. "Yeah, family lives local but she was in college down in Cork. Came back for the weekend and vanished."

"Any theories?"

"Why?" His sudden defensiveness caught me by surprise and I found myself floundering for an answer.

"Well you've got a body turning up here and from what I've read in the file, there's already a preliminary ID from a missing persons case twenty-three years ago.

The description of that missing person matches the description of the girl that went missing recently."

"There's no link between the two," he said, sounding decisive on the matter.

"Isn't that up to me to decide?"

"Actually," he answered, "no, it's not. We're looking at the boyfriend as a suspect. Fella's been acting off since she disappeared and in most cases of missing persons that are deemed suspicious, those closest to them know what happened."

"Most," I said. "But not all..."

I kept the rest of my thoughts to myself. I'd been naive to think it would be easy to walk in and work the case without any pushback. The locals never liked it when someone came onto their turf and stepped on their toes.

Nobody liked an outsider and right now, I was that outsider.

8

MY BODY SLAMMED into Zoe's and I took her to the ground, curling my body over hers protectively.

Warmth spread across the front of my shirt and I stared down into Zoe's wide-eyed stare.

There was another gunshot. It happened on the very edges of my mind, as though I was suddenly detached from the situation completely.

I lifted my head, the pain in my shoulder only vaguely registering as I noted the pulsing blue and red lights and the way they danced across the trees.

Police officers exploded from the tree line on the opposite side of the play area, their shouts somehow muffled.

I glanced over my shoulder, half expecting to see Dan standing over me, the gun aimed at my head. But he wasn't there. My eyes caught sight of the edge of his boots and I followed the line of his prone body on the ground. Even from where I sat half propped on the rain-soaked ground with Zoe still in my arms, I could tell he was dead, his eyes already glazed with the kind of grey that only death could bring, the gun still gripped in his hand.

He'd shot himself. Tried to kill Zoe and then killed himself.

Rachel stood a few feet away from him, her screams the reason everything else was so muffled.

Zoe moved, her tiny body trembling as I held her pressed against my chest. Pushing her away, I stared down at the blood that was soaking across the panda on her chest, his cheery grin stained, giving him an altogether much more macabre expression.

Zoe's teeth chattered in her head as she stared up at me, her face shock white and it was then I started to scream.

The burning in my shoulder increased, my focus slipping a little as I tried to search her for injuries.

Strong arms lifted her away from me. "I think she's shot," I said, managing to get the words out as the world tilted dangerously around me.

The adrenaline I'd been feeling was beginning to fade, leaving me exhausted and lightheaded. Fingers probed around my shoulder and I grimaced, feeling bile rush up the back of my throat.

"Can you understand me?" The voice came from above. Moving my head only resulted in the world breaking apart into streamers of light. The burning in my shoulder reached fever pitch as the last remnants of my adrenaline faded.

Someone tried to peel my coat away from my body, jostling my arm in the process, and I cried out. Darkness ate at the corners of my vision as I caught sight of the paramedics loading Zoe onto a stretcher.

I tried to tell the man kneeling next to me that she needed her doll. It was her favourite and I could see it lying on the ground nearby, abandoned. He nodded and shone a light in my eyes as another woman tried to coax me to lie down.

Alice...

Clara's voice called to me. The sound was terrifying. Fighting against the darkness that sought to suck me under, I tried to hold onto the pain in my shoulder but the world slipped through my fingers like grains of sand in an hourglass.

My sister was gone. She couldn't be calling me. She wasn't here...

Alice, where are you?

I fell into the darkness, the cold cocooning me against the pain.

There you are...

Her cold lips pressed against my cheek and then there was nothing.

9

August 24th 1996

IT'S STRANGE. Life, I mean. Never turns out how you want it to. Best laid plans and all that. Or maybe it's just me. Perhaps my luck is fucked.

I'm not very good at the whole making plans thing anyway. Every time I do, every time I think I have every possibility nailed down tight, something else comes along to screw it all up.

I'm not supposed to be seventeen and pregnant. I had plans, a life all mapped out for myself. I was going to get out of here, escape this place and live a life unfettered by the bullshit-small-mindedness of the back-end-of-nowhere-ville.

I'd go to college, study social work. I love the idea of working with kids, pulling them out of desperate situations, setting them on a better path. Watched a program on telly, a Prime Time special on the issues facing youngsters. And before the baby, I was going to help them change their lives, make sure they got a good education, found a family that loved them.

I'm one of the lucky ones. Mam and Dad are a little bit fuddy-duddy about things but they love Ali and me. We don't always have the latest gadgets but that's not really the point of family. We're happy.

And then I met Liam. Our fathers have been friends for donkey's years and the last time I saw him he'd been gangly, all legs and arms, made me think of the Daddy Long Legs that throw themselves at the kitchen windows during the summer nights.

We don't move in the same social circles. He goes to the private school, Rockwell college, super elite. Just stepping inside the door of that place costs an arm and a leg, or at least that's what Dad reckons. I tried for the scholarship but missed it by a couple of points. Irish isn't exactly my strongest subject. Not that I really care.

The convent is grand. The nuns are strict. I'm pretty sure a few of them are actually mad. Not that I blame them. If I had to live their lives, I'd go mad too.

Honestly thought, they scare the crap out of me. Alice isn't afraid of them the same way I am, it's something I've always envied about her. The ability to just switch off, ignore anyone who doesn't measure up to whatever daydream she's currently concocting.

She doesn't like Liam. Which might be funny if Mam and Dad didn't use her as the third wheel to chaperone every goddamn date we go on.

Sometimes, I wonder if maybe it was all Mam and Dad's doing, if they tipped her off to get in the way as much as possible. Or maybe she has a sixth sense for it all, popping up whenever Liam and I were got close. The prerogative of the pain in the arse little sister...

Of course part of me wishes now that I hadn't tried so hard to slip away. That I'd listened to the voice in the back of my mind that whispered it was all too good to be true. And maybe if I had, it would be different now.

I've tried to regret getting pregnant... Tried to regret the moments leading up to this but I can't do it. I don't know if I'll be a good mother. I can't help but feel I'm still too much of a child myself to look after a baby but it's not like I have a choice now.

But then that's life for you... Never is how you expect it to be. Sure, I thought I loved Liam, thought we'd be together through this... Thought he loved me.

It's a bitter pill to swallow but people make mistakes all the time. And while I can't regret this baby, I can regret giving Liam the chance to hurt me.

I was wrong to trust him. He's not one of the good guys. And the second I get a chance to get out of here, I'm gone. I don't care what he thinks, or what he does...

I owe him nothing

10

WAKING up in the hospital is not as peaceful or calm as they pretend it is in books or movies. I didn't open my eyes, see nothing but white, and wonder if I was in heaven.

It started with the sheet underneath me, digging into my lower back because there was a gather in the material. The back of my hand begged to be scratched. When I opened my eyes, I stared up at the large off-white tiles on the ceiling. The one directly over my head had the yellow and brown tidemarks that came from a leak long-since dealt with.

A metal trolley crashed in the hall outside my room and my heartbeat picked up speed, despite the painkillers coursing in my veins, making my head feel like it was stuffed with sawdust.

I started to lift my arm and pain exploded through my right shoulder blade, splintering so that it spread its fiery ache across my back and down my arm simultaneously.

"Shit!" I swore emphatically, my voice barely recognisable, sounding much more like it belonged to an old farmer with a forty cigs a day habit.

The blue and orange geometrically-patterned curtains around the bed were closed but as I lay there and stared up at the stained ceiling tile, I became acutely aware of the presence of other people on the ward with me. The sound of heart monitors and the whispered murmurings of the patients as they spoke to each other, or maybe their relatives slowly came into focus. As did the memory of how I'd ended up here.

Braving the pain, I lifted my arm once more. This time it was a little better; still painful but more manageable.

It surprised me that I'd been shot. Dan had been aiming at Zoe and I was almost certain I hadn't reached her in time. Had he changed his mind at the last moment and shot me instead? Or had I moved faster than I'd realised? Everyone knew about those cases where distraught mothers lifted cars off their children in order to free them. Zoe wasn't my child but I did care about her.

"Alice." Gerald poked his head around the edge of the curtain, the relief on his face palpable as he realised I was awake.

Speak of the devil. My granny's favourite saying popped into my head unbidden and I stifled a giggle.

"Christ, Alice," he said, pushing open the curtains and stepping inside. "When I was back at the house and I heard the gunshots, I was so worried he was going to come back to the house and—"

Typical of Gerald to think of himself.

"Officer Shaw?" The question in my voice was implicit and the moment I said her name aloud I could see a mental image of her lying on the ground, legs bent behind her crumpled body. Blood pooling underneath—

"They discharged her a few hours after admitting her," he said. "Bloody lucky she was wearing a vest. She's got some bruising and they treated her for shock but..."

Relief shot through me and I pushed the vision of her, dead, from my mind. She was fine. The shock had added details that weren't really there at all.

"Zoe," I said, pausing to clear my voice. "How is she?"

"She's fine," he said, laughing. The sound grated on me. "You know kids these days, they can bounce back from anything."

"Most kids don't have a father who tried to kill them and then had to watch him blow his brains out." My voice was harsh, harsher than I'd intended and Gerald's expression faltered.

"Christ, yeah, I know but..." he shrugged. "She seems fine. Police have spoken to her and everything.

We've agreed that she's probably blocking out a lot of the trauma."

"We?"

A sour note rose in my throat.

"Me and Jennifer," he said.

It always grated on me that he couldn't just say, 'Jennifer and me,' that he always had to put it back to front. Not that it really mattered but years of having it drilled into my head in school tended to make me pedantic about the matter. It helped that at the best of times, Gerald wasn't my favourite person in the world, Jennifer even less so.

"So you've replaced me," I said. The bitterness I was feeling fed into my words.

"I had to," he said. "You were shot. It's not like you can just hop out of the bed and— Alice what are you doing?"

As he spoke I sat up in the bed and flipped back the covers. The pain in my shoulder was almost unbearable. Tears blurred my vision as I picked at the large clear sticky plaster holding the cannula in the back of my hand.

"I'm coming back to work," I said through gritted teeth, managing to pull up an edge of the plaster. "I don't like hospitals and I'm fine anyway..." I was babbling, I thought, and cut myself off abruptly.

I tore away the rest of the plaster and the plastic tube of the cannula that sat in my vein moved, sending a weird spasm up through my arm.

"Alice," he said gently, "you're not coming back to work. You're in no fit state."

"I'm fine," I insisted, pulling the cannula free. It didn't hurt; the deep throbbing ache in my shoulder blotted it out.

"You watched a man die."

"I didn't watch him die," I said, my mind instantly replaying the sound of the shot as it rang in the early morning air. It was enough to bring a picture of Dan on the ground, eyes staring at the sky...

I shoved it away violently.

"Alice." Gerald's tone was sharp and I jerked, suddenly noticing that he'd crept closer so that now he was standing directly in front of me.

"Alice, your hand." He gestured toward the bed and I sluggishly followed his gaze down to where my hand sat against the brilliant white sheet. Not that it was white anymore. My blood was pooling between my fingers, still trickling out from the puncture wound left behind by the cannula.

"Shit," I swore emphatically and reached for the box of tissues on the bedside locker, momentarily forgetting about my arm. The second I reached for the box, pain lanced through my body, making me feel like I'd been shot all over again. Sound formed in the back of my throat but so intense was the pain that it stole every last ounce of air, leaving me with nothing to vocalise with. Sweat beaded on my forehead and my arm dropped back to my side.

"Christ," he said. "See, you're not fit to come back to work. You need to take some time to recover, get your head on straight. You're white as a sheet." He peered down at me curiously. "Do you want me to call a nurse?"

I tried to shake my head but even that was too much.

"I'm going to call a nurse and we're not going to talk about you coming back to work until you're good and ready."

He disappeared out behind the curtains, giving me a chance to draw a shaky breath in through my nose. The pain was slowly subsiding. Definitely not how they did it in the movies, I thought to myself. The hero, if he was shot, would be back on his feet in no time, capable of chasing down the bad guys and charming the heroine into his bed. There was never a scene with him sitting on the side of the bed, on the verge of vomiting because he'd reached a little too quickly for a box of tissues.

The thought drew a laugh from me that sounded suspiciously like it bordered on hysteria.

I couldn't let Gerald take my work away from me. It mattered too much to me. It was the one thing helping me get out of bed every morning. Without it...

A moment later Gerald appeared with a nurse in tow.

"You shouldn't be out of bed," she said, her Scottish accent instantly distinctive as she grabbed the cannula

I'd discarded on the bed. She tutted as she noted the pool of blood and the damp patch left on the sheets from where the cannula and I had both leaked.

Gerald grinned at me. "Must make you feel like it's home," he said cheerfully.

I stared uncomprehendingly at him.

"Tracy, here," he said nodding in the direction of the nurse. "Her accent. She's from Ireland too."

Tracy paused for a moment, her eyes finding mine. We exchanged a look, a moment of solidarity.

"Scotland," she corrected, her smile never faltering.

"Po-tay-to, Po-tah-to." Gerald laughed. "I'm not very good with accents," he said, as though that excused how rude he'd been.

Tracy nodded, her smile fixed in place but I could see the slight flinching around the corners of her eyes. "If you don't mind now," she said, "Alice, here, needs her rest."

"Of course," Gerald said magnanimously. "Tracy is right." He addressed me as though I were a small child. "You do everything she says. We need you better."

He headed for the curtain and lifted it aside, revealing the bustling ward beyond.

"Don't even worry," he said over his shoulder. "We'll take good care of Zoe and the rest of your cases. Jennifer is more than happy to take on the extra workload. I don't know where she gets all the energy from."

Anger bubbled in my veins. He knew I didn't get along with Jennifer, knew the relationship between us at the best of times was strained so why did it feel like he was rubbing my nose in it? Was I being too sensitive, paranoid even?

"I'll come visit soon."

Before I could say anything else, he left, letting the curtain drop back into place behind him.

"He seems pleasant enough..." Tracy said. I nodded and smiled but ultimately zoned out as she helped me back into bed, fixing my drip before she did my obs. My heart rate was elevated and my temperature was up.

Her level gaze met mine. "How's the pain?"

"Fine." I bit the word out. The pain was excruciating but I wasn't going to get out of hospital fast if I admitted to it.

"Look," she said, "if you need pain-relief, just say. There's no shame in asking for help when you need it. You're just stressing your body out unnecessarily."

"When can I leave?"

She laughed, a happy sound that made me like her all the more. "You've only just woken up. Doctor'll be around in the morning, he'll decide then."

I couldn't hide the disappointment from my face and she sighed. "Look, you're not going anywhere for tonight so you may as well take advantage of it. Take the pain-relief when you need it and reassess in the morning. You never know, you could be feeling a lot better."

I nodded reluctantly. I didn't want any more

painkillers; my brain was already foggy enough. But want and need didn't always make for amicable bedfellows.

"Good." She straightened up. "How about something to eat?"

I contemplated it but the nausea I was feeling was still a little too strong so I shook my head. "I think maybe some sleep instead," I said.

She gave me a sympathetic smile and then slipped out between the curtains, returning a moment later with a tiny paper tub with two pink tablets sitting at the bottom of it. She poured me a glass of water, filling the little plastic tumbler on my bedside locker before handing me the tablets to take.

Tracy watched me knock them back, making me think of another case involving a teenage boy. He had to be watched every time they gave him his medication, just to make sure he really was taking it and not holding onto it. Hoarding it so he could take an overdose.

I gave her a grateful smile when she took the glass from my shaking fingers and set it on the locker.

"The button's there if the pain gets worse or you don't feel right," she said. "Otherwise, Pamela'll be around to do your obs."

She disappeared out through the curtain and I let her go as I lay back against the pillows and waited for the medication to kick in. The moment I closed my eyes, I could see Dan's wide staring eyes and the dark stain across the soft play area, created by things that should never have been outside his skull. I didn't want to go to sleep with that in the forefront of my mind but the more I tried to fight the exhaustion, the stronger its hold on me became.

Until, finally, I slipped into a fitful sleep, my dreams a strange combination of Dan's dead eyes and Clara calling me.

Begging for help.

11

HER SKIN IS SOFT. Almost baby soft. Supple and so inviting. The invisible downy hairs on her cheeks tickle my fingers. With her eyes closed like this, I can almost imagine she's sleeping.

In a way, she is.

It's not a natural sleep, not the kind you have when you climb into bed at night and close your eyes. Pray the nightmares stay away. Just one night. Just one night free. Is it too much to ask?

It always is.

I trace the outline of purple carelessly splashed against the porcelain skin of her neck.

Why does she make it so damn hard?

I contemplate curling my fingers around her throat, splaying my fingers against that soft flesh.

With my eyes closed, I can feel her flesh give way

beneath my nails as I dig my fingers into her, gouging, tearing.

Staring down at her. I blink. The only mark marring the smooth perfection is the bruise left by rough hands.

Her eyes flutter open, the hazel so cloudy they're almost grey, confusion giving her back some of the innocence cruelly taken from her. I could wrap her in my arms, cradle her to my chest.

She focuses on my face and her jaw works, mouth shifting as she tests the strength of her gag. Muffled sounds gurgle in the back of her throat. Tears spill over tawny lashes, making me think of the blocked drain from last week.

She blinks, an attempt to clear her vision, I'm sure. Her lashes clump like the thick legs of a house spider. I could pluck them out, one by one. What would it feel like? My fingers pinch together, nails like the tip of a pair of tweezers as I grab a clump of lashes.

Her head jerks back, eyes widening further, tears coming faster. I stare at my empty fingers, too blunt, too clumsy to be suitable for the job. Next time, real tweezers. I pat her cheek, feeling her flinch beneath my touch, my stomach clenches in anticipation.

In her eyes a silent plea. It's always the same.

It starts with why and as the days whittle away it changes, morphs into something else...

End it.

"Not yet..." I whisper, pressing my lips to her cool

forehead. She tries to shy away but my hand curls around her throat once more, pinning her in place.

Taking the small brush from the yellowed bed sheet, I dip it into the powdered blush and spread it liberally across her cheek.

"But soon enough."

12

THE DOCTOR DISCHARGED me the following morning. Not that he really had a choice. He had to either agree to let me go or face the consequences of me discharging myself.

The public bathroom that sat inside the entrance to the hospital smelled strongly of disinfectant and the stronger, more acrid, scent of urine and something unmentionable. There was only so much bleach could do for such high traffic areas like this. Over time, the smell became ingrained in the places between the tiles, seeping into the grout and lurking within the vents that spilled warm air out over my head. Short of ripping the place down and rebuilding over it, there would be no destroying the cloying atmosphere.

I splashed water on my face with my one good hand. The other was strapped to my chest, immobilised and utterly useless. Getting dressed had been a lesson in humiliation and in the end I'd had no choice but to ask one of the care assistants on the ward for a little help.

The fluorescent light overhead flickered, the incessant hum that poured off it crawling inside my head like a fly intent on finding somewhere suitable to lay its eggs. My eyes were sunken, the black bags beneath them ageing me. I hadn't slept. Not a true sleep anyway. The painkillers didn't agree with me and had caused nothing but nightmares and waking terrors but without them, the pain was unbearable.

Caught between the devil and the deep blue sea.

That had been last night. Now, a prescription sat in my handbag balanced on the edge of the sink and I'd sworn when the nurse had bagged it up for me that I wouldn't take another one, no matter how intense the pain became.

I hadn't even left the hospital yet and I was already beginning to regret that promise. Picking my handbag up from the sink, I headed for the door.

Gerald stood outside the main doors waiting for me, trying to smoke his cigarette as inconspicuously as he could. Unfortunately, there had been no one else I could call to come and pick me up. I had no family here and no friends to speak of. He was the only one who actually knew I was in hospital.

His expression turned grim as soon as he saw me.

"Are you sure you're fit to be out?" he said, sounding somewhat irked. His question, coming from someone else, could maybe be construed as concern but not with Gerald. Clearly, the fact that I'd asked him to come and pick me up had seriously pissed him off.

"I told you," I said. "I'm fine. They wouldn't have let me out if I wasn't fit to go home."

"Did you tell them you live alone, that you've got no one waiting for you?"

I bit back a smart answer and nodded. It was a lie. I hadn't told them anything, not that he needed to know that.

"Well come on then," he said smartly. "I'm parked down here." He gestured vaguely in the direction of the road and I sighed, struggling to rearrange my handbag on my left shoulder.

We started to walk. Each step I took jarred my shoulder, sending tiny flares of white-hot pain down my arm and across my back.

"I'd have parked in the car park but it's too bloody expensive," he said. "A total rip-off. I don't know what they're playing at charging so much..." He blathered on and I let him, letting my mind wander as I traipsed after him, my gait slowing with every step that took us further and further from the hospital.

By the time we made it to his little red Ford Fiesta, cold sweat was running down my spine in rivulets and my teeth were beginning to chatter in my head.

"Are you all right?" he asked, taking in my appearance. "I think maybe you should go back and—"

"I'm fine," I snapped. His expression crumpled

immediately and I felt regret edging its way into my stomach. He was doing me a favour and here I was biting his head off.

"Christ, Alice, I'm just worried about you is all." He reached out and tucked a stray strand of my hair back from my face. The familiar gesture chased away any feelings of regret I might have felt a moment before.

I ducked away from his hand and gave him a tight smile.

"Sorry," I said. "I just really want to go home and curl up in my own bed."

"Of course." His voice was flat.

I'd insulted him, that much I was certain of. I pulled open the car door as he moved around to the driver's door and climbed inside. As gingerly as I could, I maneuvered into the passenger seat and tugged on my seat belt as he got the car started up.

He drove in silence, which for Gerald was most unusual. Under normal circumstances, I might have tried to make an effort to draw him out of the sulky mood he'd fallen into. But I was honestly too exhausted to do it.

"Ms Clayton asked for you," he said, suddenly breaking the silence that had stretched between us.

"Rachel?"

"Yeah," he said, putting on the indicators as we drove around the roundabout. "Wanted to know if you'd be coming back."

"And what did you tell her?" A bubble had formed in the centre of my chest, making my voice tight.

"I said you were taking some much needed time off," he said, casting a sideways glance in my direction. Whatever expression crossed my features he caught it and sighed. "You know you need to, Alice. I'm not sure why you keep fighting this."

"I'm not fighting it," I said. "I just don't understand why I need to take time off. I mean, fine a couple of days, but..."

Even I couldn't argue with needing a few days off. I could barely dress myself. I was hardly in a position to spend the day going from house to house, residential home to residential home, while also tending to the daily necessities of my caseload. Not to mention the fact that I was right-handed, which meant writing and note taking was pretty much out of the question. At least until I could figure out a workaround.

He gave me an incredulous look. "A couple of days isn't going to cut it and you know that. Deep down at least."

"But my cases—"

"There'll be new cases."

I froze. I felt like I had a huge block of ice sitting in my chest.

"What do you mean, there'll be other cases."

"Well Jennifer and I, we were talking about it and well..."

"Spit it out, Gerald."

"We were thinking, all this upheaval, it's not good for the kids so she's going to take over your caseload permanently."

"You can't do that," I said quietly.

"I don't have a choice, Alice," he said quickly. "You'll be out for months. There's physio and then there's the assessment and—"

"Wait, what?" I swivelled around in the seat, the belt catching my arm so that pain rocketed through me, squeezing tears out from beneath my lashes.

"The assessment," he said. "You're going to have to go and talk to someone before you can come back."

"That's not protocol," I said.

"No." He spoke gently, patiently. "It's not protocol but I think it'll be good for you."

"Is there something here, I'm missing?"

He sighed and parked the car across the street from my apartment.

"There have been some questions raised," he said. "Regarding the situation with Dan and Rachel and Zoe..."

"What kinds of questions?"

"We don't need to do this now, Alice, you need to rest."

"Fuck rest," I said hotly. "What questions have been raised?"

"Christ, Alice, calm down." He scrubbed his hand over his face and pinched the bridge of his nose before he continued. "Like maybe there were signs that you missed."

"Signs of what?" My voice was coming from far away, as though I'd grown detached from my own body and I was watching everything unfold from somewhere outside my physical form sitting in the passenger seat.

"The man tried to kill his wife and child," Gerald said, his voice losing the gentleness it'd had just moments before. "Shit like that doesn't just happen. There are signs and it was your job to see them."

"How could I see it when Rachel was keeping things from me?"

"Blaming others, Alice. It's not exactly admirable. You screwed up and now there's a man lying dead on a slab down in the morgue and your arm is strapped to your body because you were shot." He sighed. "Just admit you've been off your game for a while and this one slipped through the cracks."

I opened my mouth to answer him but the words wouldn't form. He was wrong, so very wrong. I hadn't missed anything. Zoe's painting of her father crying filled my head.

"I did my best," I said. "I'm not a mind reader."

He smiled at me and raw, unbridled hatred rose in my chest. I wanted to hit him, to punch him until the smile slipped from his face. Instead, I clenched my fist in my lap.

"And no one is saying you need to be," he said. "We're just worried about you is all…"

"Bullshit." I pushed open the car door and stepped out.

Gerald started to follow me but I ignored him, ignored him as he called after me, asking me not to overreact, not to be so emotional.

Of course, it was easy for him to say that. He wasn't the one being hung out to dry. It was always the same in situations like this. When the shit hit the fan, they needed a scapegoat, someone to pin it on. And apparently, I'd spun the wheel and hit the jackpot.

I fumbled in my handbag, pulling my keys free before I jabbed them in the lock and let myself into the flat, leaving Gerald outside on the road to stare after me.

13

WHEN WE GOT BACK to the Garda Station, Ronan showed me into the office I would be calling home for the duration of the case. The walls were cement blocks painted a glaring white so bright that it hurt my eyes. There was a small desk in the corner, already piled high with files and boxes. The swivel chair in front of it was old and one of the casters sat at an odd angle on the brown utilitarian carpet underfoot.

Against the back wall sat a large whiteboard. A picture of the site I'd visited just a short while ago sat in the centre, with the date the site had been discovered written underneath in neat script.

"It's not what you're used to," he said. "But it's all you're going to get here."

"It's fine," I said, eyeing the chair distrustfully. It spoke volumes about their feelings on having me here. A less paranoid person might have assumed it was representative of the lack of funding in the areas outside the capital but I'd noted the sideways glances as I'd trailed through the station after Ronan. There wasn't one person out there who looked happy to have me here.

I could suddenly understand why my predecessor had been so quick to jump at a chance of moving to Limerick, one step closer to returning to Dublin.

"Who else is working the case?"

"Everyone is," he said. "We all chip in around here. Especially on something like this."

"Aren't there other cases that need attention?"

He started to laugh and then noting the look of confusion on my face cut off abruptly. "Shit, you're serious…"

"Are there no other crimes to investigate?" I raised a questioning eyebrow in his direction.

"Course there are other cases," he said. "But come on, this is a biggie. Murder trumps everything else so everyone takes a crack at it."

I shook my head. "I appreciate that everyone wants to assist but I think it would be better if we had a defined team. That way, nothing gets overlooked or mislaid."

I tried to say it in the most diplomatic way I could but my anger was beginning to spill into my words. I couldn't help it. So far, everything was a giant cluster-fuck of epic proportions. If it turned out just like the last time I'd been put in a position of trust, then I could kiss goodbye to ever having a solid career.

He sighed. "Fine. You've got me and—" he said. I tried to keep my expression neutral. I hadn't seen him in action and my parents had always said you shouldn't judge a book by its cover. Even if that cover seemed to indicate the contents were nothing but a shallow imitation of a classic.

He poked his head out of the door. "Claire!" His shout rang out through the Garda Station and a couple of seconds later a tall, lean young woman appeared in the doorway. Her navy blue uniform made her instantly recognisable as one of the Guards.

"Yeah?"

"You've been assigned to the murder enquiry," he said.

"But I've got—"

"Pass it to someone else," he said. "You're on this full-time now. And it's, 'yes, sir.'" He turned away from her and I watched as something akin to anger flickered in her eyes.

"Yes, sir." She gritted the words out and started to leave when I spoke up.

"I'm Detective Siobhan Geraghty," I said, holding my hand out toward her.

"Garda Claire Mulcahy." She took my hand in a grip that was firmer than some male Guards I'd met over the years.

"I'm looking forward to working with you," I said.

"Pity it's not under better circumstances."

I nodded thoughtfully and let her go. She hurried from the room, leaving me alone with Ronan once more.

"That's all you're going to get as a team," he said. "The place here isn't big enough to solely dedicate anymore to it. The others will chip in as they can."

I didn't say anything else. There was no point. I knew I was lucky to get what I'd already been given. Of course, if the case grew, then I would get more resources but not until then and the more I thought about it, the more I couldn't shake the feeling that the recently missing girl and the body were somehow linked.

Crossing the room, I pulled the lid off the box closest to me. "What are these?"

"Everything we have from the original investigations into missing persons from the area," he said, moving up next to me. "These were the interviews, not that much came out of them..." He paused and I could tell there was something he wanted to say to me but he was holding back.

"What is it?"

"They made a bit of a balls out of it to be honest," he said. "Initially anyway."

I cocked an eyebrow at him. "Go on."

"Well, from the preliminary ID of the body, we think it's this girl here," he said, pulling a thick case file across the desk toward us. From inside it, he fished out a picture of a smiling young woman with striking blue eyes and sandy coloured hair. Her eyes were alight with laughter and she appeared to be grinning at someone just out of view of the camera.

"Clara McCarthy," he said. "She went missing Friday the 18th of October, 1996. Or at least that's what her sister alleges."

Something clicked in the back of my mind. "Her sister said they were walking home after a disco when Clara was taken," I said. "She was already gone three months before it hit any of the papers..."

He nodded, looking somewhat chagrined. "That's what I mean about the screw up," he said. "Initially they believed she'd run away."

"Why would they assume that?" I had a sick feeling in the pit of my stomach as I stared down at the smiling girl in the image.

"She was pregnant and people in the area were cruel," he said. "A few of the locals were interviewed at the time of the disappearance, you know to see if they could make any connection between the sister's story and Clara's disappearance, but they were all of the same mind."

I waited for him to continue and when he didn't, I turned on him. "Just spit it out already."

"There was talk of her going off to get an abortion," he said. "A friend of hers said she'd mentioned it and, well, she'd been forced to drop out of school and..."

"Why would she have to drop out of school?"

He stared at me for a moment and I had the distinct impression that he was checking to see if I was being serious with my question or not.

"Times have changed round here," he said. "There's not the same kind of stigma attached to a young seventeen year old turning up pregnant, at least not the way there was back then..."

"You're telling me she dropped out because she was forced out?"

He nodded. "She was attending the convent at the time. It's gone now, closed down a few years back, but I heard some of the stories out of that place and it would put the hairs on your head standing."

"They wouldn't let her go to school? Wasn't that a crime?"

He shrugged. "People think Ireland back then was really different to how it was fifty years ago but the church still had a hold on the local communities. And if they didn't want you, then you were out..."

"But she was a local herself right? I'd have thought they'd have looked after their own."

"But they weren't really locals," he said. "The mother's family came from the area but not the father's. They moved into their current home when Clara was ten."

"So she'd been there seven years and you're telling me she wasn't considered a local?"

He shook his head. "Round here, if you're not born and bred in the area then you're an outsider, no matter how long you've lived here. It's messed up but it is what it is."

I stared back down at the picture of the missing girl. How could they have been so cruel? So completely callous?

"So what have they got that suggests the body and this girl," I said gesturing to the picture once more, "are one and the same?"

"The clothes match and there was a single piece of jewellery recovered from the body that matches what the sister says she was wearing the night she disappeared."

Pursing my lips, I nodded as I sifted through the papers. I scanned the pages quickly. From the looks of things, the witness statements weren't much to go on.

"What changed everyone's mind?" I asked, suddenly.

"What?"

"Why did they change their minds about her disappearance? You said they thought she'd run off but something must have changed their minds."

He grabbed another box and tugged the lid off, pulling out another file that was much thicker than the one on Clara McCarthy. "This girl went missing only three weeks later," he said, flipping it open and pulling another photograph out. "On the 9th of November."

My heart stalled in my chest as I stared down at the photo, there was no denying the striking resemblance between Clara and this new girl.

"Was it a Friday too?"

He shook his head and glanced down at the notes. "No, it was a Saturday evening. She was last seen at the cinema in Waterford."

"That still doesn't explain how they linked the cases."

Ronan looked down at the file and I could tell he was avoiding meeting my gaze.

"Well they didn't," he said. "Clara's sister went to the papers when the third girl went missing. She forced the hand of the Gardaí at the time and they noticed some similarities between the cases. By that time, Clara's trail was well and truly cold."

"Christ," I said, staring at the picture of the two girls side by side. "Do you have a picture of the third girl?"

He nodded and took it from another thick file. I picked the pictures up and carried them over to the board, hanging them up one by one until all three girls stared down at us. There was no denying the similarities between the first two girls but the third looked nothing like Clara.

"We're missing something," I said, staring up at the photographs.

"What?"

I shrugged. "I don't know what it is yet but I know there's a bigger picture at play here. Wait, do you have a photo of the girl that recently disappeared?"

"I told you they're not connected. Her boyfriend—"

"Humour me."

Ronan sighed and headed for the door. I continued to stare up at the photographs, wishing the girls could spill their secrets.

He reappeared a moment later, carrying a photograph in his hands.

"Hang it up next to the third girl," I said.

Silently, he did as I'd asked and as he stepped away from the board, I felt my stomach drop into my boots.

Ronan sucked the air in through his teeth, emitting a harsh whistle of sound, his eyes trained on the board.

"Do you still think they're not linked?"

The third girl with her dark eyes and serious expression stared out at me and from the new picture Ronan had hung on the board, a fourth girl, practically a carbon copy of the third, watched us with a dark, almost accusatory stare.

"The sergeant isn't going to like this," he said, quietly. "The boyfriend is a solid suspect."

I said nothing but I could feel it in my gut, the cases were linked. The more, I stared at the images on the board, the more convinced I became.

"We need to look for others," I said, "and it's going to take more than the three of us working this to get to the bottom of it."

"What are you saying?"

"I'm not saying anything, yet," I said. I wasn't a fool. Committing to something without the proof or evidence to back it up was tantamount to career suicide but the more I stared at the board, the more certain I became. There was a serial killer at work and I had a feeling that before we would finish, there would be a lot more than four faces staring out at us from the board.

14

September 4th 1996

I WISH I was better at keeping this diary. I've always been shit at writing my thoughts down but I've got to get this out of my head.

Ever since Liam found out I was pregnant he's been acting weird. We've broken up more times than I can count. I don't want to feel like this anymore, I'm so tired of him making me feel like I'm this massive burden to him.

It's like he forgets there was two of us involved. Like I did this on purpose to ruin his life when that couldn't be further from the truth.

He told me he's been seeing another girl from Rockwell. I wanted to laugh in his face, tell him he was welcome to whoever he wanted but his father came along before I could say anything. And Daddy dearest has certainly changed his tune on our relationship since they found out I was pregnant. He told me Liam needs to broaden his horizons.

"Liam needs to sow his wild oats, Clara. He's got his whole life ahead of him. I don't want him getting tied down by fatherhood too soon."

I wanted to scream at him, what about my life but he didn't care. He thinks I'm just a millstone round his son's neck. Maybe that's all I am?

Liam said he'd drive me home and I told him I didn't need anything from him, that I'd manage just fine on my own.

I started the walk home and he came after me. Trailing me in his Dad's van, begging me to get in. I told him to shove it and he got so mad. I've never seen him so angry. He frightened me if I'm honest and my arm hurts where he grabbed it.

I can't let Mam or Dad see the marks his fingers made or they're going to hit the roof. But all I want to do is cry, to tell them the truth and let them sort it out for me... But I've hurt them enough and it's time I stood on my own two feet. I got myself in this mess, I can get myself... and the baby... out of it all.

Alice almost caught me today. I swear she knows more than she lets on, like she can see through the lies. I want to talk to her, to tell her truth but I can't. She's too young to understand. She still has this naive view on relationships. She seems to think that Liam and I will get married and we'll all live happily ever after. It's so daft it's almost laughable. But I wish it were true...

I've started looking at courses I can do at night. Mam said she'll help me with the baby, give me a chance to go back and try for my Leaving Cert and I really want to. I don't want this to be my life. I want more. I need to be more for this baby.

I need to—

15

SITTING on the edge of the sofa in my tiny ground floor one-bedroom apartment, I tried to plug my iPhone into the wall socket with one hand. I hadn't had my charger in the hospital and the phone was now as dead as a dodo.

The little battery flickered to life on the screen, bringing with it a sense of accomplishment. Weariness fought to keep me on the comfortable couch cushions but I pushed onto my feet and headed into the small kitchenette to flick on the kettle.

The place was freezing and I stared longingly at the thermostat as I contemplated my meagre bank account. If I couldn't work, how the hell was I supposed to pay my bills? Gerald had said there would be other cases but the feeling of unease in my gut suggested he had no intention of letting me come back.

There would be questions, an investigation. I was

the caseworker in charge. It wouldn't matter that I'd done my best, nor that I'd genuinely wanted to help Rachel and Zoe. All they would see was that I'd allowed a precarious situation to spiral dangerously out of control. That I'd missed something in regard to Dan and a life had been lost.

The doorbell rang, the shrill sound echoing through the apartment so loudly I jumped. The kettle started to boil as I headed for the door. Tugging it open, I met the steady gaze of the man and woman on the doorstep. They were neatly turned out, him in a suit and striped tie, she in a pants suit with a cream coloured blouse. They regarded me coolly and I knew instantly they were police. I'd worked with enough of them through the years to recognise them on sight.

However, what I hadn't expected was for two of them to appear on my doorstep.

"Ms McCarthy?" The woman asked, her London accent clipped and curt.

"Yeah," I said. "Can I help you?"

The male officer smiled and held out his hand toward me. Then noted the strap keeping my arm pinned to my body, chuckled, and changed hands. "Sorry to intrude."

I took his hand and we shook. "I'm DCI Radcliff and this," he said, gesturing to the woman next to him, "is DS Carter." He fished an ID from his pocket as he spoke and presented it to me for a cursory glance. "Is it all right if we come in and have a quick chat? It's in regards to the recent incident involving the Clayton's."

I'd been expecting them to show up at the hospital and ask what had happened but when no one had shown up, part of me had thought they weren't going to bother. However, now that they were standing on the doorstep, I couldn't help but feel a little uneasy, especially after the conversation I'd had with Gerald earlier.

"Sure," I said. "I've just boiled the kettle if you want a cuppa."

"No thank you," DS Carter said as she stepped through the door.

"I'd murder a tea," Radcliff said, his grey eyes twinkling as he waited for me to shut the door behind them.

I directed him into the small sitting area and he stood in front of the small window that overlooked the back garden, He shoved his hands into his pants pockets as DS Carter took a seat on the edge of a wooden chair I had in the corner of the room. She'd already taken a small notepad from her bag and from the corner of my eye, I caught her scribbling down a few notes.

I moved into the kitchen and set out another cup, grabbing two teabags from the cupboard before I poured the water in over them.

"Milk? Sugar?" I asked, drawing DCI Radcliff's attention back into the room.

"No sugar," he said with a smile. "Wife says I'm sweet enough but plenty of milk, ta."

I kept my smile fixed in place as I took the milk from the fridge and finished with the drinks. Once they were done, I stared down at the two mugs and realised I would have to make two trips.

I grabbed his first but I only made it to the edge of the kitchen counter before he intercepted me.

"Here, let me help." He reached past me and took both cups, carrying them into the living area, leaving me to trail after him.

He was being far too nice and it set my teeth on edge. It was entirely possible that he just was this nice but I'd seen enough police in action with the cases I worked to know he was fishing for an angle with me, trying to put me at ease. But why?

I sat on the sofa and watched as he took a gulp of the tea. His appreciative noises made the pain that was gathering in the back of my head worse.

"How's the arm," he asked, catching me somewhat off guard.

"Painful," I said. "Worse than I thought it could be."

"Are we correct in thinking the courts appointed you to the case regarding Zoe's welfare?" DS Carter asked.

"Yes," I said. "Dan had a history of drug abuse." I kept the part to myself where it was also suspected that he was a domestic abuser. Rachel had never made a formal complaint against him and without it, my saying it, was nothing but hearsay.

"Officer Shaw said you were under the impression that Ms Clayton and her partner were separated and that you were unaware of their reconciliation." DS Carter stared at me expectantly.

I took a mouthful of the scalding tea. The burning sensation as it travelled down my throat was soothing in a perverse kind of way.

"Ms Clayton only disclosed to me the morning of the incident that she had been allowing him access to Zoe outside of the supervised visitations."

'Isn't that your job though?" DS Carter said. "To know what's happening? To foresee potential issues and report them to your supervisor before it gets any further?"

"Well, I suppose but—"

"And isn't it true that you didn't make any such disclosures to your supervisor, a..." She consulted her notepad. "Mr Gerald Wilson?"

"There wasn't anything to disclose," I said. "I'm not a mind-reader. Rachel didn't tell me anything so how the hell was I supposed to know?"

DS Carter scribbled something in her notepad.

"Alice, we're not trying to upset you," DCI Radcliff said. "We're just trying to get to the bottom of all of this."

"Dan Clayton was not my job," I said, the pain in my head magnified by their questions. "Zoe was and I thought I was doing my best. I tried to protect her as best I could and—"

"No one is accusing you of anything." Radcliff said, gently. "DS Carter here is just crossing all the 't's' and dotting all of our 'i's' is all."

I stared down into my cup, suddenly unwilling to meet the accusatory looks in their eyes. First Gerald and now them.

"Can you tell us in your own words what happened that morning?" Radcliff asked.

I bit my tongue, allowing the pain to clear my head.

"Well I got the call from Gerald and—" Bohemian Rhapsody cut through my sentence and I glanced over my shoulder at the phone on the kitchen counter. The vibration alert had it dancing in time to the beat.

"Do you need to get that?" Radcliff asked but I shook my head.

"No, I can leave it."

The song ended and the phone went silent once more.

"I was going to go into the office but—"

The phone started to ring once more.

"I think you should get it," he said. "It's probably someone worried about you. You did just get out of hospital."

Pushing onto my feet, I crossed the floor and stared down at the word 'Mam' flashing on the screen.

"It's my mother," I said, suddenly feeling self-conscious. "I'll tell her I'll call her back." I answered the call with my one good hand.

"Mam, I—"

"Alice?" The female voice on the other end of the line wasn't my mother's. My heart lurched in my chest.

"Yes, who's this?"

"This is Fiona Grady," she said. "With the Gardaí here in Tipperary. I'm a family liaison officer here, working with the division for—"

"Is it Mam, is she all right? - Where is she? - Is she hurt?" I cut across her. I couldn't get my questions out fast enough.

"Your mother is fine, Alice. She's here with me. She's just a little upset and wanted me to call on her behalf."

Dread coiled in my stomach and my mouth went dry. I could feel the attention of the two detectives in my living room boring holes into the back of my head.

"I know this is going to come as a shock," she said, her words echoing from far away, as though it wasn't an iPhone I had pressed to my ear but a tin can with a string attached.

Her voice started to fragment. I caught the words, 'body,' and 'identification'. The phone slipped from my hand and clattered onto the Formica counter top.

I turned away and came face to face with the concerned expression of DCI Radcliff and DS Carter. My knees disappeared from beneath me and the ground rushed up towards me, only DS Carter's iron grip on my good elbow kept me from hitting the ground.

Pain screamed in my shoulder but it was suddenly overshadowed by the ache in my chest that was making it difficult for me to draw a deep breath.

There was a babbling noise and it took me a moment to realise it was coming from me.

"Who's Clara?" DS Carter asked. I'd thought she was a cold fish—she'd so obviously been playing the bad cop—but as she guided me over to the sofa, I could see softness in her expression. She pushed a strand of auburn hair behind her ear as she sat beside me.

"Clara McCarthy," I said dumbly.

"Why is that familiar?" DS Carter's question was directed toward Radcliff, who stood at the kitchen counter with my iPhone pressed to his ear, his expression grim as he nodded and spoke in hushed tones to the woman on the other end of the line.

What had she said her name was? I couldn't remember.

It felt like my brain had gone into complete shut down, a protective mechanism after experiencing a shock.

Knowing why I was behaving the way I was didn't make it any easier to deal with.

"Alice, can you hear me?" It took me a moment to register that Radcliff was crouched in front of me, the phone no longer in his hands.

I nodded, unwilling to speak. The incomprehensible ramblings that were swirling in my head didn't need to be vocalised.

"I've spoken to the liaison officer and she thinks it's best if you return to Ireland. I've explained the situation here and they've asked us to drop you off at the airport. Everything else will be arranged from their end."

"Clara," I said again. It felt strange to say her name aloud after all this time. I hadn't told anyone here about her, or her disappearance.

He nodded. "Do you understand what Ms Grady said to you?"

"They found her body," I said, my voice reedy.

"They've found *a* body," he corrected, "but the preliminary identification suggests it's the body of your sister. Clara."

I shot up onto my feet. My sudden movement knocked Radcliff and he hit the carpet with a soft grunt of surprise. Under normal circumstances, I might have found it funny but right now all I could think about was getting to Ireland.

"I need to see her," I said, almost tripping over the rumpled edge of the carpet as I darted for the front door.

DS Carter was there before me. The sympathy reflected in her eyes brought anger rushing to the surface.

"We'll get you to the airport," she said. "You should

pack some things first." When I stared at her uncomprehendingly, she continued. "To take with you. You'll need clothes and some toiletries."

Her words finally reached some part of me that could understand what she was saying and I turned toward the bedroom, my mind in full autopilot as I dragged a hold all out from under my bed and began piling clothes inside.

As I grabbed my toothbrush and other toiletries from the bathroom, my mind kept going back to the night Clara had gone missing. Even now, as I stared down at my fingers, I could still feel the brush of her hand in mine as she slipped away from me and I'd kept running, not looking back.

I'd let her go and now there was a body sitting in the morgue in Ireland. It couldn't be her... Wouldn't be her.

I'd let her go once. I wouldn't do it a second time.

16

THE PLANE RIDE OVER HAD BEEN the usual affair. The only discernible difference between this flight and any one of the other hundreds I'd taken home was that this time I'd ordered myself a whiskey. And then another. And another.

By the time we'd landed I was nicely cocooned in inebriation. The man who met me in the terminal, who'd said he was from the liaison team, had to steer me by the elbow to the car, just to keep me moving forward.

Thankfully, I slept for most of the two and half hour car drive. By the time we pulled up outside the house, the whiskey was wearing off, leaving me to feel like I had invited a Mariachi band to take up residence inside my skull. The wash of cold air over my face as I pushed open the car door did nothing to quell the wave of nausea that swept over me.

I stood on the tarmac outside the two-storey white house that had been my childhood home. The small windows, that only a couple years before had gotten a facelift in the form of brand new white uPVC, sat like tiny eyes in the face of a spider squatting in the centre of its web. The glass reflected nothing of the interior. It reminded me of my parents and their desire to keep family business behind locked doors. I could see the sky stretching away above us, as grey in its reflection on the surface of the window as it was in reality.

The front door was open and what had once been a welcoming warmth that beckoned me inside during my childhood now threatened to smother me.

There was a car on the drive that I didn't recognise and the thought of setting foot in the house when it was full of strangers filled me with dread. I didn't want to see anyone. I just wanted to go in, wash my face off with cold water, and take the codeine tablets that were burning a hole in the pocket of my jacket.

My head and arm had joined forces against me. The pain in both had grown to a fever pitch, so much so that I couldn't tell anymore if the whiskey had soured my stomach or if it was the pain seeking to claw its way out.

The wind carried with it the promise of rain and instead of heading into the house, I followed the path that led up the side toward the sloped lawn at the side of the house. Our tyre swing still hung from the old oak tree in the corner of the lawn and it was there my legs carried me, as though they had a will of their own.

I ran my fingers over the frayed rope and down over the tyre, the weather worn rubber blackening my fingers. Part of me had believed the memory of Clara might be clearer here. That if I stood and pressed my fingers against the swing, I might suddenly have a clear vision of her. But I didn't.

Of course, if I closed my eyes I could still see the terror in her eyes from that night. That had never left me, probably never would, but she had been so much more than that one memory.

Funny, and clever, she could make a game out of anything. She'd always had time for me. We'd shared secrets, and dreams and yet... My mind refused to conjure even one of those memories from the depths. Instead, it replayed that night over and over as if by reliving it, I could somehow change the outcome.

"Alice?" The male voice cut through my thoughts and I turned to find myself staring at Liam Donnelly, Clara's boyfriend from all those years ago. "Jesus," he said, shoving his hand up into what had been a crop of dark curly hair but was now streaked with grey. "It's been a while."

"Why are you here?" There was venom in my voice and it surprised me. I'd always kept my feelings tightly under wraps where Liam was concerned. Perhaps it was the whiskey or maybe—like the body they'd found—my feelings refused to stay buried.

He took a step back as though I'd physically hit him. His shoulders hunched and he wrapped his arms around his body. And suddenly he looked just like he had all those years ago, the same awkward teenager who'd turned up on our doorstep three days after Clara had gone missing. Eyes red-rimmed and haunted, nose running, and hair greasy. Stinking of B.O.

"I came 'cos I heard they found a—" his voice broke off and he swallowed hard, making me think the word 'body' was somehow trapped in the back of his throat.

"What, and your guilt dragged you over here?"

"I know what you must think of me..."

"Do you?" The words were heavily laced with sarcasm, the anger I'd been holding onto spilling over into my voice. "What did you argue about that night, Liam? What was so terrible that you could let her go off on her own, to walk home in the dark?"

"This was a mistake," he said, turning away.

He made it two feet before he stopped and whirled to back to me, his face a furious mask. "You can blame me all you like but I wasn't the reason she was out that night."

"What's that supposed to mean?" The words came out in on a strangled whisper.

"She wasn't feeling well. She didn't even want to go out but you did." He jabbed his finger toward me accusatorially. "Little Alice couldn't stay in," he said. "Oh no, you just had to go to that bloody disco. You had to go to that bloody disco and get pissed out of your mind." He leaned in toward me and sniffed the air. "Clearly, time has passed but you haven't changed a bit. I could smell the booze on you from the moment you arrived."

"I wasn't. I'm not—"

He laughed, a bitter sound that tore out of the back of his throat. "If you want to blame me, Alice, then fine. Go right ahead. It's nothing I haven't done myself. But I wasn't the one who ran away and left her behind. I wasn't the one who let her go."

With that, he stalked away, his long strides eating up the lawn, taking him down to the tarmac and out of the driveway. As though all the air had been knocked out of me, I took a stumbling step backward, my feet tangling with each another before they dumped me on the lawn with a dull thud.

I sat there, the cold damp earth soaking up through my jeans. He was right, of course. I was the reason she was out at all. The annoying younger sister in need of supervision. As though hitting the grass had jolted the memories loose, I could suddenly remember Clara's grimace as Mam had insisted she go with me.

"SHE'S TOO *young to go herself, Clara.*"

"*Mam, I don't feel good, my feet are killing me and my ankles are—*"

"We don't ask you to do much around here," Mam said. "So for once just do as you're bloody well asked."

"Please?" I batted my lashes and did my best to look adorable, which at thirteen, in that awkward place between childhood and becoming a woman, wasn't exactly easy.

"Fine." Clara sighed. "But you owe me."

"Yes!" I pumped my fists in the air before I turned and darted for the stairs.

"ALICE!" My aunt's voice cut through the memory sharply and I stared up at her. Imelda's dark hair was scraped back from her face into a high ponytail. Being Mam's older sister, there was a resemblance in the two women around the eyes, something they'd gotten from my maternal grandmother but standing over me, she suddenly looked like she'd aged fifty years in the few months since I'd last seen her.

"What are you doin' sitting on the grass? Your mother's been goin' out of her mind, wonderin' where you'd gotten to."

"Sorry," I mumbled, climbing unsteadily back onto my feet. "I just needed to..." I trailed off, suddenly unsure what I was supposed to say.

"I know. It's fine," she said, her eyes misting a little. She blinked away the threatened tears and her eyes fell on my arm. "What happened you?"

"I was... uh—" I cut myself off abruptly. Now was not the time to go telling them I'd been shot. Even at the best of times, my mother wasn't overly fond of the idea of me working in the UK. She'd always complained it was too far away. Too dangerous. For the first six years when I'd moved there after college, she used to send me snippets and clippings from newspaper articles she'd read about the violent crimes in the UK. As though Ireland was so much safer and if I would only just move back, nothing bad would ever happen to me.

The irony that my sister had been abducted in the country she proclaimed to be as 'safe as houses' was not lost on me.

"Broke my arm," I said. "Slipped on the stairs at work and took a tumble."

She gave my arm an appraising glance. Either she wanted to believe me or she just wasn't that interested in the truth. She nodded. "That's terrible. Anyway, come in. Your mother is waiting for you."

Imelda patted my shoulder, sending flares of pain shooting down my spine. I was overdoing it and the pain from the wound was beginning to wear me down. I could feel it. With one last look at the tyre swing, I followed her down the lawn and over to the house.

There was no point in hiding anymore. The sooner I faced whatever lay ahead of me, the better. Putting it off wasn't going to make it any better.

Pausing at the front door, I drew in a breath and tried to mentally prepare myself for what was coming. Of course, no matter how much you try to psych yourself up, no matter how many times you run this exact same scenario over in your head, there's still nothing to prepare you for the real thing.

Nothing prepares you for the grief and the anguish.

Nothing protects you from it.

And nothing can stop it.

Some seek oblivion in the bottom of a bottle or the supposed sweet relief that some medications bring but even then, even drunk out of your mind, or drugged to the eyeballs, it steels in around you. Creeping ever closer, bringing with it razor-edged grief and the narrow blade of sorrow, ready to slip them between your ribs when you're at your most vulnerable.

Like the tides, it's inevitable, whether you wish for it or not.

Sometimes, there is no getting over something; there is only getting through it.

And for some, no matter how hard they fight, it's a battle they cannot win.

17

September 10th 1996

I WAS WONDERING when Liam would come crawling back. He brought flowers and chocolates to the hospital appointment today. The nurses all thought it was so adorable, told me how lucky I was to have such a handsome and strapping young man waiting on me hand and foot.

I wanted to scream at them all, tell them what he was really like but I kept quiet. He asked Mam if it'd be all right if he came in with me for the ultrasound instead of her and she agreed...

When he saw the screen, I swear his whole face changed. I've never seen him look so amazed, like he'd just seen the face of the Virgin Mary in his toast or something. (If Mam caught me saying that she would string me up.) I wanted to tell him to cut the crap, that I knew he was just trying to make it look good but I don't think he was screwing around. There were actual tears in his eyes and I've only ever seen Liam get emotional over Tipp losing their shot at the Sam Maguire cup.

He looked at me like I'd done something miraculous and I couldn't help but feel emotional myself.

He asked what sex the baby was and the nurse seemed a little taken aback that he didn't already know. I found out right at the start, I'd intended to tell Liam but things between us soured and it never felt like the right time to share the news that he was having a son. I guess a part of me wanted to punish him for the way he was behaving... I don't know anymore, it was probably selfish of me.

When she said it was a boy... There was a moment where I thought everything between us might change, that he might decide to get involved and then he got up and walked out, leaving me alone with the nurse and the cold jelly on my belly.

I was mortified.

He caught up to me once I finished up and I was outside waiting for Mam. He seemed genuinely sorry for walking out. He couldn't explain why he did it. I think it's because he was overwhelmed. He's still so immature and this has to be a lot for him to take in. Mam said I should cut him a little slack, that boys of eighteen are not known for their maturity...

I'm not so naive. This wasn't the life he had planned. It wasn't the life I planned but it's the one I've got. I can feel the baby kicking and I know I'll do my best by him. I already love him...

Liam, I think will take a little longer to come round to the idea. He's not the worst. I refuse to believe he's all bad. He's just misguided. And maybe if he does a little growing up, it won't be as terrible as I'd first thought? Maybe he'll at least want something to do with his son when he arrives?

I won't hold my breath but seeing his face has given me at least a little more hope than I had.

18

THE SMELL of incense overpowered me as I stepped in through the front door. I slipped my shoes off, noting the small pile of trainers and other shoes already present.

There were pictures on the wall in the hall, most of them of Clara, her smile wide and eyes bright as she posed. Out of the two of us, she had always been the photogenic one. People had told her she could have been a model, which always irritated her. She had no interest in pursuing a career in front of the camera; she wanted to help people and a career in nursing had seemed most likely, at least until she'd fallen pregnant.

As I reached the end of the hall, the pictures came to an abrupt halt, the last image one of Clara and I together, arms around each other on the last holiday we'd had up in the north with Mam and Dad. We were grinning at the camera, a moment in time captured. A frozen moment of pure happiness. There were no pictures from after the time Clara had disappeared. It was as though neither of us had ever grown past that point in our lives.

Perhaps it was just that pictures after that time would show too clearly the giant hole in our family. We were broken; an incomplete circle. Making memories to mark that was simply too painful.

I stared up at the picture of the both of us, my mind refusing to accept that I was the girl in the photograph.

"Come on in, pet," Imelda said, poking her head around the door.

I gave her a small smile and nodded. Even though it had been my home at one time, I couldn't shake the feeling that I was an outsider.

I stepped from the hall into the small kitchen. The range in the corner was throwing out the kind of heat you'd expect to find in a furnace, making the sombre atmosphere in the room all the more stifling.

Dad sat at the kitchen table. He looked smaller, almost shrunken. No more than a shade of his former self. From the moment Clara had gone missing, he'd started a decline. A slow one but still noticeable to those he shared the house with. Of course, denial could do wonders and he and my mother had clung to their hope that she was still out there, still alive. Their denial was a life raft in the ocean of reality.

Over the years, Dad's hair had gone grey but as I

watched him now, I could see that it was beginning to thin too.

An untouched cup of tea sat in front of him and a half empty bottle of whiskey with the cap still off sat next to his hand. The glass tumbler—still half full with the amber liquid—was clutched in his other hand.

He raised his eyes to mine, the whites almost entirely bloodshot.

"It can't be her, Ali," he said, the pet name he had for me constricting my chest.

I said nothing but I bent over him, wrapping him my arm around him in an awkward one-armed hug. It wasn't just his hair that was thinning. There had been a time when my father had been a great hulking figure of a man. Tall and solidly-built. Not fat, by any means. The kind of build you expect to see on someone who spends all day working in the fields. A giant of a man, strong and sure. His word was law. Perhaps he had seemed like a giant at the time because we were children. Wasn't it natural to view your parents as infallible creatures, never failing, always true?

But now...

"What are we going to do, Ali?" he whispered against my hair, clutching me to his chest. "She's broken my heart."

I kept silent. There was nothing I could say to him. His grief was his own, something only he could shoulder.

He released me almost reluctantly and I pushed

back onto my feet. "I'm going to go in and see Mam now," I said.

Dad nodded. His eyes shone with unshed tears and it hurt me to see them. I wanted to turn tail and race out of the house. I'd only ever seen my father cry once before. Twice would be too much.

Pulling away from him, I moved into the living room.

Mam sat in the corner of the living room. It was smaller than I remembered, as though the walls had closed in.

"Mam," I said, my voice quiet, the kind of voice that wouldn't be out of place in a church. "I got the first flight over."

She didn't look at me. Her eyes were fixed on some point just beyond the window.

"She's taken it quite badly." A female voice piped up from just behind me and my heart leaped into my chest. I turned and found myself face to face with the owner of the voice I'd spoken to on the phone.

Her dark chestnut coloured hair was cut short, the natural curls unruly, the kind of hairstyle that gave every appearance of looking undone but in reality took hours to achieve. Her hazel eyes were kind and she gave me a sympathetic smile.

"I'm Fiona," she said. "We spoke on the phone this morning."

"Yeah, I remember." The pity in her face rankled m. It wasn't what I needed. What I needed were answers.

"You're Alice right?"

"You found a... body?"

My words seemed to penetrate at least some of the fog surrounding my mother and she let a low moan escape her.

"Maybe we should talk about this outside," Fiona said softly. "The doctor gave her something. You know, just to keep her calm, but..."

"Fine."

I followed her from the room, back out through the kitchen. She paused next to my father and patted him on the arm. "You all right, Dennis?"

He didn't answer her, just nodded, his eyes half lidded as he stared down into the now-full glass of whiskey before him. The bottle next to his elbow was a little lighter and I had to wonder just how full it had been when he started. Not that I could blame him; there was a part of me that longed to join him, to get my own glass and fill it, and keep filling it until the amber liquid smothered the guilt that was clawing at my chest.

Fiona tugged open the backdoor and stepped out onto the steps, I went after her and we stood on the patio. It had started to mist since I'd arrived. The droplets so fine I couldn't tell them apart as they landed on my skin, coating me in a damp blanket that chilled me to my bones.

"It's so good you could get home," Fiona said. "It's

important your parents have your support at this time."

I bit my tongue but I could feel a scream swelling in my chest. She was right of course. It was *good*. Yet there was a part of me, that childish, self-centred core that kept wondering who would support me? It had always been Clara and I, together against the world. We'd supported one another and when she was taken, my stability went with her.

"Are they sure it's Clara?"

Fiona shook her head. "Not entirely. Like I said on the phone, preliminary identification suggests it's your sister but..."

"What does that mean," I said, cutting over her. "What preliminary identification? Either it's Clara or it's not..."

She gave me a grim smile, more a grimace than anything else. "Its been twenty-two years, Alice. Facial identification is out of the question."

I heard her words but my brain refused to put the pieces together. There was a part of me, a deeper, more primal part of me that understood but it kept the truth hidden, as though it understood I wasn't capable of fully hearing the truth.

"The baby..." I said. "She wouldn't be a baby now."

"They've asked if you could come down to the station later and look at some photographs."

"Photographs? Of what?"

"To help with the identification," she said. "We

have some items we need you to look at. We'd normally ask your parents but..." She trailed off.

"They wouldn't cope," I said.

She nodded. "Only if you think you can do it," she added.

"Who else can?"

Fiona shuffled awkwardly and I had my answer.

A sudden thought struck me. "What if it isn't her?"

"I don't think you need to be thinking like that," she said. "You just need to focus on the next few hours and getting through them. Looking too far ahead into the future isn't helpful."

Silence returned and I didn't try to fill it.

"I'll go and make a quick phone call," she said.

"Wait!" I called after her and Fiona paused. Her expression was friendly but I could sense she was guarded just by the way her shoulders tensed when I called after her.

I drew my breath in through my nose, my stomach rolling uncomfortably. Asking the question probably wasn't a good idea but there was a part of me that needed the answer.

"You said they'd made a preliminary identification," I said. "How do they know it's her?"

"I'm not sure—"

"Please," I said. "Just tell me how they made the preliminary identification. They must be pretty sure it's her if they sent you lot here and they want us to go and look at pictures..." A sudden sickening thought popped into my brain.

Fiona sighed and trudged back toward me. "There are certain items found with the body that indicate it's your sister," she said.

"Such as?" My stomach lurched.

"Clothes, jewellery. Most notably, a necklace."

"Heart shaped," I said almost absently as my mind took me back to that night. Clara's fingers had been wrapped around the heart shaped locket, tugging and pulling at it, a nervous gesture before we'd ever left the house. What was she nervous about?

"Yeah," Fiona said. "There's an inscription on the back but until it gets cleaned up, they can't make out what it says."

My head jerked up sharply. "An inscription?"

Fiona nodded, her intelligent gaze lazering in on my question. "Clara's locket had an inscription, didn't it?"

I shook my head. "No. I bought it for her but I didn't have enough money to get it engraved," I said. "I meant to do it. I was saving up for it but she was taken before—"

I met Fiona's gaze head on. "It's not her."

19

SITTING in one of the small interview rooms of the Garda station, I stared at the fogged glass window high up in the wall. The outline of bars could just be discerned through the patterned glass and I'd spent the last twenty minutes counting the same four bars over in my mind. It gave me something to do, something other than mull over the idea that the body they'd found couldn't possibly be Clara's after all.

The door rattled and banged open making me jump. The petite woman who entered, carrying a large green file folder, wasn't much older than I was. Late thirties at most. Her highlighted hair shimmered under the florescent lights. A blunt fringe that had grown out a little too far so that it was practically in her bright green eyes framed her angular face, softening her.

The smile that had been on her face faded, her

BILINDA P. SHEEHAN

expression morphing into something more serious but still unreadable.

"Alice McCarthy?" she asked. I knew by the tone of her voice that she already knew who I was and her question was more formality than anything else. "I'm Detective Siobhan Geraghty with the—"

"I need to see the necklace," I said, disregarding any pretense at pleasantries. Under the circumstances, I figured my rudeness could be forgiven.

"Of course," she said. "But while you're here, I was hoping I could ask you a couple of questions."

"What, you mean after twenty-two years you lot are actually interested in what I have to say?"

She smiled but it was all business and never touched her eyes.

"I can't speak for anyone else involved in the case," she said, "but I'm here from the NBCI to assist in the investigation. So if you could indulge me and tell me in your own words what you remember about that night, it would be a great help."

"We were walking home together after a disco—"

"Why were you walking home? Why not get a lift with someone?"

"We were supposed to," I said, "but in the end we decided to walk it. It wasn't that far anyway." Noting the question in her eyes, I sighed. "We'd done it before and anyway, Clara used to walk home along the road after work if she couldn't hitch a lift so it wasn't that big of a deal."

She sat across from me and flipped open the large file in her hands, peering down at reams of handwritten and typed pages. From my vantage point across the table, I tried to read what was scrawled across the pages but they were mostly illegible. Only the odd word like, 'runaway,' and 'pregnant,' jumped out at me from the pages.

"Who were you supposed to get a ride with?" she said, her nose buried in the paperwork.

"It's all in there," I said exasperation causing my anger to rise to the surface. "If you can't be bothered to read the file, then why am I even here at all?"

She raised her face and observed me coolly. "Look, I'm just trying to do my job, I—"

"Your job?" My voice had an edge to it that I wasn't entirely comfortable with. "Were you doing your job when Clara first went missing and you lot dismissed her as nothing more than just another teenage runaway? Who was looking for her then? Who even gave a shit—" My voice broke down but the tears that prickled at the back of my eyes refused to fall.

Her expression remained the same. "I'm sorry you feel your concerns weren't listened to. I know this can't be easy."

"You have no fucking clue." My voice was hoarse with emotion. "Just show me my sister's things so I can get out of here."

For a moment, I thought she was going to argue with me but in the end she nodded and from the back of the file, she pulled an A4 clear plastic folder. Out of it, she took several large colour photographs.

She laid them out in front of me, one at a time and I stared down at them.

The walls closed in around me, the air thinning until I was certain I was going to pass out.

One of the photographs was an image of what remained of a pair of wide-legged blue jeans, or at least at one time they'd been blue. Now, they were dirty and faded, holes and rips where the fabric had degraded over the years. Yet, unmistakably, they were identical to the ones Clara had worn that night. Even the hem had that same ragged edge Mam was always telling her off about.

The next picture was of a tattered black t-shirt, or at least I assumed it was a t-shirt but the fabric was almost entirely broken down. There was a patch of white on one section of it, as though at one time there had been a logo. I felt bile rushing up the back of my throat as I realised why there was so little for me to identify. Twenty-two years in the ground, wrapped around the remains of a dead body, meant the natural fibres had been all but destroyed. Eaten away by the decomposition process.

I pushed the picture away and stared down at the last two. One was the remains of a shirt of some kind. It was brown now but when I closed my eyes I could see it as it had been. The blue denim shirt she'd been wearing, the one I'd noticed was ripped. My eyes snapped open once more and I searched the picture for signs of a tear in the fabric but there were too many rips to pinpoint one in particular.

I didn't want to look at the last photograph. My mind urged me to get up, to leave the room now while there was still time. The clothes could have belonged to anyone. Plenty of young women wore outfits almost identical to the one in the photographs. It didn't mean anything.

"She was wearing Converse," I said, refusing to meet Siobhan's inscrutable stare.

"We found no shoes," she said and the words hit me like a punch to the gut. I couldn't help but imagine her wandering around in her bare feet. I shoved the thought away. It was stupid and unproductive.

Why keep Clara's shoes? It made no sense.

"And this one," Siobhan said, sliding the last photograph toward me.

I picked it up, my hands trembling so badly I almost couldn't focus on the image before me.

The chain lay next to a ruler that had been put there to give an idea of size. What had once been gold was now tarnished. They'd tried to clean most of the dirt from the surface but it was still caught among the links. My heart crawled into my throat as I stared at the heart that sat at the bottom of the chain loop.

The floral pattern, although a little worn, was still recognisable. Two photographs that had at one time sat inside the locket stared up at me. Faded now, but I knew them from memory. One of Clara, the other of me. Both of us grinning. It had been my birthday present to her for her sixteenth birthday, the year before she went missing. She had worn it everywhere.

On the same sheet was n image of the back of the locket. The writing was illegible, almost a scrawl. Childish even.

"Do you know what it says?" Siobhan asked.

I shook my head and glanced up at her. "It's Clara's locket but that wasn't there when she went missing."

"Are you sure? Maybe a—"

"I bought her the locket," I said. "I never got around to having it engraved. She wouldn't have let anyone else do it."

Siobhan nodded. "You're sure?" she said. "This is definitely your sister's locket?"

My heart sank into my stomach. I hadn't wanted it to be true. There had been a part of me that had clung to the tiny flicker of hope that if it wasn't her locket then it wasn't her body. That she was alive somewhere, living her life. Happy. Content. And now that hope was extinguished, just as her life had been.

"I'm sure. It's Clara's."

20

September 17th 1996

I'M DONE with that asshole and that bitch is welcome to him. If I never see Liam Donnelly again, it'll be too soon!

21

"I'll get Fiona to give you a lift home," Siobhan said, pulling the photographs back across the table. I watched, only half listening to her prattle on as she rearranged the images into a neat stack and slipped them back inside her folder.

"What now?"

"Sorry?"

"What happens now?" I repeated the question. Ice had wormed its way under my skin and was slowly stealing the warmth from my limbs. Was this what it felt like to be dead? "Her body. When do we get it back?"

"There's an ongoing investigation," she said. "Until we've conducted our enquiries and the coroner is done with the remains, we can't release them to you."

"So she's been missing for over twenty years and even now she can't come home?"

"I'm sorry," Siobhan said. "There's nothing I can do. Fiona might have some better answers for you." She pushed up from the table and headed for the door. She paused, her hand on the handle. "If it's all right with you, I'd like to call by your parent's house tomorrow, ask a few questions."

"Will it bring her back?" I couldn't keep the bitterness from my voice.

"Nothing will do that," she said, "but it might help bring the circumstances surrounding her death to light."

I stared down at the tabletop without answering as Siobhan pulled open the door.

"Did she suffer?" The question bubbled out of me before I could stop it.

"We don't have all the information yet," she said, but I could tell she was holding something back and instinct told me it was nothing good.

"Try and get some rest, Alice," she said, leaving the room.

I sat at the table without moving for what felt like an age. Until finally, a young female Guard in a navy blue uniform poked her head around the door.

"You all right?"

"Fine, thanks," I said, pushing wearily onto my feet.

She shot me a sympathetic smile as I moved past her. My arm had started to throb once more and my eyes felt as though I'd rubbed grit in them. I needed somewhere I could lie down and curl into a ball, close my eyes and sleep until this was all over.

"I'll give you a lift home," Fiona said, meeting me in the small hall that linked the interview rooms with the main reception.

"Can you drop me in town instead?" I said. The thought of going home and watching Mam and Dad shrink in on themselves beneath the weight of Clara's fate wasn't something I could handle right now.

She opened her mouth to argue, but changed her mind and nodded instead and for that I was grateful.

WE PULLED up outside The Tobar, a bar and restaurant I'd visited many times before, as the sun started to sink behind the horizon. The lights outside made the white washed walls of the pub look inviting. It was as if I'd somehow stepped back in time. I half expected to see a pony and cart sitting outside and for John Wayne and Maureen O' Hara to come chasing out of the double doors.

"You sure you don't want to go home?" Fiona asked for what felt like the millionth time.

With a small smile I shook my head and picked my handbag up from where I'd set it between my feet.

"No, I'm fine, I'll make my own way back."

"Your mom won't be worried about you?"

I shrugged. "Doubtful, at least not with Imelda there. Plus there'll be other people calling round to the house and to be honest, I really don't want to see any of them."

She nodded. "Want someone to talk to?"

It wasn't that she really wanted to come with me; it was more a matter of form that she felt she needed to ask me.

"I'll be fine."

I pushed open the car door and stepped out into the misting rain, my hair sticking to my face as I cradled my injured arm against my body. Waving her off, I waited until the car was out of sight before I turned and made my way into the pub.

Being a Tuesday night, the place was almost entirely deserted. A couple of the local farmers sat propped against the bar. Part of me wondered if they were the same locals that had propped up the bar when I'd come in as a teenager. From the looks of them, it wouldn't have surprised me.

Pausing at the edge of the counter, I caught the barman's eye and he sauntered over toward me, his lazy grin widening as his eyes lit up with recognition.

"Alice McCarthy, as I live and breathe, fancy seeing you here." Declan propped his elbows on the bar and plopped his chin into the palm of his hand, bringing him eye level with me.

Heat rose in my cheeks. How was it possible that a guy I'd had a crush on since I was a girl in secondary school could have that same effect even now?

"If I'd known they let any old riff-raff behind the bar, I'd have gone to Henderson's."

His grey eyes twinkled as he straightened up and tossed a bar-rag over his shoulder. The white shirt he wore stretched across his broad shoulders and bunched around his upper arms. Clearly, he didn't spend all of his time stuck behind the bar pulling pints. His laughter took me by surprise and I found myself smiling in response.

"What dragged you back here? I thought you were too good for all of us now, moved on to bigger and better things across the pond."

I felt the smile wilt on my lips. The fact that he didn't know was honestly surprising to me. It had nearly always been the case that everyone knew everyone else's business. When it came to small towns in Ireland, there was no such thing as secrets.

"It's Clara," I said. "They think they've found her."

His expression instantly sobered and he leaned across the bar once more, placing a hand on my shoulder. "Oh, shit, Alice. I didn't put two and two together when I heard the news."

"It's fine," I said. "In a way I've been preparing myself for this moment from the minute she was taken."

He straightened up and cleared his throat. "Yeah, that can't have been easy." There was a sudden awkwardness to his behaviour and without him needing to say anything, I already knew what was going through his head.

No one had believed me when I'd said I was with Clara when she was taken. No one had listened to me. I'd been drinking. Just another daughter bringing shame upon our family.

And because Clara was a pregnant teenager in Ireland, they'd all assumed she'd run away. Most people knew someone who'd travelled over to England on the boat to 'deal with a problem'.

It was one of those unspoken secrets, a stain upon the country whereby women were treated like second-class citizens because of the country's strict Catholic culture.

Here, we either swept our *problems* under the proverbial rug or exported them, right alongside our beef and rich culture.

And everyone had assumed that Clara had done just that. Upped sticks and run away because she couldn't handle the shame she'd brought on her family.

And then, just like that, it had changed. Two other girls had gone, vanished in the night, just like Clara had and suddenly people were more willing to believe that Clara hadn't just run away. That perhaps I had been telling the truth when I'd spoken of her being snatched off the side of the road.

By then, it was too late and Clara's trail, not that there had been much to begin with, had gone cold.

Tears burned at the back of my throat and stung my eyes. She'd probably already been dead by then anyway.

"What are you having, anything, it's on the house?"

"Whiskey," I said. "And not the watered down crap they used to serve in here when I was a teenager."

Declan flashed a smile at me and then turned to grab a bottle off the top shelf. "You go and sit," he said. "Your corner is free."

Craning my neck, I stared at the corner booth where I used to sit as a teen. Before we were legally allowed to drink, we would gather in the corners of fields, hiding our bottles of contraband in the bushes out of sight. Once we crossed the magical threshold that lay between childhood and adulthood, we'd realised there was no longer any reason to go drinking in a ditch so we'd come in from the cold, taking up residence in the corner of the pub. For a while, we had been like part of the furniture.

I pushed away from the bar and made my way through the pub. Dropping my heavy handbag down onto the rickety wooden table, I slid into the worn seat. A newspaper lay discarded on top of the table and I scooped it up, staring down at the local headlines.

"Body found in shallow grave."

A lump formed in the back of my throat and I started to put down the paper when another article on the front page caught my attention. One small column with a grainy picture attached of a young smiling girl.

"Missing Girl's Family Make Second Appeal."

I started to read but someone had carelessly let their pint rest on the page and some of the beer-soaked words were unreadable in the gloom of the bar.

Declan set a glass down in front of me, along with the bottle.

"I haven't forgotten how you prefer to pour your own," he said, dropping into the seat opposite me.

"There's another girl missing?" I gestured at the page in front of me. Declan's expression clouded over.

"Yeah, nineteen. Her family moved here last year and she came back from college for the weekend."

"And she just vanished?"

"Went out with one of the lads one night and never came home."

Icy fingers wrapped around the back of my neck and I shuddered. "Do they think he's responsible?"

Declan shrugged. "You know how it is, people talk. But no one really knows anything. Cops hauled him in initially but they let him go without charge. Apparently, they told him not to leave the area."

"So they know something but they're not saying."

Declan shrugged and sat back on the wooden chair.

"Who was it?"

"Colm Martin." Declan pulled a face. "You don't think this has anything to do with your sister do you? I mean, he'd have been two when she disappeared."

The surname sounded familiar but I couldn't put a face to the name.

A smile touched my lips. "No, I don't think he has anything to do with Clara." Grabbing the bottle, I filled it up.

"Jesus," Declan said, beginning to laugh. "Go easy there, cowboy. There are at least four measures in that glass."

It was my turn to shrug. Pain ripped through my shoulder and I winced, gripping the edge of the sticky table as I waited for the worst of the agony to subside.

He waited until my face cleared and I stopped gritting my teeth before asking. "What happened to you anyway?"

I contemplated telling him the same bullshit I'd spun out for Imelda but as I looked up into Declan's honest face I found myself wanting to confide in him.

"Got myself shot," I said, grabbing the glass and downing the contents in two eye-watering gulps. It burned down the back of my throat, spreading heat through my core, bringing with it a kind of lazy lethargy that saw the tension in my shoulders seeping away.

The wide-eyed way he was staring at me brought laughter bubbling up the back of my throat. It didn't mingle well with the burning heat from the whiskey and the laughter quickly devolved into a coughing fit.

"Jesus, you had me going there for a second," he said. "I really thought you were serious."

Tears leaked from the corners of my eyes and I scrubbed them away with the back of my hand as I nodded. "I am serious," I said.

He stared at me like I'd just sprouted a second head. He grabbed the bottle and took a gulp straight from the neck, grimacing before returning his attention to me once more.

"You have got to be shitting me, Alice." He poured another measure into my glass and, at my raised eyebrow, topped the glass up to the top. "Shot? How the hell did you manage that one?"

"Long story," I said. "Can't really talk about it." The more I thought about Zoe, Dan, and Rachel, the more I felt the pleasant afterglow that had accompanied the whiskey begin to fade.

"Ah come on," he said. "You can't drop a clanger like that on me and not tell me what happened."

Picking up the glass, I took another scalding mouthful. Why not tell him? It wasn't as though I was going to have a job after Gerald and Jennifer were through using me as their scapegoat.

"Fine," I said, wiggling my half empty glass at him. "But you've got to keep this full."

"Deal."

"Declan!" A gruff shout went up from the bar. "Are you serving here or are we meant to fend for ourselves?"

He rolled his eyes. "Give me a minute." I watched him go and finished my drink.

From my vantage point in the corner booth, I watched him slip in behind the bar, his ready smile and easygoing manner making him popular with the patrons.

I glanced down at the edge of the paper once more and my stomach flip-flopped. Just how many girls had gone missing over the years? The headache that had been threatening all day started to build momentum.

Grabbing my bag, I pulled out a fistful of euros and dropped them on the table before I climbed unsteadily to my feet. For a moment, the pub swirled around me and I thought the whiskey was going to make a reappearance. Instead, I swallowed the acrid bile down and headed for the door.

"Alice!" Declan called after me but I raised my hand and gave him a backwards wave as I slipped out into the cold night air. At least it had stopped raining.

After a moment of fumbling in my handbag, searching for my elusive iPhone, I gave up and started down the road. It was quiet and once the pub lights faded behind me, the darkness closed in around me.

Headlights flared ahead of me and I raised my hand, trying to protect my eyes but bursts of colour swam in my vision making it impossible to stay on the road. It reminded me of the night Clara was taken. The headlights had dazzled me then too.

And then they were gone, the light fading as the vehicle turned down another road.

A few moments later, a second car pulled to a halt next to me.

Alone on the road, with the sound of the car engine in my ears, I was suddenly back at that night in 1996 with Clara. I could almost feel her hand in mine as I turned toward the ditch. This time we would get away. This time I wouldn't leave her behind and the last twenty-two years would be nothing but a terrible nightmare. She would be alive. Clara would survive.

"Alice McCarthy, get your arse in the car this minute!" My aunt's voice cut through the panic that had momentarily swamped my brain and I turned to find her standing at the driver's door of her white Citroen.

"Where did you come from?" I asked, pleased that my speech was at least steadier than my legs felt.

"Jesus, Mary, and Joseph," she muttered to herself as she came around the side of the car and pulled open the passenger door. "Get in the bloody car."

I didn't argue with her and climbed into the passenger seat, feeling her anger vibrate through me as she slammed the door.

I closed my eyes and when I opened them again she was already sitting in the driver's side and we were moving.

"Fiona told me where she left you," she said. "I can't believe how selfish you're being. You'd think you could spend more than five seconds with your mother."

I was bathed in her anger and I fumbled to buzz the window down. I needed air, to breathe, to escape.

I clicked the button and mercifully, the window opened a crack, letting the night air inside the car.

"And then I see you wandering around the roads. After everything that happened with Clara, have you no sense?" She carried on, no end in sight.

"Just stop," I said, holding my head in my hands. I needed to sleep. The whiskey mingled with the pain in my shoulder and head wasn't sitting well on an empty stomach and if she kept up her tirade I was going to redecorate the pristine interior of her car.

"What did you say?"

"I said stop. Please…"

"You were always a selfish girl, only thinking of yourself. Your poor mother and—"

I closed my eyes and pressed my face against the cold glass of the window. I felt like a teenager again, being scolded for something ridiculous. It was one of the reasons I didn't like coming back here. It wouldn't matter how old I was or what I did with my life, they would always treat me like an errant child.

The car jerked to a halt and she killed the engine. Imelda brushed my shoulder with her hand.

"I know you're hurting," she said, "but your Mam and Dad need you now more than ever."

"Thanks for the lift," I said and without another word, I pushed open the car door and stumbled out onto the drive. The house was in darkness and for that

I was grateful. I didn't want to see anyone now. My head was too full of Clara and what had happened to her. There were so many unanswered questions, I'd thought finding her might have made it easier but it hadn't.

In fact, I had more questions than ever and the not knowing was slowly crushing me.

22

Elation. I can feel it coursing in my veins like some sort of illegal high. I only tried weed once but it wasn't for me. It made my head ache and stomach knot.

It made me paranoid.

Others seem to like it well enough, though. The movies make it look harmless, fun even, but I know different. Not that it matters. Not anymore.

Alice is back. She's my drug of choice. A succour for my tarnished soul. Seeing her there on the road, stumbling around just like she had that night, it was like I'd plucked her straight from my mind, wished her into reality. Maybe I had.

Could she feel the same pull I did? Was that why she'd returned?

Not that she had a choice. Deep down I knew she would come back. I've always known it. All I did was help it along, speed up the inevitable.

Drunk.

So terribly vulnerable.

But not alone.

Is she doing it on purpose? Evading me?

Does she know I'm here?

Too many thoughts. Too many possibilities. It hurts my head. I don't need possibilities; I need action. I need certainty.

She won't leave this time. Won't run away like before. This time, I'll make her understand, make her see the truth of what I'm creating.

I always knew she would come home.

Clara's going to be so happy.

23

LIGHT LAY ACROSS MY FACE, burning against my closed eyelids, seeking a way in, a way through my lashes. The mattress was lumpy beneath my back and my head felt like someone had poured acid inside it before shaking it up like a magic 8 ball.

Noises filtered through from downstairs, the whine of a hoover and the muffled music of a radio.

Lifting my head from the pillow, I stared at the room, the unfamiliar wallpaper and pale pink lampshade slowly coming into focus. It took a moment for my brain to catch up with my surroundings and as it did, so too came the memories of the previous day.

Clara...

Just thinking her name hurt. There was a weight on my chest, crushing me into the mattress and I rolled awkwardly onto my side, welcoming the flare of pain that raced up through my arm and into my shoulder.

I'd slept with the strap on my arm all night. It was a miracle I hadn't managed to strangle myself. After the pain came a kind of numb ache that settled into my shoulder blade. A constant throbbing reminder that set my teeth on edge.

I pushed myself upright and a wave of nausea slammed into me, sending the world spiralling for a couple of seconds. The whiskey I'd drank the night before rushed up the back of my throat but I swallowed it back and rubbed my chest, a poor attempt to rid myself of the burning indigestion left in its wake.

Home... Not that this house was home for me anymore. It hadn't been for a long time.

Shortly after I'd moved out, Mam had set about the place, changing the wallpaper and dumping my bed as though trying to rid the house of any evidence that I'd ever lived there. She'd done a good job too. Nothing was as I remembered it. My old room was now the guest room. Not that they ever had any guests to stay.

I unhooked the strap that was keeping my arm in place and flexed my fingers, trying to feed a little life back into them. It took a couple of minutes but the feeling returned, slowly at first and then with a sudden rush of burning intensity that saw me curl my toes in discomfort.

The bedroom door slammed open and Mam appeared in the gap, hoover in hand.

"Don't mind me, love," she said. "Just getting a head start on the cleaning. This place is going to pot!"

She shouted over the whine of her old Henry vacuum cleaner. There was a frantic, almost frenzied energy to her movements as she scrubbed at the carpet with the head of the hoover.

"Mam, you don't have to do that," I said, crossing the floor toward her.

"Yes I do," she said. "There's so much needs doing. This place has to be spick and span and..."

I tried to take the hoover from her but she jerked away from like I'd tried to burn her.

"What are you doing, Alice?"

I held onto the head of the vacuum and tried to talk over the noise. "You should sit down. You need..."

"What I need," she said, ripping the vacuum from my hands, "is to get my work done."

I thought about arguing with her. I could fight her for the vacuum, knock her to the ground and wrest it from her control but what good would it do? I could just see it now, the two of us rolling around on the carpet as I tried to hold her down. The ridiculousness of the vision brought a hiccup of laughter and I fought to keep it in.

"The Gardaí want to come round later," I said, trying to catch her eye.

"What for?" There was an edge to her voice.

"To talk about Clara," I said.

"Whatever for?"

I stood there, staring at her as she tried to hoover

around me, unable to form the words that swirled in my head.

"Mam," I said, trying again. "They found her body. Someone murdered her." Seeing her yesterday with a blank expression on her face had been bad enough but this denial or whatever it was felt so much worse.

"Don't be daft," she said but there was a flicker of something akin to panic in her eyes as she spoke. "Move over now, let me in."

I stepped aside and caught her arm again. Beneath my fingers, her skin was paper thin, her bones sliding just below the surface making me think of the bones of a bird. She'd lost weight, either I hadn't wanted to see it, or I'd ignored it but now I could feel it and as I stared into her face I could suddenly see just how haggard she'd become.

Her hair, which was normally neatly combed, was frazzled and unkempt. The bags beneath her eyes made her appear drawn. Her face was wan and pale.

"Mam, you need to listen to me..."

"No, Alice," she said, her voice high and thready.

"Mam, Clara is dead and cleaning isn't going to bring her back." There was a cruelty to my voice that I hadn't intended and I regretted the words as soon as they'd left my mouth.

"No, I don't, I don't. I can't. You can't make me. You can't, you can't!" Her voice grew higher and higher until she was practically screaming the words at me.

I tried to hold her, to comfort her but she flung the

hoover at me suddenly, her eyes wide and frightened as she bolted from the room.

There was a slam as she disappeared into her bedroom and then nothing.

I clicked off the vacuum cleaner, letting the silence close in around me, almost suffocating in its entirety. It had been the same after Clara disappeared. The constant cleaning, the denial, the screaming.

Closing my eyes, I tried to crush the memory down inside. I didn't want to remember it, didn't want the memory of the look in my mother's eyes. The blame.

I crossed the hall to Clara's room. My fingers hovered over the doorknob but I couldn't bring myself to turn it. Perhaps I was just as bad as my mother. Staying out of Clara's room was a form of denial, a way of insulating myself from the truth.

I spun away from the door and headed for the stairs, taking them two at a time until I reached the bottom. Panic clawed in my chest, fighting to escape. The voice in my head, the same one from the night Clara had been taken thrummed in my head, urging me on.

Run. Run. Run. Run. Run.

Shoving open the back door, I burst out into the morning sunlight and stood on the porch, drawing lungfuls of air into my body. There was no heat in the light that danced across my face. There was never much heat in the Irish sun. If we were lucky, we got a week of temperatures in the mid twenties. For the first day everyone ventured out as if they were sun worshippers starved of the light. Twenty minutes was all it took for the uninitiated skin to crisp, changing from a pasty white to a lobster red. The shops would run out of aftersun and aloe vera gels and by day two everyone would begin complaining about the heat and the farmers would be on their knees praying for the rain to return.

When the rain did return—and it always did, this was Ireland after all—and the mercury dropped back to a more normal range, the country would let out a collective sigh of relief before once more bemoaning the cruel twist of fate that saw them living in a country where it rained 99% of the time.

"How are things this morning?"

I jumped at the sound of Imelda's voice and jerked my head up from the silent contemplation I'd fallen into.

"She's cleaning again," I said.

"Well that's good..." Imelda trailed off as she noted the look on my face.

She stood next to me, in companionable silence but I could sense there was something she wanted to say.

"Thanks for last night," I said.

"About that." She twisted her fingers around the strap on her handbag, almost a nervous gesture. "You know your Mam has a lot on her mind right now, she doesn't need..."

"It's fine, it won't happen again." My voice was flat, my head beginning to throb.

"I just mean..."

Turning away, I pushed open the backdoor and stepped back into the kitchen. There had been a time when the room would have been warm. The range in the corner was nearly always lit when Clara was here. At times the heat in the small room was almost unbearable. Now, it sat cold and unlit. Like the forgotten carcass of some great fiery beast, perched in the corner of the room. Seeing it lit yesterday had been an aberration. Perhaps Fiona had done it; Imelda knew better than to interfere.

The telephone in the hallway rang, the shrill sound echoing in the unnatural silence of the house.

"Hello?" My father's voice, quiet and uncertain, cut the jarring ringer off as he picked up the phone. "I'm not sure, I... No, I..."

Standing in the kitchen doorway, I watched his expression crumble as he listened to whatever was said on the other end of the line.

"No, she was..."

Crossing the hall, I snatched the phone from his hand and pressed the receiver to my ear.

"Do you think your daughter's death is in any way connected with the other missing women?"

"How about you fuck off?" I said, pouring as much bitterness into my voice as I could. They were goddamn vultures, the lot of them. Always claiming to be on your side, always claiming they wanted to help when in reality all they wanted to do was grab their next big headline.

"Is that Alice? Can you tell me if—"

I slammed the phone down.

"You shouldn't speak to them like that, love," Dad said, the tremor in his voice betraying just how much the call had upset him. "They're only trying to help."

"I think maybe you should let the answering machine pick up any other calls," I said, touching his arm gently.

The phone started to ring once more and he reached for it. "It could be important," he said.

"And if it is, they'll leave a message and we can get back to them." I took his arm and steered him toward the kitchen.

"I'll put the kettle on," Imelda said, hovering in the doorway.

Directing him to the table, I sat across from him, noting the dark circles beneath his eyes. "Maybe you and Mam should take a trip to see Dr. Lennord," I said. "You know, have a chat to him about..."

"All that ape wants to do is drug us to the eyeballs," he said. "After the way he treated your mother the last time..."

I nodded. It was a silly suggestion. Dad hated the family GP. He'd resented him ever since Dr. Lennord had suggested we have Mam sent into hospital after Clara's disappearance.

There was a knock on the front door that saw Dad climb unsteadily to his feet. Grabbing his arm once more, I shook my head. "It's fine, I'll get it." I had visions of him standing at the front door, flash bulbs going off in his face as he stood there frozen like a deer in headlights.

"No, love, I can…"

I pushed him back onto the kitchen chair. "I said I can do it, Dad. Just sit and drink your tea."

He didn't fight me, which suggested he was far more worn down than I'd realised.

Leaving him in the kitchen with Imelda, I headed for the front door and tugged it open. There was no one on the front step and the driveway was empty. Dad's car sat abandoned near the door and Imelda's car was parked close behind. From what I could see, there was nowhere else for anyone to hide.

Turning, I started to shut the door when something on the doorstep caught my eye.

My heart stalled in my chest, my breath catching in the back of my throat as I stared in disbelief at the white rabbit statue that sat in the centre of the old brown welcome mat.

Some of the paint from his little red waistcoat had worn away, exposing the white pottery beneath and the hands on the large pocket watch in his grasp ticked sluggishly, making me think the batteries inside were on their last legs. Crouching down, I tentatively reached out, my hand trembling as I brushed the tips of the white rabbit's ears.

The memory of Clara handing the box to me filled my head. Her grin wide as she watched me rip away the balloon covered paper.

"You won't be sleeping in anymore," she said, as I pulled the white rabbit alarm clock from its box. The rabbit had always been my favourite character from Alice in Wonderland. Clara had gotten the clock for me as a present, a sort of consolation prize for the fact that I couldn't go with her to Irish college for the summer. It was going to be the first summer we'd spend apart.

The rusty alarm ripped through the silence and I jumped, spilling backwards in the front door, I landed on my ass in the hallway. My heart thumped wildly in my chest, my breathing ragged as I stared down at the white rabbit that had started to vibrate on the welcome mat.

"What the hell is that?" Imelda asked, appearing behind me in the hall.

I scrambled to my feet and snatched the rabbit from the mat, flicking the switch on the underneath so that the alarm once more fell silent.

"My old alarm clock," I said, unable to tear my gaze away from the rabbit.

"What's it doing on the doorstep?"

I pushed onto my feet, my legs suddenly felt like

the bones in them had been replaced with jelly. "I don't know."

Imelda stared down at the rabbit, clutched in my hands. "Well it must have come from somewhere," she said. "It can't just have walked onto the mat itself."

I shook my head. "I don't know." It was the truth. The last time I'd set eyes on the clock, I'd been a teenager and the alarm had sat pride of place on my bedside table. Then one day it was gone. No one knew where it was. It was as if it had suddenly come to life and hopped away.

Only now it was back and I had the distinct impression that whatever secrets the white rabbit had, he wouldn't share them with me.

24

September 18th 1996

How can one person misjudge another so utterly and completely? I think I must have dickhead printed on my forehead.

Sarah says I'm too naive for my own good but I don't think it's naivety. I want to believe that people are capable of goodness in this world. I want to believe that not everyone is out only for themselves. And every time I think I'm coming close to discovering true goodness in the world, something else ruins it.

Sister Rosario has decided I'm a poor example to the others in the school and has asked me to stay home for the rest of my pregnancy. Mam was livid but I told her to leave it. Kicking up a fuss isn't going to make this any better. And anyway, if I stayed they'd only find new ways to make my life miserable.

They said they'll send my work home for me with Alice but I'm thinking I'll just drop school completely. I'm old enough now anyway and I could get a job. I'm going to have to do something to support myself for when the baby comes. Things are already tight enough for Mam and Dad without an extra mouth to feed.

I told Sarah and she said I could always go to England and get it dealt with. I told her not a chance but I can't say I haven't considered it.

I never wanted this baby, I didn't choose it but now that I have it, I think I kind of love it. But if it wasn't here it would be easier... Does that make me a terrible person to think that? I suppose it does but I'm so tired all the time and my eyes hurt from crying. I thought life was going to be different.

I hate myself for being so stupid and believing Liam. How could I have thought he was one of the good guys?

Sarah said she saw him in town yesterday with Anne-Marie. She's perfect for him, her parents have a share in Coolmore and Liam loves horses...

Sometimes I wish I was ~~dead~~.

25

SCOOPING up the sandwich from its paper wrapping, I stared down at the files spread across the white bedspread. Going through the old files was taking longer than I would have liked but I needed to be thorough. Someone had to be; the mess they'd initially made of the case was criminal.

A knock on the bedroom door made me jump and mayonnaise plopped onto the paper-towel in my lap.

"Shit," I swore under my breath and set the sandwich down on the bed. Light Mayo my ass. Grabbing another couple of napkins I scrubbed my fingers clean of the greasy condiment that had dripped down over my hand. Tossing the used napkins in the bin underneath the dressing table, I pulled the door open and found myself face to face with Ronan.

"What are you doing here?" I asked, cocking an eyebrow at him.

He raised a white bag and grinned sheepishly at me. "Thought after the run in you had with the sergeant you might fancy a Chinese."

As he moved the bag, the scent of chow mein wafted out and my mouth began to water. I glanced over my shoulder at the pathetic sandwich on the bed, the lettuce wilting out from between the bread.

"Come in." I stepped aside, letting him in the door.

He glanced around the room and nodded approvingly. "Not bad."

"Seriously?"

He nodded. "Yeah, I thought they'd have stuck you in a B&B, or had you bed in with the sergeant."

The thought of having to stay with Sergeant John Mills was enough to bring an unladylike snort of laughter spilling from me. Ronan grinned in response.

"Not a fan then?" I asked, making some room on the dresser, so he could begin unpacking the bag.

"He's fine," he said, somewhat cautiously. "Strict and he tries to be fair."

"But?"

Ronan shrugged. "I guess he's just a little old-fashioned, like a relic from a bygone era."

I knew what he meant. Sergeant John Mills was a good man, I had no doubt about that. And he seemed to care about the case. But there was a wariness about him. I got the feeling that he thought my presence would somehow blow the case out of proportion.

Perhaps he felt I would upset the delicate

ecosystem that existed, trampling over relationships and bonds that were as deeply rooted as some of the mountains that surrounded the county.

And considering the way he'd blown a gasket earlier today when I'd told him my suspicions about the most recent missing girl and her connection to the cold cases, well it hadn't exactly put us on the best of terms.

"Why is he so resistant to the idea that the cases are linked?"

Ronan shrugged. "Maybe because he's so old-school? He doesn't like to jump to conclusions, he tends to follow leads to their logical conclusions and in this case he believes the boyfriend is the most logical conclusion."

"But he's wrong," I said.

"But you have no proof of that," he said.

"All you have to do is look at the girls to have all the proof you need. I don't believe in coincidences, Ronan, in this line of work, relying on that kind of policing gets people hurt. Or worse."

He shrugged. "It's your case, you can overrule him if you want to."

I nodded and chewed my lip thoughtfully. I could overrule him. I was technically in charge but I was also here as a courtesy. The sergeant had asked for my intervention. He'd really asked for the intervention of the NBCI and I knew if I pushed him too far it wouldn't be long before he'd go complaining to my superiors.

With cases like this, it was vital you kept the local lines of enquiry sweet. A political minefield if ever there was and I didn't exactly have the best reputation when it came to juggling the feelings of the local Gardaí.

I caught Ronan studying the newspaper I'd left on the top of the dresser. The photograph of Joanna Burke, the most recent girl to disappear, stared up out of the front page as if she dared us to find her.

"Do you think the reporters are right?"

There was an almost imperceptible tightening in Ronan's shoulders and I knew I'd struck a nerve. The only problem was, I had no idea why.

"About what?" His tone was deliberately light, as he set the silver trays out and popped the lids free. The room was quickly filled with the rich scent of noodles and spices.

"That it's a serial killer at work," I said.

"I didn't think we were allowed to admit that out loud."

"We're not," I said, it felt wrong to deny the possibility that the deaths were the work of a serial killer but I had strict instructions from the higher ups not to entertain the notion, at least not publicly. *"Talk like that creates panic, Siobhan, and we have enough of that already."*

Ronan nodded. "Well, what do you think?"

"I think it's more than possible," I said, grabbing a tray of noodles and plopping back on the edge of the bed. I folded my legs up underneath my body as I pushed the plastic fork into the food and twisted, watching the brown strings wrap around the tines. "There's a similarity between the girls. Not just in their looks but also in the manner they went missing. That shouldn't be overlooked."

Ronan sat in the chair next to the window and picked at his food, seemingly lost in thought. "It's a long time though," he said. "I mean, why go quiet for all those years?"

I shrugged. "Could be any number of reasons, I guess. I don't really know. Maybe they were in prison..." I trailed off as my phone started to buzz from somewhere on the bed. Setting the tray of noodles down, I started to search, pulling the papers and folders up in a haphazard fashion as the phone's ringer increased in intensity.

It cut off suddenly and I swore under my breath as I pulled the phone free from beneath my crisp white pillows.

"Expecting someone?" Ronan asked, his barely concealed curiosity drawing a smile from me.

"Not that it's any of your business," I said as I scrolled through the missed calls log. I could feel Ronan's anticipation as he waited for me to finish but I had no intention of saying anything else. It simply was none of his business and that was all there was to know about the matter.

"You were saying?"

"Nothing," I said, half distracted by the number. It

wasn't one I was overly familiar with and it took me a couple of minutes to place the area code.

"Limerick," I said.

"What?"

I glanced up and found Ronan leaning forward, elbows on knees, his hands hanging loosely down.

"Limerick," I repeated, gesturing to the phone. "Don't recognise the number but it's a Limerick area code."

Hitting the redial button, I pushed the phone to my ear and waited. It was answered after the third ring, the man on the other end sounding like he'd crawled out from beneath a pile of clothes, or maybe newspapers.

"Yes," he said, the most unenthusiastic answer I'd heard in quite a while.

"I've got a missed call from this number and I'm—"

"Siobhan Geraghty?" The voice was now suddenly interested and I could almost hear the man on the other end of the line straightening up his glasses and rearranging his tie.

"Yeah, Detective Siobhan Geraghty," I said. "And you are?"

"Sorry about the confusion," he said. "I'm Dorian Whittiker. I work for the regional forensic pathologist's office. I was going to send you an email."

I paused, waiting for him to continue but the silence on the other end of the line dragged.

"Right," I said. "Well I'm here now so what did you want to talk to me about?"

Dorian coughed awkwardly and I found myself wondering if it was more a nervous tic than any real attempt to clear his airways.

He hesitated, and I could almost imagine him casting about the room, looking for a jolt of inspiration that would never come. "I was hoping you might be willing to drop in for a chat over some of the results we've got." There was a triumphant sigh once he finished.

"What kind of results?"

"Oh." His voice dropped, all triumph fleeing in the face of my quick response. "This would go much better if you could come by the office," he said. "I'll be here until ten and...I could meet you."

Glancing at the clock on the bedside table, I did the mental calculations in my head. It would take more than an hour to get up to Limerick and it was already nine forty.

"Perhaps in the morning," I said. "I'm coming from Cahir so I won't make it up there before you leave."

Dorian sighed, as though I had inconvenienced him greatly. "Fine. 9am sharp."

"Do you have a confirmation on the identity of the body?" I thought about the meeting I'd arranged with Alice McCarthy. At least if I could bring her and the family a positive confirmation, it might help with some of the uncertainty. I couldn't begin to imagine what it was like to be in their shoes. What must they be thinking?

"I'm still waiting on some results," he said, but I could tell there was something he was holding back.

"What is it?"

"I'll talk to you in the morning. Goodbye detective." The line went dead and I found myself staring down at the black screen of my phone.

"That is one kooky bird," I said more to myself than Ronan.

"State pathologist's office?"

I nodded. "The regional office," I said. "He didn't want to tell me anything over the phone."

"What did he say?"

I hesitated. What had he said? Nothing, if I was perfectly honest. I'd learned nothing new from him, other than he struck me as someone who suffered with social anxiety. Although maybe it had more to do with the fact that it was a phone call. I'd read somewhere that the more people fell into the trap created by social media and the lure of the smart phone, the more they became incapable of simple conversations on the phone.

It was easier to write a text or an email. The written word gave them the opportunity to plan out in minute detail exactly what they wanted to say without any of the awkwardness or pregnant pauses that came with collecting their thoughts in real time.

"He wants to meet tomorrow," I said. "He's waiting on some other results but there's definitely something he wants to talk about."

"And he gave no clue what it might be?"

I shook my head and picked up the now cold noodles. "Nothing. I asked him if he had confirmed the ID for the body but..." I shrugged. "He wasn't exactly comfortable on the phone."

Ronan grinned. "Was it Dorian?"

I nodded. "Yeah, how did you know?"

"Went to school with him," Ronan said. "His family comes from out the Mitchelstown road. Poor guy wasn't exactly the most popular at school. Too smart for his own good and some of the other guys didn't like it."

"They bully him?"

"If you call forcing him to use his school uniform to mop out the urinals bullying, then yeah," he said. "I guess you could say that."

I suddenly had a vision of a young awkward teenage Dorian standing in the boy's bathroom, his socks sodden as he tried to fish his school trousers out of the urinals. It wasn't a pleasant thought and I felt bad for being curt on the phone.

"You weren't one of the bullies, were you?"

Ronan's expression was pleasantly blank as he met my gaze. "I didn't help them," he said, "but I didn't help Dorian either so I suppose in a way..." He looked away and stuck his fork back into the tray of food in front of him a little more forcefully.

"What do you make of the necklace?"

The sudden about turn in the conversation left me grasping at straws for a moment.

"Clara's locket?"

He nodded and shoved a forkful of rice into his mouth.

"It's weird." I held the tray of noodles as I tried to scramble my thoughts into something a little more coherent than the jumble they currently existed in. "People make mistakes though," I said. "Alice doesn't remember getting it engraved but maybe Clara got it done herself."

"Seems a bit odd," Ronan said, taking another mouthful of rice before he grimaced and sat the tray down on the dresser.

Stretching, I followed suit and left my own tray of food next to his as I climbed to my feet. The room was small enough that when I stood at the end of the bed, my leg brushed Ronan's arm.

His eyes darkened for a moment and I half expected him to reach out toward me. Without waiting for him to say anything, I moved around the bed, standing next to the en-suite door as I shuffled the photographs of the body and the clothes on the bed. I found what I was looking for and stood up, acutely aware of the way Ronan's dark gaze followed my movements.

I stared down at the image of the necklace. "What if it's not the same necklace?"

"You said Alice was certain it was the same. She

said she'd bought it herself, right? You'd think she'd know."

"It's been twenty-two years," I said. "It's possible she was mistaken." I was clutching at straws but nothing else made much sense.

"I guess, until we know what's written on the necklace everything else is just speculation," Ronan said finally. "Why would the killer engrave the necklace?"

I shrugged. "I don't know... we're missing something and I don't like feeling that way." Glancing down at my watch, the realisation that it was so much later than I'd first thought struck me.

"I better get some sleep," I said. "Dorian wants me up there at 9am sharp."

"I'll come with you," Ronan said. "I'll even give you a lift if you fancy."

I hesitated remembering just how uncomfortable I'd been with him in the car earlier. It wasn't just him either; it was most people. They all had somewhat of a death wish, or at least that was how it felt to me.

"We'll get there faster if I drive," he said. "I know the area better."

"Fine." I took the rest of the takeaway boxes and proceeded to bag them up. The thought of leaving them overnight in the tiny bin in the corner didn't exactly thrill me. The place was going to stink.

"I'll walk down with you," I said, as Ronan slipped his jacket on. The momentary expression of surprise that crossed his features disappeared as quickly as it had appeared.

"I'm a big boy you know," he said playfully, "I can walk myself out."

I raised the takeaway bag, the gesture self-explanatory and his grin widened.

"Anyone would think you were trying to get rid of me," he said.

And in a way I supposed I was. I liked him, he was easy to chat with, and so far he hadn't looked at any of my theories about the case as though I was utterly losing my mind. He also didn't appear to mind that I had arrived to effectively take over his position of authority. Most of the men I'd dealt with in the past resented it when I was promoted over them. Almost as if by virtue of being female I belonged in a lesser role, perhaps one that saw me in the kitchen making cups of tea for the real detectives. They weren't all like that, but enough of them to leave a lasting impression on me.

We took the stairs down in companionable silence and I waved Ronan off before finding a bin to dump the bag of leftover food. Sitting out at the back of the hotel, I pulled my phone out of my pocket and dialled Paul's number from memory. He answered on the third ring and the sound of his voice washed over me like a balm.

"Hey babe." His voice was thick with sleep and for a moment I felt a little guilty for waking him.

"You're in bed early."

"Got an early start," he said. "A raid on. Have to be in the office by 3am."

"You got a break then?" He'd been working a drugs case for the last month and every time he'd mentioned it, there had been no breaks at all but then that was the nature of police work. One minute you were buried up to your eyebrows in dead ends and the next, if you were lucky, it all fell into place.

"Yeah, Jimbo had surveillance watching the place, caught some suspicious movement in and out of the property. Looked like a fairly large shipment came in so we're going to move on it while it's hot."

"That's great." I was happy for him, genuinely so, but there was a small part of me that felt a little jealous that no matter what happened, it always turned up roses for him. I had no doubt that if he'd been the one assigned to the Clara McCarthy case, he would already have someone in custody.

It was a petty thought to have and the moment it popped into my head, I felt heat creeping into my face. Shame setting two spots of colour high on my cheeks. Not that Paul could see them. He was still babbling about what they hoped to find on the raid.

"How's it going your end?"

"Fine," I said, almost noncommittally.

"Come on, babe, you can tell me about it. You know my lips are sealed right?"

I wasn't worried about him spilling the beans to someone he shouldn't; he wouldn't jeopardize a case in that way. No. I was more concerned that if I did tell him the details that he would start pointing out obvious errors that I'd made.

"I should let you get back to sleep," I said, quickly. "Can't have you falling asleep in the middle of your raid and blowing the whole op."

He laughed, the rich sensuous sound sending a shiver of warmth racing through my body.

"I wish you were here," he said. "The bed is too empty without you."

"Cold too I should imagine," I said.

"The worst..."

"I love you," I said, blurting the words out as a wave of insecurity washed over me. It didn't happen often but when it did it always left me feeling cold.

"Love you too, babe," he said. The line went dead and I stared down at it for a couple of seconds, feeling suddenly foolish for the insecurity that still fluttered inside me. Pushing it away, I made my way slowly back up to my room. It felt smaller than it had when Ronan was here, as though the walls had shrunk in further, drawing in toward the bed, crowding me out. Pushing the notes and files to one side, I slid beneath the covers and flicked off the lights, trying to imagine that I was back in my own bed. I tried to make myself believe that I wasn't alone in the bed, that Paul was next to me, his breathing heavy as he slept.

But I was alone.

The sudden knowledge that if I screwed up, that if I

made a mistake we would find another body slammed into me. The Sergeant, John Mills might not believe that Joanna and the others were linked but I knew they were. I couldn't quite explain it. Call it a gut feeling but whatever it was I was positive of it. And we were running out of time.

26

I TRY to concentrate on the words on the page but they blur into one another and I realise I've read the same sentence over at least twenty times. The rhythmic sound of the bedsprings mingled with the animalistic sounds of flesh on flesh keep drawing me back to the room.

I keep my back to the door, letting them get on with their game. They think I don't know what passes between them, that I don't know about the times when I'm not here and he visits her.

Not that I can blame him; she is beautiful. I knew he'd want her as much as I did the day I saw her in the paper. Wide hazel eyes, long silky brown hair, a smile that hid more than it hinted at. No, I'd known the moment I laid eyes on her what she was, what she craved.

And I'd been right.

A part of me registers the guttural grunt as he finishes. Setting the unread book aside, I climb to my feet and wait. The murmur of words spoken causes the hairs on my arms to stand to attention in anticipation. My tongue slides across my dry chapped lips and I fight the urge to worry at my fingernails. They're already ragged, I can't have them bleeding at the wrong time.

The sound of his fly grating as he slides it closed speeds my heartbeat. He appears in the doorway, framed in the half-light thrown by the bedside lamp. His eyes dark, unreadable as he sees me watching but his mouth isn't in shadow and I can see the self-satisfied smug grin quirking his lips. An unspoken challenge of sorts. *'Let's see if you can do better...'*

The nod of his head is almost imperceptible but I've seen it so many times before, I'd know it anywhere. He exits, taking a sharp right as he heads for the kitchen, giving me the privacy I need.

My turn...

27

RONAN PICKED me up as promised from outside the hotel and the journey was surprisingly smooth, despite my nervousness over his driving ability. A couple of times on the ride up, I'd caught him watching me from the corner of his eye as though he couldn't fully make up his mind just what I was thinking.

I wasn't worried about him figuring out my dark secret. Cars frightened the shit out of me. It was one of the many reasons I loved living in Dublin; everywhere I needed to go was within biking distance and anything further than that could be reached with the Luas or the bus. It wasn't every form of transport that panicked me either. Just the cars. I could take a bus or a train just as well as anyone else. But getting into a car was a special type of hell and taking on this case had been a baptism of fire of sorts with the constant need for vehicular transport.

The building we parked in front of had, at one point in time, been a beauty. The red brick walls were covered in an acidic green ivy and wouldn't have looked out of place on the front cover of some glossy campus prospectus for an elite university. However, on closer inspection, I could see the ivy had grown ragged, almost woody in parts and the bricks beneath were starting to break up. The minerals had leeched out, covering the red with spots of white and cream so that it looked less like a prestigious building and more like the acne prone face of a teenager, who'd spent a little too much time squeezing that which they should have left alone.

"Not what you were expecting?" Ronan asked, catching me in the act of appraising the building as we approached it.

"I don't know," I said, somewhat honestly. "I guess I expected it to be newer..."

"Wait until you see the inside then," he said. "They were awarded a huge grant last year. Three hundred million or so and rather than building some huge modern eyesore, they decided to pour it into kitting this place out with state of the art gear."

The doors were one of those huge carousel affairs and Ronan went first, pushing the door to get it moving. I hopped in behind him as it started to move forward of its own accord. It spat us out in a large sprawling marble entry hall. The huge domed ceiling above our heads was made entirely of glass and I could

BILINDA P. SHEEHAN

see the pale blue sky, with its traces of white clouds overhead.

"Can I help you?" A clipped female voice cut through my admiration and I caught the eye of the woman behind the marble desk that took up pride of place in the middle of the floor. Her brown hair was scraped severely back from a thin, almost gaunt face. She had the look of an academic, her wan complexion telling me she spent more time cooped up among stacks of books rather than outside in the sunlight.

"We've got an appointment to see Dorian Whittiker," Ronan said smoothly producing his identification and a smile that would have melted any other woman in an instant.

The woman behind the desk peered disdainfully at his badge before turning her attention on me. "And yours?"

I pulled out my own identification and presented it to her. She took more time over mine and I couldn't help but wonder if perhaps she was a little surprised by my credentials. Finally, she glanced up at me, her gaze opaque and unreadable.

"He's expecting you," she said. "Second floor, third corridor down. You'll have to buzz for them to let you in up there."

Ronan's smile was once more wasted on her and she turned her attention away from him with a half grimace. She only had eyes for her books and within seconds, she was caught up entirely in the texts laid out on the desk in front of her.

My low-heeled boots made an odd echoing clip as we crossed the white marble floor. Ronan beat me to the glass lift and the doors whooshed open smoothly. He punched in the floor number and grinned at me as the doors slid silently shut.

"She was cheery," he said. "Don't know why you'd do a job like that if it was only going to make you miserable."

"I don't think it was the job," I said. "I think it was our intrusion."

Ronan snorted and the doors slid open, admitting us to a long narrow walkway. I gazed over the glass railings and caught sight of the woman at the front desk watching our progress.

"You don't think she could hear us, do you?" I asked, feeling suddenly paranoid.

Ronan shrugged and pushed open a set of double doors. "Don't know," he said. "Don't care. Wouldn't have killed her to give us a smile."

I stared at him for a moment, suddenly unsure when he'd morphed into such an arrogant asshole. The woman at the desk owed us nothing at all, especially not a smile.

"Seriously?"

Catching the tone in my voice he paused and glanced over his shoulder at me. "What?"

"A smile? She could have given you a smile?"

"Yeah, what's wrong with that?"

"You sound like a chauvinistic pig," I said. "She didn't throw herself at your feet grovelling because you deigned to smile at her and suddenly she's the problem?"

A cloud crossed his expression for a moment and then he rolled his eyes at me. "Whatever," he muttered. "Didn't have you pegged as one of them."

I let it go. Arguing with him, here and now was a pointless exercise. I wasn't his mother, and it wasn't my job to teach him what was rude and what wasn't. If he couldn't tell the difference, there would be another woman who would have no problem putting him in his place.

At the end of the long white corridor, which made me think of so many of the descriptions of the long tunnel those who'd had near death experiences spoke of, we reached another set of double doors. The windows were blanked off and a large keypad and buzzer sat on the wall, alongside what looked suspiciously like a camera.

Ronan pressed the buzzer and a voice distorted by static cut through the silence.

"Can I help you?" The disembodied voice asked. Despite the static, I recognised the clipped tones of Dorian Whittiker instantly.

"Siobhan Geraghty," I said, cutting over Ronan before he had the chance to speak. "Detective Siobhan Geraghty. We spoke on the phone last night, you asked me to come down. Said you had some information for me pertaining to the case I'm working."

There was a moment of silence and then a buzz came from somewhere deeper in the building. The door clicked and a green light flashed on the panel. Without needing to be told, I pushed the nearest of the doors and it folded in on itself, permitting me admission to Dorian's inner sanctum.

I'd thought the hallway we'd been standing in had seemed sterile but in comparison to the one I now found myself walking down, the other had been positively grubby.

The walls were a brilliant white, the kind that hurt your eyes. It matched the high gloss white tiles on the floor. Even the grout between each tile was a perfect glowing white. Dotted along the walls at regular intervals sat signs. Some of them yellow with large symbols indicating the need for caution and care. Others were a more normal white, with small black writing that insisted on hand washing to prevent the spread of contaminants.

At the end of the hall there was another set of double doors. They were silver and chrome, heavy doors that opened electronically as we approached. The room beyond was set up much like I'd have imagined a laboratory. Well if the laboratory had belonged to Frankenstein.

A large stainless steel table dominated the centre of the room. A small stand that gleamed dully in the harsh lighting sat near the head of the table, which was currently unoccupied. Judging by the way the steel gleamed wetly—as if it had been recently hosed down —I guessed that the table had been occupied recently.

Dorian, or at least I assumed it was Dorian, seemed to melt out from somewhere near the back wall. It took me a moment to realise that he hadn't actually materialised from the shelves but out from behind them.

Just beyond the chrome shelves lined, which were lined with all manner of bottles and fluids, sat another large metal desk. The only bodies dissected and examined on this table however, were microscopic in nature. Dorian was dressed in a white lab coat, his lanky frame barely filling his clothes, making him look like a little boy caught playing dress up in his father's clothes.

His dark hair flopped over into his intelligent brown eyes as though he'd just raked his fingers through it. Judging by the way he was fidgeting with the pen grasped between his long slender fingers, he probably had. Dark bags sat beneath his eyes, making me wonder when he'd last had a decent night's sleep. Despite his naturally sepia brown complexion, the fluorescent lights gave him an ashen undertone that drained the warmth from his face.

"You're late," Dorian said, managing to sound both irritated and somewhat frightened. "I called the station but they said you were already on your way up here- and then I didn't know when you would arrive so I had to hang around and wait and—"

I glanced surreptitiously at my watch as he babbled.

"It's only nine fifteen, Dorian," Ronan said. "Traffic was heavy. You know how it is when you get near the city."

"No," Dorian interjected, shoving his black-rimmed glasses back up the bridge of his nose. "I account for the traffic so I leave on time."

"I'm sorry we're late," I said, casting a sideways glance at Ronan. "It was my fault."

"You should set your alarm for half an hour earlier," Dorian said, his attention pinning me in place.

"Pardon?"

"Your alarm," he said. "On your phone. I assume that's what you use. Everyone nowadays uses their phones instead of a real alarm clock. You should set it for half an hour before you're due to get up. That way, by the time your real alarm goes off, you'll be more alert and more apt to get up on time, thus preventing you from wasting anymore of my time."

"Dorian, mate," Ronan said. "Chill. It's fifteen minutes..."

"It's not just fifteen minutes though," Dorian said, and this time his voice was a little shrill. "It might be fifteen minutes to you but I have things that need doing. Things you wouldn't hope to understand and—"

"You wanted to talk to me about the case," I said. "I'm here now, what have you got for me?" I cut him off mid-stream and for a moment Dorian looked as though he was going to argue with me. His body was taut, tension buzzing through his veins as he stared at me with eyes like big black buttons.

"Sorry," a female voice said, coming from somewhere on the opposite side of the room. I turned and a petite young woman pushed open a side door. In her hands she carried a large tray of what appeared to be vials of clear liquid. "He gets like this when he drinks to much coffee," she said, crossing the room.

"I do not get like anything when I drink coffee—"

"Yes you do," she said patiently as though speaking to a small child. There was a slight accent on her words.

"You're American?" I asked, meeting her gaze curiously.

"Canadian actually," she said with a smile that didn't entirely reach her eyes. "I get that a lot though, moved over here when I was twelve so it's softened a lot."

I nodded.

"I do not get like anything when I drink coffee!" Dorian cut in as though the subject hadn't even changed.

"Well have you told them you got the necklace all cleaned up?" She cocked an eyebrow at him, a clear challenge.

"Well I didn't have the chance, I—"

"No, because you were too busy berating them for getting here late."

She turned her attention back to me once more and held her hand out. "I'm Rosie by the way," she said. "Finishing up my schooling with a little work experience here in the lab with Dr. Whittiker."

We shook hands. She seemed a little old to be doing work experience but I didn't say anything about it.

"I'm Detective Siobhan Geraghty, with the NBCI," I said. "And this is my colleague, Detective Ronan McGuire, he's from the Clonmel branch."

Ronan I noted gave her a wide charming smile and Rosie seemed to straighten, warmth lightly colouring her cheeks as she returned his smile with a flirty one of her own.

"I managed to get the necklace clean," Dorian said, cutting through the sudden awkwardness. "The engraving wasn't a professional job, far too crude. Even sloppy."

"What does it say?"

He gestured for me to follow him and I did so, in behind the shelving units in the corner of the room. It seemed like an odd set up for an office and as though he could sense the question on the tip of my tongue he said, somewhat sheepishly. "I get claustrophobic in the room they said I could use as my office. Rosie suggested I set up my office out here instead."

"Good call," I said, noting the way the shelves left

an impression of open space whilst still affording him the privacy necessary for an office.

The necklace was in a plastic evidence bag, clearly labelled with the case number in block lettering. Scooping it up from the counter, I twisted the necklace into the light and stared down at the writing. Dorian hadn't been kidding when he'd said the engraving was sloppy. There were deeper indentations in the metal that made me think whoever had done it, their hand had slipped a couple of times, denting the locket.

"It looks like it was written by a child," I said. Alice would have been thirteen when her sister went missing. She'd assured me the locket had no engraving before Clara disappeared and I hadn't thought she was lying.

"Do we know what it says?" I asked, studying the words. The only word that really jumped out at me was the 'I'. Everything else was jammed together.

Without saying a word, Dorian handed me another slip of paper.

Who in the World am I?

"Is this a joke?" I asked, facing Dorian once more.

"I—No, it's—"

"It's no joke," Rosie said. "That's what it says."

"Why would they write this on it?" I stared down at the scrawl. Now that I knew what it said, it was a little easier to put the pieces together and I could almost make the words out, if I squinted really hard.

"It's from Alice in Wonderland," Dorian said.

"From Chapter 2, The Pool of Tears. Alice ponders on whether she is truly herself. She thinks she might have been changed out for one of the others. One of her friends."

I stared at him, a sick feeling curling in the pit of my stomach.

"And that's not all," Dorian said, sounding a little more confident than he had a moment before. "We gained access to Clara's dental records. We were lucky in that she didn't have the best of teeth. She had worn braces, and they were removed only two months before she disappeared."

He pressed a button on a lightbox on the wall, illuminating an x-ray of a set of teeth. He lit up a second box and another x-ray appeared. I was no expert but even to my untrained eyes, the teeth looked different.

"What are you saying?" There was a tightness to my voice that I hadn't expected.

"I'm saying it's not Clara McCarthy," he said stiffly. "The dental records don't match. We'll get the DNA back and it'll confirm what I'm saying here."

"Then if the body isn't Clara's, who is it?" I stared down at the necklace once more. Whoever had done this was playing with us.

"From examination of the other missing women from the same time period, the x-rays from this body matches most closely with Evie Ryan."

I recognised the name immediately. I'd looked over her case file the night before. She'd gone missing three weeks after Clara, on Saturday the 9th of November. I'd even commented on the resemblance between the two girls. Same height, same build, same hair colour. It wasn't a coincidence. Evie had been chosen for her appearance, I was certain of it. I couldn't prove it, of course. Not unless the killer suddenly decided to pop up and give us a complete signed confession with all the gory details over how and why they'd taken the girls in the first place.

"There's more," he said. "This wasn't the original burial spot of the body."

His words were like a slap of icy water.

"What?"

"The soil there is far more acidic with a pH below 3.2 we wouldn't have such an intact skeleton if she'd been buried there the entire time.

"Not to mention the lack of adipocere. It's present on the body and the clothes but the surrounding soil where the body was found is clean. There's also have very little bone splintering. I would have expected much more due to the constant freeze and thaw cycles evident in the soil samples we took."

I stared at him uncomprehendingly. I had an idea of what he was saying. He needed to stop blinding me with science.

"English, please," I said. Dorian stared at me as though I was suddenly the one speaking a different language. "Pretend I'm a complete idiot and break it down for me."

He sighed and jammed his hand back through his hair before once more straightening his glasses on his nose. His expression told me he considered me a complete idiot anyway and I could tell he wasn't exactly full of confidence for my ability to solve the case.

"The victim wasn't originally buried in the woods where you found her. She was interred somewhere else and very recently, like in the last week, dug up and moved to the woods... Any longer than a week or two and I would expect to see more animal disturbance and distress to the bones and clothes."

"So you're telling me, it's not Clara, but another girl Evie. She's dressed in Clara's clothes, even has the necklace Clara's sister gave to her. But this one has a new engraving on the back that seems to be taunting us. And what's more, the burial site isn't the original. She was dug up from somewhere and dumped in the woods."

Dorian nodded. "That's it exactly."

"My guess is that she was dug up and placed in the woods so you would find her," Rosie said.

Dorian turned on her, his dark eyes flashing with sharp anger. "We can't know that," he said. "The evidence can only tell us she was moved, not the why."

"Come on," Rosie said, pulling a face. "You don't bury someone for twenty-odd years and then suddenly dig them up and dump them in the woods, on a path that's by all accounts quite popular, if you don't want the body to be discovered. Evidence or no, I say your guy wanted her found... And the necklace seems to back it all up."

She wasn't wrong but then neither was Dorian. The evidence couldn't expressly tell us the reason for the moving of the body but Rosie's interpretation was pretty close to what I was thinking myself.

"Is that everything?" I sighed, frustration thrumming in my veins. It was still early and yet I felt as though I'd just pulled a double shift.

"It's all we've got until the DNA comes back," Rosie said.

"What about cause of death on the body you do have?"

Dorian lips twisted into a grimace, making him look like someone who'd just tasted something particularly unpleasant.

"There's evidence of blunt force trauma," he said, "but..."

"But what?" I was beginning to sound snappy and I tried to soften my words with a smile instead.

"Damage to the vertebrae of the neck and the clavicle. What tissue samples we managed to take suggest strangulation. However, the body is in such a state of decomposition it's difficult to tell which injury was the actual cause of death. They're both significant enough to cause death. There are signs of torture..."

Torture wasn't uncommon but judging by the way

Dorian's face appeared to pale as he mentioned it I could only guess at the severity of it.

"Such as?" I dug my fingernails into the palms of my hands in an attempt to keep my emotions in check.

"Spiral fracture to the left femur," Rosie said. "Extensive scarring on the bones, made by an as yet unidentified blade. Fracture to the wrists of both arms. Dislocation of the right shoulder, fracture to the jawbone and orbital bones consistent with repeated blows. Some of the fractures had time to begin healing before they were re-broken."

"What does that mean?" I had an idea but I needed to hear her say it.

"It's possible she was kept for some time before he decided to murder her..." Rosie said. "Her injuries are consistent with prolonged imprisonment and torture."

"That's enough," Ronan said, I glanced at him over my shoulder and he'd started to stalk away across the lab.

"I need a full report," I said. Rosie's expression was grim as she nodded.

"You find it difficult to listen to," she said, calling after Ronan. He halted and turned back, his face ashen.

"It's suffering," he said. "I know she suffered, I'm not sure why I need the gory details of it all."

I opened my mouth but Rosie beat me to it.

"That's nice for you," she said, without any trace of bitterness. "You can walk away. It must be nice that you can choose not to hear how these women spent their last hours or days. That you can decide it makes you too uncomfortable. Where was their choice?"

"That's not the point, I..."

"But it is the point," she said and this time there was the barest hint of anger in her voice. "That's exactly the point. If you're going to catch this bastard, and let's be honest, that's exactly what he is, then you need to hear their suffering. No one is asking you to endure it. They've done that for you. By walking away, you're denying them, denying their existence, denying that their pain mattered. They've already been silenced, they don't need *you,* the one who's supposed to be on their side, to do it all over again."

He sighed and turned on his heel, the sound of his shoes echoed through the lab before the door clicked open and the sound of his clipping shoes faded down the hall.

There was a moment of silence, finally broken by the awkward sound of Rosie clearing her throat.

"Sorry about that," I said.

She shrugged. "I guess sometimes we forget that people aren't as good as we want them to be."

The only answer I had for her was a small smile. There wasn't anything I could say that hadn't already been said. Whether Ronan liked it or not, whether it made him uncomfortable or not, Rosie was right. The victims—the ones we were supposed to be working on behalf of—had no choice in their suffering. And I'd long felt that the least I could do for them was act as their witness.

I couldn't save them from the fate that had befallen them but I could do everything in my power to bring those responsible to justice.

28

I sat in the living room, hands wrapped around the ceramic cat shaped mug. The rabbit alarm sat clock on the coffee table in front of me.

Ever since I'd found it waiting for me on the doorstep, I hadn't been able to tear my eyes away from it. It was important, that I was certain of but how, or why? That was a lot more difficult to understand.

It had been gone for so long, I'd initially wondered if perhaps I'd been mistaken about it, if I'd misremembered an important detail about Clara giving me the clock.

I hadn't. And one quick glance at the back of the rabbit's pocket watch, to the place where I'd scratched my initials into the surface as a teenager told me I wasn't mistaken. It really was mine. The white rabbit had come home.

"Alice?" The familiar voice made me jump. Turning, I found myself staring up into the blue eyes of a woman standing in the kitchen doorway. She shuffled awkwardly, shoving a strand of hair back behind her ear, a self-conscious gesture that felt as familiar to me as her voice.

"You don't remember me?" she asked, sounding hurt.

Her name hovered on the edges of my mind, like a picture that refused to come into focus.

"Sarah," she said. "I went to school with Clara and—"

"You used to babysit me," I said, the memory flooding back.

"That's right," she said, her smile wide and genuine, brightening her face considerably, making her look younger.

"You were friends with Clara," I said with a smile of my own. "I remember. The pair of you were thick as thieves and you wouldn't let me come with out with you." That had been before Clara had met Liam. Before she'd gotten pregnant, before she'd been forced out of school.

"It used to drive you mad," she said. "Got us into so much trouble with your Mam."

We laughed together. It was nice to remember Clara in a time before everything started to go wrong. Part of me knew it wasn't right to think of it like that but I couldn't help it. There was still a part of me that felt almost betrayed by her. It was a stupid, childish part of me but I couldn't shake it off. We were supposed to grow up together, have families, watch each other grow old.

She hesitated, twisting her fingers round in the beige cardigan she wore. "I heard…" she trailed off, her eyes sliding away to dart around the room before they came to rest on my face once more. "I heard they found her." Her voice was little more than a hoarse, hushed whisper heavy with emotion.

"They seem to think they have," I said, swallowing past the dry lump in the back of my throat.

"You don't sound convinced," Sarah asked, taking a step into the room.

"No, it's not that," I said, looking down at the patterned carpet. I could still remember the day Mam had had it fitted. Clara and I both had thought it looked like something that belonged in an old folk's home. Of course, we never said that. Mam had been so pleased with it that to say anything negative would have been cruel.

"Do you mind if I sit?" Sarah asked, breaking through my thoughts.

"Yeah, go ahead," I said, gesturing to the chair opposite me. "Do you want a cup of tea?"

She shook her head and I fought back the relief. I didn't want to get up. I still didn't entirely trust my legs, not after they'd refused to hold me up when I'd found the white rabbit clock on the doorstep. For some reason, they'd turned to jelly and I wasn't still sure if they'd returned to normal yet. Not to mention the pounding headache. It hadn't improved. In fact, it had worsened. Dehydration from the hangover and the stress, most likely. It would pass eventually but right now, just thinking was enough to make my brain throb.

"Is it possible the police have made a mistake?"

I jerked my head up, meeting Sarah's curious gaze. "I don't see how they could," I said. "They asked me to identify some of her things and..." I shrugged, a sort of numb feeling spreading through my neck and shoulder as I moved my injured arm without thinking.

"I'm so sorry," Sarah said, dropping her gaze to her hands. Her fingers were completely knotted up in the front of her cardigan now. "We always thought—or maybe hoped is a better way of putting it—that Clara would come back. That she'd turn up one day and..."

"It's a nice thought," I said. "But I think I knew deep down it was never going to happen. Someone took her that night. I was there. I saw it happen."

"Of course," Sarah said. "I never meant to suggest..." She trailed off and smiled awkwardly. "I'm sorry, I came over here to see if I could help and I think I'm just making everything worse."

I shook my head and tightened my fingers around the mug in my hands, an attempt to soak up every last drop of heat radiating through the ceramic.

"No, I'm the one who should be sorry," I said. "I'm just feeling a little delicate."

"I heard you'd enjoyed yourself in the pub," she

said, her smile widening. "It's good to switch off, even if it's only for a short while."

That was the problem with small places; everyone always knew everyone else's business. There was no escaping it. No matter how much you tried to keep to yourself, there was always someone lurking around a corner, waiting to catch you out and spread the gossip to all who would listen. I'd hated it when I'd lived here and now that I was back, I hated it even more.

I returned Sarah's smile with a tight one of my own.

"What happened to your arm?"

"Oh, you didn't hear that then?" I asked. Sarah's expression crumpled, telling me I'd allowed some of my bitterness to seep out.

"I should go," she said, climbing to her feet unsteadily. "I didn't mean to intrude. I'll—"

"Sarah, I'm sorry," I said, setting the cup on the table in front of me. "I shouldn't have said that. It's just..." I shrugged helplessly and my shoulder sent a painful warning down my arm.

"Dick said I shouldn't come here," she said. "That I'd only be poking my nose in where it wasn't warranted. He was right."

"He wasn't. You're not," I said, reaching out toward her. I caught her hand and her fingers reflexively closed over mine. "I shouldn't have been cruel. I'm sorry."

She sniffed, her eyes glassy with unshed tears. The guilt I'd been nursing intensified.

"Well if you're sure I'm not bothering you," she said, edging closer to the seat once more.

"You're really not." I meant it. There were many things I disliked about being back but Sarah wasn't one of them. She was my connection to Clara, a chance for me to feel even closer to my sister. I couldn't just throw that away, not over a bloody hangover and a desire to play my cards close to my chest.

"You're still with Dick, then?" I asked, desperately hoping my voice stayed light.

Sarah smiled and ducked her head, her fingers once more straying to the edge of her cardigan. "Yeah," she said, almost shyly. "We got married and everything."

"You were lucky," I said. Sarah's head snapped up, her eyes boring into mine and I hastily added. "You know, knowing he was the one. Some people don't ever meet the one they're supposed to be with, never mind meet them when they're still in school."

She laughed, tucking her hair back behind her ears. "I suppose we were," she said. "I think I always knew he was the right one. You know?"

"I don't," I said. "I haven't been that lucky."

"So there's no one, then?"

I shook my head. "Nope. Foot loose and fancy free," I said. "That's me."

The look she gave me was loaded with pity and I couldn't help but feel my hackles rise. I wasn't particularly bothered by my single status. In fact, I kind of enjoyed it. Gerald had once joked—after I'd turned down his offer of a date—that I was married to the job. Like a nun committed to social work instead of God.

"I'm sorry," she said, again. The constant apologies grated on me but I pushed the uncharitable thoughts aside.

"Don't be," I said. "I like it, means I've got more time for my work."

"I heard you were in social work," she said, wrinkling her nose. "I don't think I could do that job. I think it would break my heart too much."

"Why?" I couldn't stop the question from popping out of my mouth.

"Well, there's a lot of breaking up of families, isn't there? I mean, I don't think I could do that. Family is so important."

"Well, yeah, but sometimes families fall apart," I said. "It's not our goal. We want to keep them together, help them get back on their feet when they're struggling. It doesn't always work. Not everyone is cut out to be a parent."

There was a flicker of something dark in Sarah's eyes and it was gone as quickly as it had appeared but I'd seen it. I was certain I'd seen it, and whatever it was, sent a trickle of discomforting ice down my spine.

"Well, I can't relate," she said. "I can't imagine my life without my, Ali," she said, the pride in her voice undeniable.

"You've got a daughter?"

She nodded, her expression brightening further. "She's ten next month," she said. "Growing up far too fast for my liking though."

I smiled and nodded along with her but it hurt to hear her talk about her family. It wasn't that I begrudged Sarah her happiness but there was a part of me that thought it should have been Clara's life and Clara's children I was hearing stories of. She'd deserved a chance to be happy, the opportunity to grow up and get married. Instead she'd been in the ground all these years because someone decided to steal her life away from her.

It wasn't fair and it wasn't right.

Anger started to build in my stomach and without thinking, I hopped to my feet.

"I'm sorry, Sarah, I've just remembered, I've got an errand I need to run for Mam. I'm so sorry but I've got to go."

She stared at me in surprise.

"Oh, yeah, of course," she stammered, sounding somewhat bewildered. "I'll let you get on." She climbed to her feet and headed for the door.

"If you need anything, Alice," she said. "Any help with the preparations. I'm here for you."

"Thanks—"

"I wasn't there for Clara when it mattered," she said, her voice cracking over the words. "But if you need me, I'm here now."

She turned on her heels and hurried from the

sitting room, leaving me to stare at her retreating back. My mind puzzled over her words. What had she meant when she'd said she wasn't there for Clara when it mattered? They'd been best friends. They'd shared everything. Was there something Sarah wasn't telling me? Was there something she knew?

If there was, I intended to find out.

29

After Sarah left, the morning was taken up with a steady stream of visitors. It never ceased to surprise me just how quickly news spread in a small community. People came and went, expressing their sympathies that Clara had been taken so young. They were like vultures gathering at a corpse. Perhaps it was unfair of me to think of them like that but when you're forced to stand there and listen to a constant stream of platitudes, any patience you might have had quickly disappears.

By lunchtime, my headache had grown to epic proportions and I escaped up to my bedroom. Lying back on the bed, face covered with the floral pillow, I tried to blot out the thoughts milling in my head.

"Alice!" Imelda's voice floated up the stairs and I tried to ignore it. Maybe then they'd all go away.

The door banged open, making me jump and I

peered out from beneath the edge of the pillow to see Imelda framed in the doorway. She was pale, the circles beneath her eyes standing out in stark relief. As I stared up at her in that moment, I realised just how much she'd aged. The strain of Clara's discovery was clearly taking its toll on her.

"What's wrong?" I pushed the pillow aside and sat up, the movement triggering the pain circuits in my brain to light up like a Christmas tree.

"The Gardaí are here," she said. "Two detectives. They said they want to speak to all of us."

Shoving myself up off the bed, I followed her down the stairs and found myself in the doorway to the living room. The house was quiet, only the ticking of the grandfather clock in the hallway broke the silence with its steady rhythm. There was something else too: an answering tick, half a second out of time with the big timekeeper in the hall. I scanned the living room, my eyes coming to rest on the white rabbit with his pocket watch held aloft.

I hadn't been able to bring myself to take it upstairs to my room. There was something off about it, something that curdled my emotions in the pit of my stomach like cream that has gone sour. Despite being a gift from Clara, it was now tainted. It had gone missing just before she had and now it had returned just after her body had been found. The rational part of my brain knew the rabbit hadn't really done those things itself but the more primal part of me, the instinctual side of my nature, was sure the two things were connected in some way.

Mam sat on the sofa, staring out of the window, her gaze blank and unseeing. Dad had persuaded her to take one of the tranquillisers she'd been prescribed. Looking at her now, I wasn't sure what was worse; the silent blank staring or the frantic obsessive persona that had entered my room this morning like a whirling dervish. They were both terrible. Neither was the woman I knew or recognised as my mother but then a part of me believed *that* woman had disappeared along with Clara.

It was as though the man who'd taken Clara taken my mother too, leaving in her place something unrecognisable. What was left seemed to be raw, unbridled emotion in the guise of a human being. A changeling. And I knew, even if nobody else did, that it wasn't my mother. It wasn't the woman who soothed me to sleep when I was sick, or held me when the nightmares were too real for my childish mind to comprehend.

But wasn't that grief's modus operandi? It's signature? It stole away the ones you loved, ripping them from your arms and heart. Leaving you to struggle in the dark, dank, void alone. And in that void, it didn't matter how loudly you screamed, no one could hear you. No one wanted to hear you. They were too caught up in their own emotions to notice you drowning in the silence of yours.

Dad was next to her, his own expression one heavy with concern as he watched his wife closely. Seeing the two of them together caused the ache in my chest to increase. I knew how he felt. He wanted to make it better, to fix the problem. After all, wasn't that what he was supposed to do? Wasn't that his job? And he was good at it... Or he had been, before...

He was good with his hands. Capable and strong they never faltered, never failed him. Whenever there was an issue at home, like the time the drains had backed up, or the central heating had packed up working, he'd jumped into action. In his element, righting the wrongs and fixing the issues...

Only this time, there was nothing he could do about it.

And I could see it written on his face, like someone had taken a black pen and written his thoughts across his forehead.

I knew how he felt, not that I could tell him that.

But I wanted to make this better too. I wanted to go back to that night and fight harder. In my dreams a thousand times since she'd disappeared, I'd felt Clara's hand slipping from mine and every time I held her tighter. Securing my fingers around hers, taking her with me.

Saving her...

But my dreams weren't the reality I found myself in now, no matter how much I wanted them to be.

"Alice." Detective Siobhan Geraghty stood up, her

mouth a moue of displeasure. "I was just introducing myself and Ronan here and telling your parents why we've come here today and—"

"When can we get her body back?" Mam asked, her eyes suddenly snapping into focus, like someone had just flipped the lights on inside.

"That's just it," Siobhan said. "In circumstances like this, we need to hold onto the body for a little longer. At least while the investigation is ongoing."

"No." Mam's voice was the firmest I'd heard it in a long time. She levelled a glare at the detective Siobhan had introduced as Ronan. He seemed to wilt a little under her stare.

"She doesn't belong there," Mam continued. "She needs to be here, with her family, where we can look after her." Her voice cracked, taking with it another piece of my heart. "I don't want her there alone. She doesn't belong there..." She trailed off, her defiant expression crumpling.

I knew what she meant. I wanted Clara home as well. It had been too long and she belonged here, with us. The rational side of me knew it wouldn't be the same; she was bones now, not the flesh and blood sister I'd known. But the primal side of me pushed those thoughts aside. If we could just have her home, everything would be all right, it told me.

"We've just come back from speaking with the pathologist," Siobhan said, trying again with her gentle placating tone that only grated on me. "Despite the positive identification of Clara's belongings..." She glanced up, giving me a small sympathetic smile. "We now believe the body is not that of your daughter, or sister," she added for my benefit. "This is dependent on the DNA of course but the dental records, we have, are very clear on the matter."

Her words hit me like a bucket of icy water and I felt my body take an involuntary gasp of air, like I was resurfacing from beneath the surface of a frozen lake.

I stumbled and without thinking, thumped the edge of the doorframe with my arm. The pain was enough to bring the world back into focus with a sharp jolt. Tears blurred my vision and I dashed them away with the back of my hand as I tried to wrap my mind around Siobhan's words.

It wasn't Clara. They hadn't found Clara...

"I don't understand," Dad was speaking, his confusion evident. "You tell us you've found her and now you're saying it's not her at all... How can you do that?"

"I can't imagine the distress this must be causing you all," Siobhan said. "But when we initially told you about the body we did say it was dependent on the findings of the pathologist. We went on the preliminary identification from the items found with the body in question, which led us to believe it was in fact your daughter Clara. But—"

"She's not dead," Mam said, her voice quiet, almost contemplative.

"That's not what I'm saying, Mrs McCarthy. As it

stands right now, your daughter is still a missing person but—"

"So she's not dead then," Mam said again, her eyes focusing in on the detective's face. There was a shrewd intelligence glittering in her blue-eyed gaze, one I recognised only too well.

She looked now at the detective, the same way she'd looked at me after I tried to tell her Clara had been taken. A combination of disbelief and rage, the part of her mind that Clara's disappearance had awakened, peeking out, her attempt at protecting her mind from the terrible truth.

To others it might have sounded stupid. Why couldn't she face the truth? Her daughter was gone, most probably dead. But they didn't know her as I did. She was the type of person always prone to imagination. When we'd been children, listening to her stories before bed had been our favourite way to fall asleep. We didn't need bedtime fairytale books. Not when Mam was on hand to conjure the most imaginative of tales from her mind.

I'd certainly inherited her ability to conjure up my own amusements and as I'd grown older and Clara had disappeared, what had once been an asset became a curse.

There wasn't one scenario Clara could have faced that I hadn't already thought of. In the early hours of the morning, before the sun rose was the best time to conjure the kinds of horrors that would have most sane people running for the straight-jackets.

"I can't answer that with any certainty," Siobhan said firmly. "However, I have to take into consideration all the elements in play."

"How did they get her clothes?" The question left my lips before I had the chance to truly think about what I was saying.

"That's one of the queries I've got," Siobhan said. "How certain are you that the clothes you saw, were the clothes your sister was wearing at the time of her disappearance?"

An image of Clara screaming and terrified popped into my head. Closing my eyes, I scrubbed my palm against the rough surface of my jeans, a pathetic attempt to rid myself of the ghostly brush of her fingers my mind liked to remind me of.

"I'm positive," I said. "That's what she was wearing when she was—"

"Shut up!" Mam screamed at me as she hopped to her feet and launched herself across the living room toward me.

"Shut up! Shut up! Shut up! Shut up!" She chanted the words over and over. I expected her to hit me, to lash out with the pain she was clearly suffering. But either she couldn't, or didn't want to. Instead, she stood over me, fisting her hands, her nails digging into the soft flesh of her palms, leaving bloody half-moon prints in their wake. Her eyes were wild.

"Ita, stop it please, it's not Alice's fault." Dad wrapped his arms around her frail shoulders but she refused to budge. She stared down at me with eyes that blazed with her rage and something else, another emotion I'd never noticed before. Terror.

"She wants her dead," she said, the words tumbling from her mouth. They hit the air, detonating inside my head with deadly accuracy. "She keeps saying she's gone, Dennis, she said it from the start and even now, when they know it's not Clara she still can't leave it."

"Mam," I said, straightening up in the doorway. "This isn't what I wanted... I want Clara home as much as—"

"Don't say her name," she said. "Don't you speak her name to me."

I bit back the hurt and anger that rose in the back of my throat. It was always like this. In her eyes, only she was allowed to talk about Clara, to reminisce about her.

Pushing past her, I escaped out into the hall and made for the front door. I wasn't sure where I was going but I knew I couldn't spend another moment in the house.

"That's it, Alice." My mother's voice drifted after me. "Run away. Run away and leave us, just like you left Clara."

My tears traced down my face, in hot angry rivulets as I slammed the door behind me, the glass rattling in its frame the same way my heart rattled in my chest.

30

"JESUS, THAT WAS HARSH," Ronan said, scrubbing his hands back through his hair, causing it to stand to attention.

I said nothing as I climbed silently into the passenger seat. I waited for him to start the car. He didn't say anything else as he started the engine and we drove out onto the road.

The countryside whipped past and I kept my gaze trained on the horizon, my fingers curling and uncurling into fists as we took a turn a little too fast for my comfort.

I was no stranger to grief. Spend long enough in the job and you get to witness first hand the raw unchecked emotions that came to those loved ones left behind. Knowing all of this never made any of it easier and watching Mrs McCarthy fly off the handle today at her only remaining daughter had been a lesson in keeping my tongue in check. No one, not even Alice would have thanked me for intervening on her behalf.

I'd seen families torn apart by loss, forced to watch the disintegration of relationships in real time as the case progressed. The only difference with the McCarthy's was that the disintegration had already occurred long before I'd ever made it to their living room. From what little I knew of Alice, she'd moved away as soon as she was old enough to strike out on her own. It had been she who had dogged the Gardaí over her sister's disappearance. Her parents had taken a backseat, letting her chase and cajole, plead and threaten, with the powers that be, all so her sister could be categorised among the ranks of the missing. It couldn't have been easy for her. When you looked into her eyes, you could almost see the toll her sister's loss had taken on her. Pain and guilt, a nasty combination for anyone to bear but she hid it well. She was probably the type to bury it deep inside, keeping it from the watchful view of those around her.

Perhaps, if I'd had to live with a mother like that, I would have done the same.

Not that I could blame Ita McCarthy either.

Her daughter was gone. It was a grief I couldn't even begin to fathom.

The English language was a miraculous thing. In its infinite wisdom, it gave us words for the loss of our loved ones.

Losing parents left you an orphan, a lonely word

that conjured images of gaunt, hollow eyed children desperately bereft of love.

Losing a partner made you a widow, or widower, depending on your role in the partnership. A crushing loss that saw your soul cleaved in two, one half forever lost and forced to wander. It wasn't something I could imagine.

But the loss of a child... That type of loss was too great to imagine. So huge that not even the English language, which had given us so much, could do justice by giving a name to that kind of agony.

Death was long supposed a natural occurrence. It would come to us all in time.

But the loss of ones child, that was unnatural.

The child was never supposed to go before their parents.

And today, in that living room we'd witnessed the aftermath of that balance which had been so carelessly disrupted all those years ago.

And it was a loss Ita McCarthy had had to endure for all these years. No doubt, she blocked it out, pretended to herself that it wasn't true, that her child wasn't missing, wasn't dead. A form of survival because at the end of the day how was the human mind supposed to overcome something so terrible?

"Are you all right?" Ronan's voice cut through my thoughts and I jerked with the sudden realisation that the car had stopped moving.

I glanced over at him. The Garda station was silhouetted behind him.

"I'm fine," I lied. "Just thinking about the case is all."

"I can't get Mrs McCarthy's reaction out of my head. She was so—" he paused. "Cruel." His forehead creased with consternation.

"She can't help it," I said. "She's hurting. When that happens you lash out at those nearest and dearest."

"She's going to drive her daughter away," he said, saying the very thought I'd had myself.

I shrugged. "Not our problem. We can't fix their familial issues," I said. "All we can do is try and get the answers they need so they can begin to make sense of their lives."

"Do you think they will?" His question took me by surprise.

"I don't know," I said, carefully. "Some make it back to each other. And then others..." I trailed off and Ronan nodded.

"Yeah, I know," he said. "Same thing happened with my Mam's sister and her husband."

"What happened?" I didn't want to pry but there was something in the way he spoke that suggested he wanted to talk about it.

"Auntie Eileen had a little one die," he said, gruffly. "Cot death. One minute everything was fine and the next Ben was gone..."

"I'm so sorry," I said and even as I said it, I knew the

words were woefully inadequate but there was nothing else I had to offer him. I couldn't take his pain away for him. I couldn't fix it. The tragedy was long passed.

He shrugged, a non-committal move of his shoulders that hid a multitude of thoughts. "Auntie Eileen split from Frank not long after," he said. "He'd been the one to put him down you see and she couldn't look at him. Blamed him, in her own way." He glanced up at me. "She didn't mean to, she knew it wasn't his fault, knew he loved the bones of Ben but still…"

I nodded. I did understand. I'd never experienced it but it was too common a reaction to the tragedy the loss of a child brought. I'd seen it happen too many times before.

"So what's the next move now?" he said, abruptly changing the subject.

"We're going to have to talk to Evie's parents."

"They've been informed," Ronan said, taking me by surprise.

"When?"

"Sergeant Mills knew the family personally, he wanted to be the one to break the news to them."

I nodded without saying anything. It made sense and while hearing the news from a friend wouldn't make it any less cruel, it was still kinder than hearing it from a complete stranger.

"I'd like to pull Alice McCarthy back in," I said, suddenly. Ronan jerked his head up and caught my eyes with his.

"Whatever for?"

"Well for one thing, Evie was wearing Clara's clothes when we found her body, not to mention the positive ID we have on the necklace. I want to hear in her own words what happened the night Clara went missing."

"It's in the statement," Ronan said.

"Have you read that thing?" I couldn't quite keep the edge from my voice. "For god's sake they wrote on the bottom of it that Clara was clearly a runaway."

"They didn't know any better," he started to say before I cut him off.

"That's not an excuse, Ronan. They dismissed Alice's statement of events because she'd been drinking the night before and they thought she was concocting a story to take the heat off her own behaviour."

Ronan said nothing, allowing me to vent. "Show me a teenager who hasn't indulged in a little ditch drinking in their time, how many of them created violent stories where their sisters disappeared to cover up a little underage indulgence?

"And they couldn't account for the scratches and bruising on her arms but they didn't investigate it further either." I sucked in a deep breath. "Face it, they screwed up back then and her statement is as good as useless. We need to hear from her, if she's willing to go back over it, what really happened that night. Maybe then, it'll give us a way forward because right now, we've got nothing."

"We've got a body," he said. "Why are you so hung up on the McCarthy case?"

I sat back against the seat and closed my eyes. Why was I hung up on it? The answer, at least to me anyway, was pretty simple.

"She's the first," I said quietly. "There's a pattern of behaviour here, you can see it in the photographs and the likeness between the girls."

"There's a similarity in the first two but not the other three."

"But the other three, including Joanna all look alike," I said. He was right of course. Perhaps, the first two girls were an anomaly. I didn't believe it myself but I couldn't dismiss it either. I needed more proof and so far that seemed to be pretty thin on the ground.

Ronan stared out the window once more. "I'm not doubting you," he said. "But don't you think maybe we're scrabbling a little too desperately in the dark here?"

Scrubbing my hands over my face, I shrugged. "What choice do we have? Until we have more to go on, we have no choice but to scrabble around in the dark, until something shakes loose."

The phone in the car started to vibrate making us both jump. I reached for it at the same time that Ronan did, our fingers brushing before I could jerk my hand back.

He stared at me curiously for a moment before he picked the phone up and took the call. His expression shifted, closing off as he nodded.

"We'll be right there," he said before he hung up.

"They've found another body," he said.

"Where?" But I already knew the answer.

"A few metres away from Evie," he said.

"Is it Clara?"

"Didn't say but," he swallowed hard, his Adam's apple bobbing in his throat. "They think there's more than one."

I clenched my hands, my short fingernails biting into the skin of my palms. "Forensics on the way?"

Ronan nodded.

"Then let's go," I said. "It's time something started to shake loose around here."

31

HER EYES ARE CLOSED when I enter the room. Feigning sleep or perhaps unconsciousness. On her stomach, face turned away from me. But it's just another lie. The tensing of her shoulders tells me that as my footfalls catch her ear.

The bone of her right arm protrudes through the skin as it lies limply on the sheet next to her. The bloodstain underneath is already drying.

The skin below my elbow itches where my own scar sits. So faded, I'd almost forgotten it existed until now.

I don't waste a second; I don't have that kind of luxury.

Her eyes slide back in her head, her muffled moan trailing off as I roll her quickly and efficiently in the bed, sliding the plastic sheet beneath her body with practiced ease. The sheet is a necessary precaution for what comes next.

When I finish with her, she stares up at me with wide fever-bright, frightened eyes. I can't even remember when she stopped pretending to be asleep and I'm too caught up in my purpose to care.

But she's different to the others. They broke faster, gave up quickly. Like animals beaten into submission. But not her. Oh, she pretends it's there, cringes at all the right moments, leaking tears, causing the carefully applied eyeshadow to smudge. At least the mascara is staying put. No one likes panda eyes.

But despite her obvious agony, the look I crave—a silent plea to end it all—is just not there and I have a dark feeling in the pit of my stomach that she's not going to give it to me either.

"Do you want to die?" I whisper the words against her ear and she struggles against the rough rope holding her down. Pain sends a shock through her that stiffens her spine as she moves her broken arm. At least I know she's not so far gone that she can't still feel pain. Of course, she will reach a point where delirium will steal even that from her.

And I don't want to wait until that happens. What I need from her has to happen soon or I'll lose my chance.

There's panic, the smell of her fear an intoxicating scent that would drive him into a frenzy if he were here in the room with us. But it's just her and me at the moment and I'm not so moved by the bodies adrenaline soaked response to terror. That's not what drives me.

I search her gaze but all I can see is a kind of defiance. Almost daring me to try and end her. It's something I understand. The drive to survive. I've been doing it all my life. Was that what I saw in her when I found her picture? A kindred spirit of sorts? It sounds absurd.

Placing one knee on the bed, I straighten up. The knots in my back from my time spent working on her fail to loosen.

"If I walk out of here now, he'll come back and we both know that of the two of us, you'd prefer me to be in here. I'm by far the nicer..." I finger a braid, running my thumb over the silken strands and she flinches. "But there's another way..."

I meet her gaze head on, offering the mercy the others before her craved.

And instead of gratitude, I see anger light her hazel eyes. She thrashes on the bed, screaming against the gag still secure in her mouth.

My head begins to thrum, mouth dry as I watch her flail. Sweat beads on her skin as her movements slow. She'll pass out if she keeps this up.

She collapses onto the bed, the air sliding out of her body, leaving her on the plastic sheet like a deflated balloon. I don't have enough time. My window of opportunity is closing, taking with it everything I had hoped for her. Rage boils in my chest as I stare down at her.

Sucking in a deep breath, I leave the room; ignoring the curious look he gives me as I head for the shed. At least he knows not to go back into her without my permission. And by the time I'm done, she'll wish she had given me what I needed.

By the time I finish with her, she's a masterpiece. Even he looks at me differently when he sees her laid out on the plastic sheet. A mixture of shock and awe.

I strip off the protective gloves and drop the now empty bottle of caustic soda into the sink. It had been far more effective than even I had anticipated. They won't find anything on her now.

The thought that something I've done could have such far-reaching consequences gives me a thrill but it isn't enough to make up for the disappointment. She died defiantly and for that she has my grudging respect.

I watch, downhearted, as he wraps her carefully in the plastic sheet. He stole from me what I needed, stole my chance. I've given him everything, shielded him from his own idiocy and he repays me like this? By ruining what little pleasure I have left?

As I watch him, I know I hate him.

32

By the time we arrived in the car park, back where I'd originally started with the case, the evening was beginning to draw in.

Forensics were in the process of setting up several large lights that flooded the area with a bright white glow, illuminating the ground with an eerie cast.

The plastic sides of the large white-walled tent in the middle of the trees flapped noisily, creating eerie noises that carried and echoed through the trees. The wind that was gradually building around us whipped my hair into my eyes as we traipsed across the gravel.

Ronan lifted the yellow tape and I slipped underneath, grabbing a pair of gloves and plastic covers for my shoes. I eyed the spare coveralls on the table, held down by a large rock someone had scrounged from the edge of the pathway.

"You'll have to put one of them on too, if you're

planning on getting a look-see at the bodies," Rosie's muffled voice cut through my quiet contemplation and I jumped.

I wrinkled my nose in disgust as she drew down the mask she was wearing and folded her arms over her chest. She was already wearing the white coveralls, the hood drawn up so that her hair was completely encased. The way the wind puffed the white overall around her, made me think of a toddler wearing a padded snowsuit.

"Seriously?" I couldn't keep the irritation from my voice.

"Pathologist says no one comes in or out of here without one of them on," she said, pointing one gloved finger in the direction of the pile of coveralls.

"Fine." I sighed and dumped my bag and notebook down on the table. Scooping up a coverall I tossed it in Ronan's direction.

"You want me to go in there?" He didn't even try to disguise the surprise in his voice.

"Of course I do," I said. "Two sets of eyes in this case, are better than one. And anyway," I continued, "I trust your judgment. Who knows what wild goose chase I might have us running down if I didn't have you there to rein me in."

He didn't miss the thinly veiled sarcasm in my voice, which made him pull a face at me before stripping off his black coat. The muscles in his back strained against the thin material of his powder blue shirt as he bent over to pull the coveralls on over his clothes.

I followed suit, studiously avoiding looking at his broad shoulders. Not that it was an easy thing to do, especially when he swore under his breath and stumbled on the path, almost tipping himself into the bushes lining the pathway as he hopped around on one leg in the coveralls and one leg out.

He regained his balance without needing any input and finished dragging the coveralls over his clothes. I zipped mine up the front and straightened as Rosie thrust a white mask in my direction.

"I'm fine thanks," I said, waving it away. They only ever made me claustrophobic and short of breath. There was something about breathing in the same warm air that sent my brain into overdrive.

"You're going to need it," she said. "It won't be much protection but it's something at least."

"I don't understand," I said taking the proffered item.

Her lips thinned, an expression that had more in common with a grimace than a smile.

"You will." Her words were cryptic and I fought the urge to shake the truth out of her.

"You said bodies," Ronan asked, taking a mask of his own from the box of them on the table.

"Doesn't miss much, does he?" Rosie said, stepping off the path into the trees. "I can see how he made detective."

"Come on," Ronan said, beginning to argue, he trailed off as Rosie stalked past the tent and entered the dense scrubby brush.

"Through here," she said. "Mind the ground it's quite soft and there's a lot of roots to get caught in."

"Who found the site?" I kept my voice light and businesslike, keeping my mind trained only on setting one foot in front of the next but no matter how hard I tried, I couldn't stop myself from speculating.

"Dog walker," she said. "Just like before." I could sense there was more she wanted to say but she seemed to be holding herself back.

"Why didn't we know about this before?" Ronan asked the question that was hovering on the tip of my tongue.

"Because it wasn't here then," she said.

"So he was back," I asked, my head jerking up as I scanned the surrounding trees, as though if I searched hard enough I might spot him, lurking, observing our reactions to his handiwork.

The smell hit me first and I stumbled, my covered boot sinking into the water logged earth.

"Jesus Christ," Ronan muttered, sounding every bit as sick as I felt.

This was no old burial ground. Whatever we were about to walk into, it was fresh...

Nausea crept up on me, stomach twisting into complicated knots, eyes watering, mouth salivating as I clamped a hand over my lips, struggling to keep my gag reflex in check. The last thing I needed to do was vomit all over the crime scene. It was one thing for a man to do it, to lose his lunch over a decomposing body, but something else entirely if I did it. A male officer would find himself the butt of the station's jokes for a while and for a while, every subsequent case that involved a body would cause his comrades to regale each other with stories of his rookie mistake.

If I did it, the teasing and banter wouldn't be light-hearted. There would be talk of how I was unfit for duty. They would consider me a liability. Whispers and innuendo would be rife amongst the others. The teasing and jokes would take a sharp turn away from lightheartedness and straight into cruelty.

People liked to kid themselves that there was no sexism on the job but the old boy's club was as alive and well today as it had ever been. In this job, if you wanted to keep your place and you were female, you needed to work twice as hard as your male compatriots. Solve twice as many cases, work doubly hard at fitting in. The slightest flicker of emotion on the job would earn you a title of hysterical, a woman incapable of keeping her emotions where they belonged.

Balling my hands into fists, I sank into the feeling of my nails biting into my palms as I gritted my teeth and shoved aside the roiling of my stomach.

Ahead, there was another small clearing and the CSIs had set up another round of floodlights. The bright white light bleached the ground, exposing every little detail surrounding the scene. A hunched over figure was crouched next to what appeared to be a pile of rags. It took my eyes a second to make sense of what I was looking at and when my brain finally caught up, I wished for the ignorance I'd initially been afforded.

The body lay on the ground, face—or what little remained of it—staring up at the sky. The white slip she wore was almost pristine and clung to her swollen flesh. Someone had taken the time to strew wild-flowers over her, the purple and blues of the blossoms a macabre parody of the bruises she wore.

A broken doll carelessly discarded by a child in a hurry.

"Jesus Christ." Ronan breathed the words out, the horror conveyed in his voice matching the turmoil churning inside me.

"Do we know who she is?" My voice was detached, cool even. Ronan glanced at me, his hooded gaze giving nothing away.

"There's no ID," Dorian said, surprising me as he turned around and stared up at me from behind the mask he wore. "No personal effects."

I crossed the small space, careful to keep to the edges of the scene. The ground was already soft, the last thing I wanted to do was accidentally slip in on top of the body and destroy what little evidence Dorian might be able to recover.

Halting near the edge of the makeshift grave, I stared down at her. Decomposition had taken a firm hold thanks to all the open wounds. The left arm was swollen. Purple and black bruising stood out along the already discoloured flesh and near the elbow, I could see the bone protruding through the skin.

Her eyes were open and staring. A grey film clouded the colour of the irises but if I were to guess, I'd have said that at one time they'd been hazel.

The lower half of her face was a ruined mess of raw meat, the lips and mouth a gaping wound that made my stomach clench painfully.

"Chemical burns," I said, more to myself than any of the others standing nearby.

"Looks that way," Dorian said. "I won't know anything definitively until I get her back to the morgue."

Her fingers were blackened with death but the gel nails stood out, the bright shell pink colour almost offensive against the backdrop.

"You're thinking it's Joanna?" Ronan asked, cutting through my contemplation, his voice muffled behind the mask he'd clamped over his mouth.

"She's missing," I said. "She fits the type he seems to have. It looks like her but until we get a positive ID, I don't want anyone breathing a word of this. I don't want a repeat of the McCarthy case."

Ronan nodded and returned his attention to the body.

"Someone cared for her," I said, noting the poorly

applied make-up and the delicate braids in her hair. "She wasn't just dumped here, she was placed here..."

"Where are you getting that from?" Ronan asked, his gaze darting from my face to the body.

"They've taken some time over her appearance," I said. "She suffered, there's no doubt about that, but there's an attempt to hide the worst of her bruises around her face." I took a breath and regretted it instantly. "The body is clean, even the soles of her feet." I pointed to her freshly painted toes and the bare clean feet that pointed towards the path we'd just come from. "It almost looks like she's been laid out. And the flowers..."

I stared down at the remains of the young woman. She had been beautiful; I'd seen it in the photographs. There had been something about her that not even the camera could fully capture, but you could see it, lurking beneath her eyes. The killer had tried to destroy it, done his level best to crush it from her but despite the agony he'd put her through, he hadn't succeeded. He'd tried to destroy her beauty and failed.

"It reminds me of that painting," Ronan said, cutting across my own thoughts. "You know, Hamlet's girlfriend. She's in a river and there's all these flowers floating alongside her and—"

"Ophelia," I said simply. "I'm not sure who the artist is but I saw it a few years ago in London. The Tate I think."

"It's a Sir John Everett Millais painting," Dorian interrupted. "And you're right, it is in the Tate."

"How do you know all this?" Ronan asked. "I can barely remember last weekend's footie results, never mind remember obscure painters and paintings."

Dorian seemed to contemplate the question for a moment before he finally shrugged. "I have an eidetic memory," he said finally. "There's not much I forget."

"Well it certainly seems like a handy talent."

"It's not always so pleasant," Dorian said darkly, returning his attention to the body. "There are certain things I have witnessed, I would much rather forget."

I knew exactly what he meant. The scene laid out in front of me wasn't something I would shake free of easily. In fact, I could almost guarantee it would haunt my dreams for a long time to come.

"You said we had bodies," I said, breaking the silence.

Dorian glanced up at me. "We do," he said. "She's not alone in here."

For a moment I wasn't sure if I'd misheard him. I scanned the scene but whatever he was referring to was so well hidden that it couldn't be seen from my vantage point.

"It's older," he said. "The body that is. I don't think it's an original site, just like the last girl. It's a shallow burial, directly beneath this body." He indicated a section of soft muddy ground he'd excavated from beside Joanna. To my untrained eye, what was in the hole looked like the gnarled roots of one of the many trees surrounding us. Leaning a little closer, I realised it was the ribcage of another victim.

"Shit," I said under my breath.

"So, two then?" Ronan asked.

Dorian shook his head. "I've got reason to believe there's another next to it," he said. "I won't know for certain until I get them all out."

"Russian dolls," Rosie said, her sudden input making me jump. "He practically buried them one on top of the other in there, like those Russian dolls you can get where they all nest inside each other."

"How long is it going to take to ID them all?" I had the beginnings of a headache forming in the centre of my skull. This had gotten a lot more complicated in a very short space of time.

"We'll try and speed it up as much as we can," Rosie said. "But we don't always get lucky with dental records and DNA takes time."

"I know," I said. "Best case scenario?"

"Best case," she said thoughtfully. "We might have something for you tomorrow night."

"I can't keep this out of the media until then," I said. "The families need to be notified and I don't want to give false hope to anyone else."

Rosie shrugged. "It's the best we can do," she said. "We'll send some stuff to Dublin and they might be able to fast track it but even then, everyone is working to capacity."

I nodded. It was all I could ask of them. I knew they were working to capacity and to expect miracles from them was unfair.

"Just get it to me as soon as you can," I said. "I'm going to have to warn the families involved but I'll try and hold off as long as I can. If the press gets hold of this..." I blew out a long breath. They'd have an absolute field day with it and would treat it all as proof of the existence of a serial killer. Not that I thought they were wrong but sensationalist headlines only led to panic and right now we needed everyone to keep their heads.

With one last look at the body we believed to be Joanna, I turned away. Her family still had hope she would return to them alive. When I broke the news to them, I would rip it all away.

The killer had succeeded at one thing; he'd successfully stolen the hope of all the families involved. He'd taken their children and murdered their futures.

And if I didn't find a way to stop him soon, he was going to do it all over again.

33

MY LEGS CARRIED me down the road and away from the house as my tears ached to find release. Not that they would fall. I'd cried enough down through the years over my mother's treatment of me.

Part of me wondered if she truly hated me the way she seemed to or if it was simply the misguided anger she felt over Clara's disappearance finding an easy target in me.

Not that it made any difference. It all hurt the same.

Time passed and still I walked. The mist had become a steady drizzle, soaking in through the thin jacket I wore so that my clothes were plastered to my skin. I didn't care. I was out of the house, away from the oppressive atmosphere that sought to stultify my mind.

It wasn't until I came to the crossroads that sat opposite the local garage that it dawned on me I'd walked all the way into town. My throat scratched and my eyes felt gritty as I watched the cars moving in and out between the petrol pumps like slow waltzing couples. A perfectly coordinated dance.

Patting my pockets, I noted the satisfying jingle of change in my jeans and crossed the road.

The bell over the shop door chimed, heralding my arrival. I shivered involuntarily, the sudden blast of heat a stark contrast to the chill that clung to my wet skin. I ignored the curious stare from the clerk who looked like he wasn't long out of the classroom and crossed to the alcohol shelf that sat at the opposite wall. They'd moved it since I'd last been in here. When I'd been a teenager, the bottles of vodka and whiskey had lined the back wall. Cheap vinegar tasting wine had sat on the carousel shelving next to it, usually with a large yellow sign overhead proclaiming it to be the offer of the week. It had been easy to slide a bottle or two under your jumper and slip out unseen.

Judging by the way it now sat under the watchful eye of the attendant in his high-vis jacket, they'd grown wise to our tricks. Stealing a cheap bottle now would take a lot more ingenuity than we'd had to employ in our day.

Not that I needed to steal it now.

"Jesus, Alice, what happened to you?" Declan's friendly voice cut through my perusal of the liquor section. Turning, I found myself face to face with him and the skeptical expression he wore on his face.

"I needed a walk," I said, ignoring his obvious concern. The last thing I needed from him, or anyone for that matter was pity and sympathy.

"So what, you thought heading out in the rain was a good idea?"

"We did worse when we were teenagers," I countered, grabbing a bottle of vodka from the shelf. The unpronounceable Russian brand name on the label ensured that what little change I had in my pockets would cover the cost. "Anyway, last time I checked, a little rain never killed anyone."

From the corner of my eye I could see the smile that lurked at the corners of his mouth.

"Shouldn't you be keeping your arm dry or something?"

I gave him an incredulous look as I passed him and set the small bottle on the counter.

"What century are you from? I'm not some fragile woman to be kept in doors for fear of a sniffle."

Declan's chuckle warmed me despite my damp clothes.

"Eight-ninety-nine," the clerk said ringing the bottle up.

I pulled the coins from my pocket and let them spill across the counter, judging by the paltry amount of euro coins I had in the pile, I was going to come up short.

"Twenty on pump two and that," Declan said from over my shoulder. He thrust a wad of paper money in over my head and let it drop onto the counter next to the vodka bottle.

The clerk pulled a face. "You should have told me that first," he said. "I'll have to cancel this and ring it all up again." There was a whiney note to his voice that didn't endear him to me.

"I'm sure you'll live," Declan said, ignoring the bitter look the teenager shot him.

"I don't need you to pay for my drink," I said, as the clerk slipped the bottle into a paper bag and set it back on the counter.

"I know that," Declan said, grabbing the bottle before I could stop him. "I just thought it was only fair to pay for my half is all."

He sauntered toward the door and tugged it open, an infuriating smirk on his face as he waited for me to follow him.

Scooping up my coins I shoved them back into my pocket and followed him with a glare.

"If I'd known you were going to muscle in on it, I'd have picked a bigger bottle." I threw him a dirty look as I moved out past him and his laughter followed me onto the forecourt.

His car was the only one at the pumps at the moment but even if the place had been full, I'd still have known it was his.

"You got it," I said, eyeing the black Ford pick-up with more than a little envy. Even when I'd known him in school he'd spoken of getting himself a big pick-up style truck. I'd never understood the attraction at the time but looking at the monster that sat next to the pumps I could suddenly understand why he'd been drawn to it. Most people from the area favoured 4x4's, a necessary vehicle for farming. But Declan's truck looked much more versatile.

"Still paying it off," he said, running his hand possessively over the bonnet. "Runs like a dream though." He jerked his head toward the cab. "Go on, hop in..."

I had a moment of hesitation as I stared at the truck and then back to Declan's smiling face. Clara had been offered a lift the night she'd been taken. Of course, thinking Declan had anything to do with Clara's disappearance was more than a little ridiculous. We'd both been little more than kids when she was taken.

Tugging open the passenger door, I struggled up onto the step.

"Need a hand?" Declan teased as I teetered in the door of the truck.

I flopped inelegantly onto the leather seats and grinned triumphantly at him. "Told you, I'm not some fragile little woman."

"Never said you were," he said with a grin as he headed for the driver's door.

I pulled the door shut and surveyed the view I had from the passenger seat. The cab was positioned high up, giving me a bird's eye view of everything around me.

Declan climbed in next to me and passed the still bagged bottle of vodka over the centre console.

"Want a lift home?" he asked, starting the truck up. The seat beneath me instantly started to warm and I suddenly wondered if my clothes would begin to steam.

"Any chance you could take me to Galtee woods," I said. "The car park..."

His smile faded. "You sure that's a good idea?"

"Honestly, I'm not sure of anything anymore but I want to see the place where they found the bodies..."

He stared out the window for a couple of minutes before he nodded. "Fine."

We drove in silence for a few minutes and when Declan did finally speak, his voice was more than a little strained.

"They sure it's Clara?"

I shook my head and then realised he couldn't see me. His gaze was pinned securely on the road ahead, almost as though he was afraid to look in my direction.

"Actually, they don't think it's her at all."

"What?" He glanced at me and the car wavered before once more correcting its course. "What does that mean?"

I filled him in on what the detectives had told us and he listened without uttering a word of interruption, for which I was grateful. The thought of having to repeat myself, or dwell to closely on just what the pathologist's findings could mean filled me with dread.

"Shit," was all he said as I finished up. "I'm sorry, Alice."

I bit the inside of my cheek as I stared out the window, my fingers knitting over and back on themselves.

"I think when they told us first I was relieved," I said quietly. "That sounds awful, doesn't it? Like maybe my mother is right and I'd rather Clara was dead than still out there somewhere."

"I don't think that's awful," he said, driving onto the road that led up toward the car park. We rounded a corner and the trees were suddenly illuminated by the flashing red and blue lights of a Garda car.

"Shit," Declan swore and hit the brakes hard, the seatbelt jerking against me as it kept me from exploding out through the windscreen. "What the hell? They were done up here…"

The Garda sitting in the car stepped out and slowly sauntered down the gravel road toward us.

"Road's closed," he said, his voice authoritative.

"What's happened?" I asked, leaning over Declan toward the open window.

The Garda shoved his hat back from his forehead, scratching at his hairline, his eyes slid over my face before returning to Declan's.

"What are you two doing up here?" There was no denying the curiosity in his voice.

"Have they found another body?" I answered him with a question and his expression darkened with irritation.

"I think you two should get gone, before I haul you both in."

Declan nodded politely. "Of course, Guard."

The Guard stepped away from the driver's side of the car before Declan slammed us into reverse.

"Wait—" I demanded. "Why are we leaving?" I struggled to pull my seatbelt free of its moorings. "If they've found another body I want to know..."

My stomach clenched painfully as the trees crowded in around the car. What if Clara was here, somewhere, waiting to be found? They'd found the other girl and she'd been wearing Clara's clothes, it wasn't hard to believe my sister was still here...

What if they were here because they had found her?

A chill, which had nothing to do with my damp clothes, crawled down my spine.

"We can't stay here," Declan said. "They'll drag us into the station and—"

"I don't care," I said, pulling the seatbelt free and flinging open my car door.

"Christ, Alice!" Declan swore as he hit the brakes. The car came to a jerky halt, the engine stalling. Silence rushed in to fill the void. Ahead, I could see the flapping white tape with the word Garda blazoned in blue, blocking the rutted road that wound up into the trees.

I was out of the car before he could stop me, my feet slapping the ground with each step. The Guard who had greeted us, turned at the sound of my echoing footsteps. His mouth became an 'O' of surprise as I closed the gap between us and slipped past him.

"Hey!" His shout went up behind me but I didn't care.

Footsteps crashed behind me and I was suddenly transported back to that night, the night Clara was taken. The footsteps gaining ground at my back belonged to the one who had taken her. My breath grew ragged in my lungs but I pushed on. She was here, I knew it. I could feel it in my bones. I just needed to reach her. If I could do that, then everything would be—

A body slammed into me, driving me into the dirt. A knee pushed in the centre of my back, forcing me face down onto the muddy, puddle-strewn path that ran alongside the road.

Someone grabbed my uninjured arm, pulling it sharply behind my back. Under normal circumstances, it would have hurt but it was no comparison to the violent agony in the shoulder I'd been shot in. Pain seared through my brain and I tried to scream but there was no air in my chest and the sound left me in a panicked wheeze.

There was a commotion of voices behind me but

they were drowned out by the beating of my heart and the hissing of the rain that had started to fall.

"Hold still..." The one holding me down grunted as I fought his grip. I felt the cold circle of metal close around my wrist and I knew what was coming before it even happened.

I tried to tell him not to pull my other arm, to warn him but the words wouldn't come.

The howl that ripped from me then was more animal than human, the sound reverberating off the trees. Fire spread from my shoulder and down my spine, darkness eating at the edges of my vision as the one holding me down twisted my injured arm behind my back.

I let the darkness take me, grateful for the oblivion it promised. It was a safe harbour from the pain that exploded through my nerves and threatened to send me over the edge into madness.

34

"SIOBHAN!" Ronan's voice carried over the patter of raindrops on the plastic tent, cutting through my silent contemplation of the scene.

Two bodies sat in bags nearby, their remains carefully collected from the hole they'd been dumped into. Dorian was crouched over the third set of remains, his expression unreadable behind the white mask he wore.

"What is it?" I turned to Ronan who had paused next to me, his mouth ajar as he stared at the skeletal remains in the grave. The bones stuck up at odd angles. The only thing holding it all together was the plastic the killer had left beneath it. Unlike the other bodies, this victim had no clothes to keep the pieces in place. A lead weight sat in the bottom of my stomach as I found myself wondering if perhaps the lack of clothes was an indicator of just whom the body belonged to.

After all, the killer had used Clara's clothes for Evie's burial.

"Ronan," I said, prompting him once more as I touched his arm.

"Sorry," he said, scrubbing his hand over the dark stubble that had started to sprout on his jaw. "We've got a problem out here."

"Well what is it? I'm a little busy right now..."

"Alice McCarthy," he said, and the discomfort in the pit of my stomach grew. "She's out front."

"So, tell her to go home," I said. "We don't have any new information for her and this is no place for her to be right now..." I trailed off, noting Ronan's grimace and the way he ducked his head to keep from meeting my gaze.

"That's the problem," he said. "I'd have told her that but she went and got herself arrested and in the process she managed to somehow end up getting hurt and—"

"What?" The word exploded from me before I could stop it.

Dorian looked up at me. "If you do not mind, Detective, those of us working here need peace and quiet. If you could take your outbursts elsewhere it would be appreciated."

Grabbing Ronan by the elbow, I dragged him away from the entrance to the tent and out into the open.

The mist had gotten heavier, the wind kicking the icy droplets up beneath the hood of my jacket.

"How the hell has she gotten arrested and hurt?"

"They think she was drinking and tried to run past the Guard on the parameter. When he tried to stop her..."

"Shit," I said, pinching the bridge of my nose with my thumb and index, an attempt to stall the headache building behind my eyes. This was the very last thing we needed. I could just imagine the headlines now and they weren't pleasant.

The officers in charge of this case in the past had already screwed it up four-ways to Sunday. We didn't need to add assaulting the victim's family members to the list of mistakes.

"Show me," I said.

Ronan nodded and started back through the trees, before he'd taken more than two steps however, he paused and glanced back at me over his shoulder.

"How many bodies do they think are in there now?"

"Still just three," I said. "That we know of. The latest is in a mess."

"Any reason why that might be?"

I shrugged. "Honestly, I have no idea. I'm hoping it's just because the body was disturbed from its original resting place and that it was damaged in transit. Otherwise we're looking at a dismemberment which is a departure from the norm."

Ronan nodded and in the harsh lighting cast by the floodlights, I could see how pale he looked. Of course, he was new to all of this. He'd worked one murder before this case and I couldn't begin to imagine that it had come even remotely close to the horror that this case had conjured.

I'd worked my share of murder enquiries but never anything like this. It didn't matter how many bodies you saw, it still couldn't prepare you for the harrowing experience of standing witness to the discovery of a victim of a violent crime.

He said nothing and I didn't try to comfort him. There was no point. I'd learned a long time ago that there was nothing to be said that could possibly bring comfort. There was only one thing we could do that might bring a little peace and soothe the night terrors; bring the monster responsible for these crimes to justice.

It wasn't always possible but I'd be damned if I was going to let this go without a fight.

He'd gone dormant for thirteen years but if it was Joanna in the ground with those two other bodies—and I had a feeling it was—then whoever was responsible was clearly getting warmed up for some sort of final showdown. And whatever plan they had in mind, I knew I needed to catch them before they could finish.

Otherwise, we were going to need a lot more body bags.

35

IT'S ALWAYS hard to say goodbye. No matter the situation, goodbye is just one of those words that tends to stick in the throat.

Letting Joanna go was no exception.

She'd been special; there was no doubt in my mind about that. Her determination and spirit had been unique. If I'd had the time, I could have broken her and it would have been glorious to behold.

But *he* was always too eager.

Like a bull in a goddamned china shop, his lust rampaged over their flesh, sating his carnal needs. I despised him for it.

Girls like Joanna deserved so much more than he could give them.

Back when I'd been as blind as he was, back when I still believed we could create together, their suffering at his hands meant something. They had carried the burden of his violence as a necessary evil for something greater. Or at least there had been a time when I'd believed that to be true.

We had worked seamlessly together, two halves of one great machine, creating something perfect.

And he had ruined it.

Just like everything.

I'm not someone to be rushed. My work matters. I'm not driven by some base emotion like him. I have no need to penetrate their flesh with mine. What I give to them and what they give to me in return is beautiful. The antithesis to his monstrous violation.

But Joanna...

Even thinking of her now brings a lump to my throat. So much potential wasted.

Not that I'm not proud of what I've accomplished.

The awe he'd felt when he'd seen what I'd done with her quickly passed, replaced with rage when he realised I'd stolen his plaything away.

I felt the result of that rage quick enough. But every punch he'd landed had been met by my laughter.

It was laughable that he thought they were his—that he could do with them as he pleased—when in actuality they belonged to me.

I chose them.

I picked them carefully.

They're mine.

But he can't see it. His short-sightedness makes me despise him.

He thinks he can hurt me but he's wrong.

The bruises he left on me will fade, just as they have done in the past.

I hold all the power.

I'm stronger than he is.

Smarter.

And when I take Alice, he won't have a say. I'll make sure of it. She is mine—always has been—and it's high time for me to collect.

36

It could only have been a couple of seconds before I came around. I was still on the ground, the pain in my shoulder intense enough to seal the air in my lungs. But thankfully, the pressure that had caused the pain in the first place was now gone.

"Alice!" Declan's voice carried over the sound of the rain hitting the ground around me.

"I didn't know." The male voice came from somewhere nearby.

"It's your job to know these things." I would have recognized the stern authoritative female voice anywhere.

I lifted my head and found myself staring into Declan's concerned gaze.

"Shit, are you all right?" He reached out toward me, the brush of his hand against my arm sending a warning flash of pain shooting down my arm.

"Don't touch me," I said, my voice croaky.

He withdrew from me as though I'd physically hit him. Under normal circumstances, I might have felt bad but as I lay on the ground, another wave of pain was building in my shoulder.

"Don't try to move Alice," Siobhan said from somewhere to the side of me, her tone soothing and compassionate. "There's an ambulance on the way." I couldn't see her face but I could see her heavy-duty black boots that were still caked in orange mud.

Ignoring her command, I slipped my good arm beneath my body once more and pushed upwards. My hand slid and I dug my fingers into the freshly churned gravel and muck. The front of my body came away from the earth with a wet sucking sound, I was soaked to the bone, not that it mattered. The second I lifted myself from the ground, the wave of agony crashed over my head once more. Lights that were too bright to belong to the Garda car parked behind me exploded behind my eyelids.

The pain passed, leaving a sickening spasm of pins and needles in my arm.

"Christ help her," Siobhan's voice echoed in the silence. Strong hands wrapped around my waist as another pair of arms slipped beneath my chest, hoisting me to my feet.

I bit back the grunt of pain that hovered in the back of my throat as I found myself face to face with the female detective.

"Get her a blanket." Siobhan barked orders as though she'd been born to give them and within seconds I was wrapped in the scratchy blue blanket carried in the boot of the Garda car. It wasn't my first time feeling the rough fabric beneath my finger tips and I pulled it a little tighter around my shoulders, remembering the morning after Clara had been taken.

The Garda car had halted beside me on the side of the road as I'd stumbled back towards town. They'd spoken to me, asked me for my name, my address, but I'd been so cold, my lungs still aching from the river water I'd inhaled and my brain had refused to piece the information they required from me back together.

There was just one name on my mind and I repeated it over and over, my voice too hoarse and worn for them to make it out.

It hadn't helped that I'd smelled like a bloody liquor shop and although I couldn't remember everything they'd said to me, every question they'd asked, I could remember the knowing look they'd passed to one another.

"Alice, what are you doing here?" The question was innocent enough but I'd known enough police both through Clara's case and my work in the UK that I wasn't so easily fooled. No matter how innocent, there was always an agenda with these people. They were always working an angle, looking for the slightest crumb of information, no matter how small.

"This is where they found the first body," I said,

twisting around so I could get a look at the path that wound up into the trees but Declan's broad shoulders blocked my view.

"But it wasn't Clara," Siobhan said gently.

"But she could might still be here and when I saw the cars and…" I trailed off. It sounded ridiculous and deep down I knew it was ridiculous. What could I do? I wasn't a detective. I wasn't even law enforcement.

The flash of the ambulance lights lit up the trees as the vehicle drove along the bumpy road.

"I don't want to go to hospital," I said wearily.

"How about we let the paramedics make that decision?" Siobhan's words were meant to be kind but they just felt like another kick in the teeth. I'd made a fool of myself, pulled people away from doing their jobs. For all I knew, Clara was up there and here I was flailing around in the mud and crying because my arm hurt. It was pathetic… I was pathetic, perhaps my mother was right?

I'd always thought her behaviour toward me was borne of her pain. I hadn't considered the possibility that it was actually borne of the truth. That she could see through me for what I really was. A spoilt little girl throwing a tantrum every time she didn't get her own way.

From the corner of my eye, I spotted Siobhan signalling to the paramedics so that they hurried in my direction.

"You got here fast," Siobhan said.

"We were the ones who responded to the initial call here." The male paramedic who'd reached us first spoke. "There was nothing we could do up there but until the doctor makes the call we've got to hang around..." Siobhan nodded and I found myself following their conversation with more than a little interest.

For an ambulance to get called, whoever they found up there couldn't have been dead that long. Certainly not for as long as Clara had been missing, anyway. I pushed the thought aside, not wanting to entertain anything so morbid. The childish part of me still wanted Clara to come home to us, alive and well but with every day that passed that part of me grew smaller and smaller. I didn't think it would ever completely disappear but it was small enough now that I could shut its whisper out of my head.

"So what happened to you then?" The male paramedic asked, his smile wide and filled with genuine warmth as his eyes swept over me in assessment.

"I'm fine," I lied, ignoring the throb of my arm that set my teeth on edge.

"She took a spill," Siobhan said, talking over me as though I wasn't there at all. "The Guard with her said she appeared to have blacked out for a few moments."

"Well, we'll get you looked over, shall we?" The male paramedic said, guiding me back toward the ambulance.

I shook free of his gentle hold and turned toward Siobhan once more. "Who have you found up there?"

Her lips thinned, practically disappearing as the colour in her face faded.

"When we know something, Alice, your family will be the first to know."

"That's not what I'm asking," I said, taking a step toward her. "Please. Please, have you found her up there?"

She opened her mouth to answer and I knew it would be the same old line the Gardaí had been feeding my family for years. '*Leave it with us. We know how to do our jobs. As soon as we know something, you'll be the first to know.*'

And we had done just that. We'd let them get on with their jobs, gave them the space they needed, all the time hoping and waiting for the day to come when we'd get the call. Waiting for them to find her.

I was so tired of waiting.

Siobhan hesitated, whatever she saw in my face causing her pause.

"We don't know who we have up there," she said, ignoring the look of disbelief on the face of her male colleague. "We have to wait for forensics to identify them but as soon as I know anything..."

"Even if it's not Clara?"

"I'll still call," she said gently, pressing her hand to my good shoulder. "No matter what, I'll call. I promise."

It was as good as I was ever going to get.

I let the paramedic move me toward the ambulance and away from the flashing lights and cordon tape set up by the officers working the scene.

I climbed unsteadily up the steps and sat down gratefully on the trolley in the back. Declan hovered uncertainly near the doors, his expression unreadable beyond his obvious concern.

"Actually, Alice," Siobhan called after me, hurrying down the path toward the back of the ambulance. She paused at the doors giving Declan an awkward smile as he moved out of the way.

"When they discharge you, could you give me a buzz?" She held a card out toward me and I took it. "I think it's about time, you and I had a proper sit down chat about everything that happened the night Clara went missing."

"You've already got my statement from the night," I said flatly. I'd been hoping she was going to tell me something after all and now that I knew she wasn't, I was too tired to hide my disappointment.

"I know that," she said. "But I want to hear it from you and it'll give me a chance to ask questions that might not have been asked at the time."

My head whipped up but her expression was inscrutable, her smile polite and professional.

"What kinds of questions?"

"We weren't in possession of all the facts when your sister went missing," she said. "We know more now. And anything you can add to the picture we're building of the one responsible for these crimes, the faster we can put a stop to them."

Her statement left me with more questions than answers and I realised as she stepped away from the ambulance that it was deliberate. She knew how I felt about the Gardaí and the way they had treated my sister's disappearance and she had fed me with just enough information to ensure I would call her. It was smart and under different circumstances, I might even have respected her for it. But as the paramedic in front of me shone a light in my eyes, I couldn't bring myself to summon the energy it would take to care that she was manipulating me.

Instead, I watched as she jogged back toward the woods and the place where my sister might be.

Would they look after her?

37

"DETECTIVE GERAGHTY." A female voice pulled my attention back to the scene. "Dr. Whittaker is ready to move the bodies," Claire said as I reached the edge of the wooded pathway.

"You can call me Siobhan," I said with a tight-lipped smile.

She nodded but I could see the hesitation in her face and I knew without her having to say anything to me that she would never call me by my first name. Had I been too hard on her? Scolded her too much for turning up late to the briefing when it clearly wasn't her fault?

"Tell him I want a word before he leaves." As she turned away, I called after her. "Claire, how long have you lived in the area?"

My question seemed to catch her off guard. Her expression—a mixture of curiosity and concern—let me know that whatever else she thought of me, trust definitely wasn't top of her list.

"I've lived in Tipperary my whole life," she said. "Well not exactly this area."

"How so?"

"Well the county was broken into two districts at one point. North and South Riding," she said. As far as I was concerned, she may as well have been speaking double Dutch. I'd lived in Dublin my entire life and to my shame I'd never really strayed outside the cities limits. Preferring to keep my professional and personal life safely ensconced in what I considered to be my comfort zone.

"I live in what used to be North Tipperary. Close enough to feel like home," she said with a small smile, "without having the over familiarity of home."

"So you don't know any of the people from the area then?"

"No," she said. "Sergeant Mills is your best bet in that department. He knows this place like the back of his hand. He's lived here his whole life."

That was part of the problem. He knew everyone a little too well and I had a feeling that the kind of knowledge he would bring to an interview would be more of a hindrance than a help.

"Actually," I said. "I think you'll be perfect."

Her smile was hesitant. "What for?"

"I'm going to swing by Mr Donnelly's house tomorrow for a chat and I'd like you to come with me."

The uncertainty in her eyes was palpable. "I thought you were working closely with Detective McGuire," she said. It took me a moment to realise she was talking about Ronan. When had I become so comfortable with him that I barely recognised his official title when it was used?

"We are," I said. "But I'd like you to join me on this."

"Fine." Her ascent was abrupt. I let her stalk away up the path, watching until she disappeared into the tree line. And as I watched her retreating back, I couldn't help but think I'd misread the entire situation.

I caught up with Dorian as he was finishing up in the makeshift shallow grave. A collection of sample pots lay out on a large plastic tarpaulin spread out on the ground. Staring into the hole, I watched Dorian's boots churn up the orange mud. The soil was waterlogged and each time he raised a boot, the ground protested loudly as though it didn't want to let him go.

"You wanted to ask me something?" His voice was contemplative as he scooped up one of the pots and stared in at the orange soil within.

"Is there anything you can give me, anything you can tell me about the bodies?"

"All three are female," he said without the least hint of humour. "I won't know cause of death until I can carry out an examination of the bodies."

"And the third," I asked, "she was—" I broke off, hoping the right words would pop into my head. It felt so wrong to describe the state of the remains as being a mess but it was the only word that came to mind. What I'd seen of her, had been a jumbled mess and I needed to know if we were looking at experimentation on the killer's behalf or if the disturbance of the primary burial site had caused the skeleton to break up.

Dorian set the container he'd been examining aside and stared up at me. "From the brief examination of the bones," he said. "There does appear to have been some dismemberment involved before the decomposition of the soft tissue."

"Jesus..." I breathed the word out, scrubbing my hand over my face as I turned away and stared into the darkness of the tree line. "Can you tell if the marks occurred after or... before she died?"

"It's not uncommon," he said. "It's more unusual to find the bodies intact, particularly in a case like this."

"Really?" I turned on him, the rage I felt finally bubbling to the surface. "You talk about them as though they're not even human."

Dorian looked up at me, a mixture of confusion and pity in his eyes.

"This is my job, Detective, making it personal won't make me any better at it. Truthfully, it will only compromise my ability to work through the information."

He was right and I was being unfair, laying my own thoughts and feelings at his door instead of dealing with them myself.

"I'm sorry," I said, turning away. "Let me know when you've got something."

He called after me but I ignored him and instead headed back down the path away from the crime scene. I'd seen more than enough for one night. I just needed to trust that Dorian would do his job and do it well. But if I was honest that wasn't what I was struggling to believe.

Could I do this? Could I take the strands of this case and weave them together in time to find whoever was responsible, before another girl was lost?

38

WE SET the operations room in one of the larger offices in the Garda Station. Two of the walls were covered in large whiteboards, the third dominated by a corkboard capable of taking all of our case material and then some.

Sitting in the black swivel chair I'd managed to beg from the main office, I stared at the six photographs Ronan had placed on the board. We'd only managed to find one other girl that fit our parameters; Anne Marie Shields. Just like the other girls, she had gone missing while making her way home after a night out with friends, in December 2005.

The smiling faces of the missing women stared accusingly out at me, taunting me, daring me to find them and the one responsible for their disappearances.

"There has to be more to this," I said, leaning

forward so that my elbows rested on my knees. Cupping my chin in the palm of my hand, I squeezed my eyes shut, my brain instantly conjuring an image of the girl in the woods.

"Well we know he's active again," Ronan said grimly.

"These can't be his first attacks," I said. "Someone like this doesn't graduate straight to murder, especially not like this."

"What do you mean?"

"There's no forensics and how much do you want to bet, Dorian won't find any forensics on this body too?"

Ronan's corrugated brow, betrayed none of the emotions I knew lurked beneath the surface as he surveyed the images before us.

"So what, you think there are others we don't know about?"

"At the very least I think we should be looking at reports of rapes before Clara McCarthy went missing."

"Sorry I'm late." Claire appeared in the doorway, face flushed from exertion.

Glancing down at my watch, I nodded disapprovingly for her to join us. "The briefing began ten minutes ago," I said. "if you don't wish to work with us on this then you can—"

"The Sergeant needed me to run some paperwork over to Cahir," she said, her words rushing together. "He said it couldn't wait."

Pursing my lips, I said nothing else. I knew she wasn't lying. The sergeant didn't approve of me or my investigation. It only made sense that he would use the officers I'd been assigned for his own purposes. Of course, treating Claire like she was nothing more than a glorified errand boy smacked a little too much of the usual chauvinistic bullshit I'd grown accustomed to in the force.

"You've been assigned to this investigative force," I said. "In future if he has an errand he desperately needs doing, tell him you're off limits and if he's got a problem with it, he can come and find me."

Two spots of colour appeared on Claire's cheeks and she ducked her head before I could try and read her thoughts.

With a sigh, I stared down at the sheaf of papers clutched in my hands.

"Claire, any chance you can do a little digging into reported rapes in the area before Clara McCarthy's disappearance in October 1996?"

She nodded and scribbled furiously in the notepad she'd pulled out. "Anything else? What about petty offences?"

"Such as?"

"You know the sort; trespassing where there was an element of being a peeping tom or nicking personal items."

I thought about it for a moment. It wasn't a bad idea.

"You can check it out but I've got a feeling any of the crimes he'd have committed in that arena would have been done when he was a juvenile and those records are always sealed."

She nodded and chewed the tip of her Bic pen thoughtfully.

"Ronan, I want you to contact the families, see if we can't get them back in here to have another chat. We don't need more statements but I think the chance to ask our own questions on the matter might be helpful..."

"Some of the families have moved away," he said. "And some of the parents have passed..."

"Is there anyone, a sister or brother... aunt or uncle even?"

He gave me a grim smile. "I'll find someone," he said.

"I've been going through the old interviews in the Clara McCarthy case," I said. "Alice mentioned something interesting over Clara's boyfriend but when I checked the files you'd given me, I couldn't find his interview transcripts or tapes?"

For a moment Ronan looked surprised but he recovered quickly. "I'll have another look in the file room," he said. "Maybe they were mislabeled."

"I'm going to talk to her friends," I said, more to myself than to anyone else. "At least the ones who gave the main statements. See if anything has changed in the years since."

"You really think the McCarthy case is the key to cracking this, don't you?" There was no accusation in Ronan's voice, just genuine curiosity.

"It was the beginning," I said. "Not to mention the fact that the killer seems to be communicating with us."

"How is he communicating?" Claire asked. She'd been so quiet, I'd practically forgotten she was in the room.

"The necklace," I said jerking my chin in the direction of the board where we'd hung the crime scene images. The photograph of the now cleaned up necklace sat there, larger than life, the scrawled message a reminder that the killer was so much cleverer than we were. He'd sent us on a wild-goose chase by dressing Evie in Clara's clothes, made fools of us. It spoke to an emotional intelligence and awareness not usually present in killers who were so vicious in their methods of execution.

Some might consider the word execution a poor choice to describe a killer of this nature. They weren't executions in the typical sense. This was no gang retaliation and it certainly wasn't committed as a weapon deployed in active warfare. But in a way they were executions nonetheless. It had been an attempt to annihilate the person he'd captured. Destroy and erase the lively beautiful women he had chosen as his victims. Assassinate their characters and their spirits.

He'd gone silent for thirteen years but he was back

and I knew he wouldn't stop, not until he was caught or killed.

Whichever came first.

"How do you know that was meant for us?" Claire asked, catching me off guard.

Dragging my head up from the papers I'd been studying, I stared at her.

"What do you mean?"

"It feels personal," she said carefully, as though suddenly afraid she was about to say something wrong and would find herself on the wrong end of my sharp tongue. "Too personal for it to be meant for us lot?"

I stared up at the image of the necklace once more and the message scrawled across the back.

"Who in the world am I?"

She was right. How had I not seen it before? The message was far too personal. I'd studied the case files of other killers who had communicated with the detectives involved but in all those situations the messages had been far more general. Nothing as specific as this. Nothing as personal as a question that wasn't really a question scrawled across the back of a locket. A gift between sisters.

"Any ideas about whom it might have been meant for?" It was a general question, meant for either of the officers present.

Claire sank in on herself, her shoulders rounding defensively. "Sorry," she said, her voice leaden. "I didn't mean to make a stupid suggestion it just occurred to me and—"

"It wasn't stupid," I said. "Not at all in fact, quite the opposite. And my question was genuine. Who was the intended recipient of the message? Who would know what this meant?" I gestured to the board and the image we were all focused on.

"Evie's boyfriend?" Ronan suggested helpfully, "maybe her mother?"

"Maybe it has no connection to Evie at all," Claire said, emboldened by my encouragement. "It's written on Clara's locket."

"Is there any indication that Clara and Evie knew one another? The girls were taken very close together, just weeks between disappearances and there's no denying they both look quite a bit alike."

Ronan shook his head. "From everything I've looked at, there doesn't appear to be any connection between the two girls," he said.

I blew out a sigh and stared at the pictures. "That doesn't mean there wasn't one. All we can do for now though is keep looking for the piece we're missing."

Ronan and Claire scribbled furiously, the scratching of their pens on paper the only noise that broke the silence.

"I went through the statement Alice made when Clara first went missing. In it she mentions a white panel van. But when I went back through the files I couldn't find any information the officers at the time dug up on locals in the area who might have had vehicles matching that description."

"That's an easy one," Ronan said. "They didn't look into it. I tried to find that information myself before you got in on this and there's nothing to find."

"Why would they have ignored something like that?"

He shrugged. "Honestly, your guess is as good as mine."

"Could it have anything to do with the other missing files?"

"It might. I'll have to see what I can dig up."

"Right, keep me informed," I said, climbing wearily to my feet.

"Where are you off to?" Ronan asked, his head coming up so that his eyes met mine.

"I'm going to talk to the Sergeant Mills," I said, steeling my resolve. "Try to convince him to reassign the officers who were working on Joanna's missing person's case, to our murder enquiry."

"And if he turns you down, we'll have another case and still no more help," Ronan added the wry remark without any hint of the usual smile that clung to his lips.

"I've got to try." I felt my shoulders shrug an act of belying the nervousness I felt.

I held back the words that hovered on the tip of my tongue. An explanation. How part of me felt like I owed it to the girls to find more resources for their case. They deserved to be found, deserved to be brought home and reunited with their families. We had failed Joanna by not catching this bastard sooner. I didn't want another girl to suffer at the hands of this maniac because I hadn't tried a little harder to swallow my pride and ask for help when we needed it.

That wasn't something I could live with.

39

AFTER A QUICK CHECKUP from the ER doctor and a refusal to stay overnight for observation, I found myself back outside the hospital.

Aunt Imelda's car was idling next to the curb. I'd called her as soon as I knew I was free to go. She hadn't said much on the phone.

While I couldn't see her expression in the dark interior of the car as I crossed the road, I could already imagine the frosty reception I was about to get.

Pulling the car door open, I slipped into the warmth and prepared to get an ear bashing. Instead, she pulled away from the curb without a word.

The tension inside me ratcheted up with every moment that passed.

"Aren't you going to say something?"

"Why bother?" she asked, keeping her eyes on the

road ahead. "It's not as though it's going to stick inside that head of yours."

"What's that supposed to mean?"

She sighed. "I know things aren't easy for you right now, but..."

"But I need to think of my parents," I said, cutting her off before she could say the words aloud.

"You make it sound like a bad thing."

It was my turn to sigh. Turning in my seat, I stared out through the fogged window, my finger creeping up to write the name 'Clara,' on the glass.

"It's not a bad thing," I said. "But it's all I've listened to since she left. 'Think of your parents suffering...' What people seem to forget is that I lost her too."

"I know you did," she said. "You two were always close."

"I was with her when she was taken," I said. "I heard her screaming. She's gone because I couldn't hold onto her hand."

The words caught in the back of my throat, wrapping themselves around the rapidly forming lump there.

"No one is blaming you."

"I'm blaming me," I said vehemently, drawing a sideways glance from my aunt. "And after today I know my mother certainly does."

"She doesn't, not really. She's just upset."

"No." I shook my head. "You don't need to make excuses for her. I've always known she blamed me. It's because I came home without Clara. She might even think I let her get taken to save myself."

Imelda shot me a shocked look. "That's not true, Alice. You were a child. You were never to blame."

I turned back to the window. I'd lived with this guilt longer even than I'd lived with my sister. What would she be like now, if that night had been different? Would we still be close? I'd gone over a million questions about her in my mind since that fateful night.

"I should have gone back for her," I said. "I knew she was vulnerable, slower, because of the baby. But I didn't go back..."

"You were trying to survive, Alice," Imelda said, in her usual no nonsense voice. The same one she used on her fifth class students in the primary school. "Don't ever apologise for that. If you hadn't then your parents would have lost both their daughters."

"I think Mam would have preferred that," I said. "I think she would know how to deal with that grief better. This way—" I shrugged, glad to find the shot they'd given me in the hospital was still keeping the pain at bay. "She doesn't know how to love me anymore because I remind her of what she lost."

"She still loves you." I could hear just how unconvinced even Imelda sounded about the whole thing.

"I got over it a long time ago," I said softly. Watching as the letters of Clara's name glistened in the half-light.

Imelda said nothing else as she drove me home

and for that I was grateful. In this life you had to take small mercies where you found them. And the silence she granted me gave me time to think.

What if Clara really was up in those woods? Maybe not in the newest grave but somewhere up there. Alone.

The urge to go up there once more was strong. Not that it would do me much good. I'd just end up stumbling around blindly. Probably end up getting lost on the Galtee's and have to get rescued. That would really help the situation.

My phone buzzed and I drew it out of my pocket, staring down at the message.

"I hope you're all right? -D."

I started to type back a response and paused.

What was I supposed to say to him? Chances were, he thought I was some sort of lunatic. Not that I could blame him for thinking that, the way I'd run at the Guard was definitely suggestive of someone with a few screws loose. But the need to know if my sister was up there had washed over me and I hadn't been able to help myself.

This whole case had opened so many wounds I'd one thought closed for good.

I shoved the phone back into my pocket as Imelda parked the car in front of the dark house.

"I was worried the place might be crowded with people," I said. "Like it was earlier."

Imelda shook her head. "No. A few people called

after the Gardaí came this morning but I told them to put the word out not to call. I think you all just need some time to wrap your heads around everything that's going on." She pressed her face into her hands. "I'm not even sure I've begun to process this whole mess myself. Part of me just wants it all to be over."

There was nothing I could say. She was right. We all needed it to be over. As much as I wanted Clara to be found well and alive, I knew it would never happen. She'd been gone for far too long. If she were still alive, she would have found a way to get back to us by now.

But my parents needed to believe she was still out there.

What would happen to them once that belief ended?

"You want me to come in with you?"

I shook my head. "Nah. I'm just going to go to bed. It's been a long day."

There was a moment of awkward silence as I tried to find the words to thank her for everything she'd done.

"I'll see you in the morning," she said. "I'll come over first thing and see Ita."

"I'm sure she'll appreciate it."

"She won't." Imelda gave me a rueful smile. "But I'll do it all the same."

I nodded and stepped out of the car.

Pausing, I waited for her to drive away, the sound of the gravel beneath the car tyres oddly comforting.

Sucking in a deep breath, I turned my head up to look at the sky. It had stopped raining, the clouds thin enough to reveal the stars.

My breath came in small clouds and still I stood there until the cold crept into my bones, numbing the sensation in my limbs.

"Where are you?" The question slipped out before I could stop it. Not that I expected an answer, it didn't stop me from wanting one though.

Clara wasn't here. And there would be no answers tonight, divine or otherwise.

The house was silent as I crept up the stairs, making me think of all the times I'd done the same thing when I was a teenager. Moving softly along the hall, I avoided the old creaky floorboard, deftly stepping around it to avoid alerting the whole house to my presence.

One night, three years after Clara had gone missing I'd snuck back into the house after meeting with my friends. I'd been drunk—too drunk—and one misplaced step had drawn my mother out into the hall.

I could still remember the hopeful note in her voice as she'd called Clara's name. And even though I'd been drunk, I could still remember the look of disappointment that had swept over her face when she realised it was me and not Clara at all.

That expression had stayed with me and it was that expression I'd recognised in her eyes when she'd looked at me earlier.

Pausing next to my bedroom door, I stared at Clara's closed door. Curiosity getting the better of me, I crossed the hall and pushed the door open and stepped inside.

Even in the dark, I could see everything had been left exactly as Clara had left it. Flipping on the light, I stared over at the rumpled bed sheets and the clothes that sat discarded on the chair next to her bed.

Nothing had changed. If I hadn't known better, I would have sworn that Clara had just stepped out and would be returning at any second.

Crossing to the dressing table, I sat on the white plush stool in front of her mirror. The surface was cluttered with make-up, hairpins, and bottles of body spray. Scooping up the one nearest to me, I pressed it to my nose and inhaled deeply. It was amazing the way scent could instantly transport you to another place and time. White musk, Clara's favourite, or at least it had been.

Would she have still worn it now? Or would she have found another scent?

People grew and changed all the time; I certainly wasn't the person I had been back then.

Pushing up from the stool, I crossed to her wardrobe and pulled the doors open.

Surprise rocked me back on my heels as I stared in at the neatly plastic wrapped items hanging from the rail.

It wasn't Clara's doing, that much was for certain.

My hand drifted over the plastic wrappers, static causing the hairs on my arm to stand to attention.

I'd thought my mother had left it all untouched. I'd been wrong. The clothes weren't the only oddity; despite the apparent disarray of the room, I hadn't found one speck of dust. Clara had been gone more than twenty years. There should have been some dust.

The air in the room became stale and I crossed hastily to the door. Escaping out into the hall, I pulled it shut as quietly and as quickly as I could. There was something terribly oppressive about Clara's bedroom. It made me feel as though I might suffocate if I spent too long in there, as though it wasn't just the clothes that were wrapped in plastic.

With a backwards glance at Clara's room, I headed for my own, escaping into the veritable solitude of the alien room I had once called my bedroom.

The further away from Clara's room I got the more I realised the sudden sensation of being suffocated had come because the bedroom felt more like a tomb than anything else. It was no longer Clara's bedroom but a relic, a monument erected to her memory. We had no tombstone and no grave marker. Instead we had a bedroom. A crypt wherein memories of Clara were kept entombed.

I sat on the side of the bed and glanced around at the unfamiliar wallpaper, which drew a smile from me. My mother had mourned the loss of one daughter by doing everything in her power to erase the one left behind. If I were a more generous person I might have found it ironic but I was too tired to truly care. Rolling back onto the bed, I closed my eyes and let the darkness take me. Perhaps sleep would bring me the peace I sought.

40

SITTING OUTSIDE THE GARDA STATION, I pulled my phone out of my pocket. There was one message a single thumbs up emoji from Paul. At least one of us was having a good day. I could still hear Sergeant Mills' voice in my head telling me there would be no others joining the team. Lack of funds and resources. The usual political bullshit.

How he could sit there and keep a straight face after seeing the pictures from the crime scenes was beyond me. Every time I looked at them, I felt sick to my stomach. Just knowing there was someone out there capable of that kind of cruelty left me cold.

And yet, Sergeant Mills hadn't so much as batted an eyelash at the attempted annihilation of the most recent girl's body.

I hit the call button and raised the phone to my ear.

Paul picked up on the second ring, sounding more than a little out of breath.

"Hey, baby, you get everything wrapped up down there?"

"I keep running into a brick wall," I said. "We need more people and every time I ask for them I get shot down in flames. Sorry, am I interrupting something?"

"Not at all," he said. "Just give me a second to go somewhere a little more private."

"Why where are you?"

"The gym." I could practically hear the smile in his voice as he said it. There was the sound of a door sliding closed and then he came back on the line.

"Give Donovan a call," he said, sucking in a deep breath. "I'm sure if you explain it to him he'll send more people your way."

"We both know if I call him in, he'll take me off lead and put someone else on it. I can't afford to lose this, Paul, not after the last time. As far as Donovan is concerned if I can't get the locals to cooperate then I'm a liability."

"That's not true," Paul said.

"Yeah," I said. "It is."

"Well how close to solving this thing are you?"

I sighed and pressed my hand against my face. How was I supposed to explain it to him? The case wasn't the straightforward cold case it had been painted as. Especially not now that we had a new victim to deal with. The presumption had been that whoever had been committing these murders had gone to ground. Or maybe gone to jail for some offence or other. But now they were active again.

"Siobhan?"

"Yeah," I said. "Look I'm sorry. I'm just tired and it's been a rough day."

"You know if you were here, I could help you unwind."

"I'm sure you could," I said, with a smile.

"Siobhan!" Ronan's voice interrupted the call and I turned to see him waving at me from the door of the Garda station.

"Got to go," I said. "Duty calls."

Paul sighed. "It's fine, babe, I've got a ton of paperwork left to sort through here anyway after the raid."

"I'll call you later," I said.

"Sure thing." The line went dead and I slipped the phone back into my pocket.

"Sorry," Ronan said as I joined him on the steps into the station. "Didn't mean to interrupt anything."

"It's fine. I was just finishing up anyway."

"Any luck with the sergeant?"

My expression must have said it all because Ronan gave me a rueful smile. "Yeah, I did say he would balk at the idea."

"Have you found something?" I asked, choosing to change the subject rather than go into a blow-by-blow account of my failed meeting with the sergeant. I already felt crappy enough without reliving the moment over.

"You said you couldn't find the interviews pertaining to Liam Donnelly, Clara's boyfriend at the time of her disappearance."

"Go on," I said, prompting him.

"Well, I went back into records and looked through everything we've got and you were right. The records are missing. There is a listing that says he was interviewed but the tapes are no where to be found."

"Why would that be?"

Ronan shrugged. "Could just be a clerical error."

"Or, it could be someone trying to hide something."

He nodded. "I thought he warranted a second look anyway, so I've asked him to come down to the station first thing."

"Good thinking," I said.

"Yeah..." Ronan scuffed the toe of his shoe against the curb making me think of a young boy rather than the grown man he actually was. "So do you want to grab a drink or something?"

I shook my head. "If it's all the same with you, I think I'll just head back to the hotel and grab some shut eye. The day has already been far too long."

He gave me an awkward smile and nodded. "Sure, I can see that."

There was a sudden tension to the air that hadn't been there a moment before and I had the feeling that something had shifted between us. Ronan turned and headed back into the station before I could say anything else, leaving me to stare after him.

I couldn't afford to let my thoughts wander from the case at hand. It was too important to screw it up by letting my personal life interfere and I had a feeling that if I had gone for the drink with him, things would get a lot more complicated.

Things were already complicated enough without adding to them. Heading back into the station, I gathered my things from my desk and stuffed the files and notes I'd been working on into my bag.

Ronan was across the room, one hipped propped against her desk. He chatted animatedly with her and I watched from the corner of my eye as she smiled coyly up at him.

Grabbing my jacket from the back of my chair, I slipped into it. Noting the way Ronan leaned down toward Claire to push a stray lock of hair back behind her ear.

Without a backwards glance, I strode out of the station and called a taxi from the steps.

The case was definitely beginning to get to me when I found myself getting bothered over the behaviour of a colleague. Tomorrow would be better. It had to be; things certainly couldn't get any worse.

Or at least I hoped it couldn't but there really was no telling where cases like this were concerned.

41

PUSHING through the station door the next morning, I balanced my paper cup of coffee on the pile of files I was carrying and flashed my I.D at the guard on the desk. He waved me through and I gathered up my things.

"Siobhan!" Ronan said, catching up to me as I dropped my files back down on the desk. "Liam is here."

"Great," I said, sliding my notes out from the bottom file. Grabbing the paper cup, I followed Ronan down to the interview room.

Stepping into the room, I ran my gaze over the man behind the table. He was nervous, his leg hopping up and down beneath the table as he drummed his fingers on the tabletop.

"What's this about?" he asked, not bothering with the usual pleasantries exchanged during these types of situations. "I wake up this morning with a Guard outside my front door, demanding I come down the station."

I shot Ronan a sideways glance but his gaze was trained on Liam.

"Mr Donnelly," I said, sliding into the seat opposite him. "My name is Siobhan Geraghty, I asked for you to come down to the station so we could discuss the disappearance of a young woman by the name of Clara McCarthy."

If I had thought Liam had been nervous before, I'd been mistaken. The colour drained from his face and he leaned forward in his chair.

"I had nothing to do with it," he spat the words at me.

"I never said you did," I said, keeping my voice measured as I flipped open Clara's file. "But you were her boyfriend at the time of her disappearance, is that correct?"

"What does that have to do with anything? I told you lot everything I knew at the time when she was taken. Its been twenty-odd years, why can't you lot find someone else to pin it on?"

"I'm not trying to pin it on anyone." I met his gaze head on. "I just want to get to the bottom of her disappearance."

Liam sighed. "Yeah, we were dating," he said. "Sort of, anyway. When she got pregnant Clara became a little unstable. Hormones or something..."

"What does sort of mean?"

"Clara wasn't exactly one for monogamy."

"Was Clara seeing someone else?"

Liam looked away. "If she was, she never admitted it to me."

"But you thought she was?" I asked, picking up on the note of discomfort in his voice.

"Look, I told them then and I'll tell you now. I don't know if she was seeing someone else. There were rumours but I..." he trailed off and dropped his gaze toward the surface of the table. "I tried to ignore them."

"How did it make you feel?" Ronan asked. "Finding out the she might be seeing someone else behind your back."

"I just told you, I tried not to listen to the rumours," he said.

"But she was pregnant," I said. "How could you not listen?"

"I loved her." There was a stark honesty to his words that tugged at my heart. There was no doubt in my mind that he knew more than he was telling us but he was telling the truth when he said he loved Clara.

"But we broke up a few weeks before she went missing."

"How come nobody else knows this?"

"Because I was trying to get back with her. She was having my baby... A boy."

"And what did Clara think of your attempts to win her back?"

"She seemed to be open to the idea of it but—"

"But what, Liam?"

"We fought."

"When?" Ronan couldn't keep the anticipation from his voice.

"The day she went missing. She didn't want to go out but her sister was desperate to go to some teenage disco. So I said I'd come with her. Keep her company."

"And what did you fight about?" I could feel the tension in the room begin to climb as soon as I asked the question.

"What does it matter? I told you, I had nothing to do with her murder."

"Clara is still a missing person," I said carefully.

"Don't give me that bull," he said angrily. "We all know she's dead. You found her fucking clothes on a dead body. How do you think they got there if Clara herself isn't dead?" His voice cracked a little at the end.

"Mr Donnelly, we're trying to find out what happened to her. Anything you can tell us that might help with our enquiry would be greatly appreciated." I left out the part where I was beginning to think he was somehow connected to the death of his girlfriend. Without proof, I had nothing at all. Not to mention the fact that I couldn't connect him to any of the other missing girls. It wouldn't stop me from looking into him though. No stone would be left unturned.

"She said she'd met someone else," he said quietly.

"Said she had no interest in getting back with me. I lost my temper."

"And what happened?"

He glanced up at me. "Nothing. She got out of the car and walked away. I didn't see her again after that."

"You didn't go after her?"

Liam shook his head. "I was hurt. I thought about going after her but..." He looked down at the surface of the table once more. "I'm not proud of my behaviour from that night. I regret not going after her, maybe if I had she would still be here and my son would—" He buried his face in his hands as he choked off.

"Is there anything else you can remember from that night, Liam?"

He shook his head. "No, I went home and to bed."

"Is there anyone who can verify that?"

His head snapped up sharply. "What do you mean?"

"Anyone who can verify that you went home and to bed that night?"

"Am I a suspect?"

I contemplated telling him the truth but I knew that if I did, he would get himself a solicitor faster than I could get the words out.

"We're just trying to eliminate everyone close to Clara at this time."

"I'm sure my dad saw me," he said. "I'll have to ask him but when I do, I'll get him to call into the station if you'd like." It was a challenge. He was waiting to see if I really would push him for an alibi but what Liam didn't know was that I had no intention of letting him get away with anything. If he knew something, I would get to the bottom of it. And if he was involved in Clara's disappearance, then I would find out.

"That would be great," I said.

"Have you spoken to her sister yet?" There was no denying the hostility in his voice when he spoke about Alice.

"Why? Should we?"

"She's a complete basket case. When Clara first went missing, she accused me of being involved."

"And why would she do that?" I kept my smile firmly fixed in place but I didn't like the insinuation he was making. Alice had been little more than a child when her sister went missing. There wasn't a chance that she was involved in Clara's disappearance.

"I don't know," he said. "She said Clara was upset. But Clara never told her jack shit."

"Well," I said, climbing to my feet. "Thank you for coming in Mr Donnelly. I think that's all the questions we have for this time. If we have anymore, we know where to find you."

He pushed up from the table, the sound of the metal chair legs scraping back against the floor.

"Just one last thing," I said as he made his way to the door. Liam paused to look back at me.

"Do you know anyone in the area who owned a white van around the time of Clara's disappearance?"

A flicker of unreadable emotion flitted through Liam's eyes as he stood framed in the doorway. "No," he said. "Sorry. I don't."

"Well if you can think of someone," I said. "I'd like you to let us know."

"Why are you looking for a white van?"

"Because when Clara was abducted, Alice remembers seeing her getting bundled into a white van."

Liam nodded. "Sure," he said. "Anything I can do to help."

"We'd really appreciate that."

I let Ronan escort him out as I sat back down at the interview table once more. There was something he was keeping back, that I was certain of. The only problem was, I couldn't put my finger on just what it might be.

When he returned a moment later, I turned to face him. "Any luck with digging up something on the missing files?"

He shook his head. "I tried to contact the Garda who initially led the investigation but I keep running into a brick wall."

"Any particular reason?"

Ronan's expression was a grim one. "The best I can figure is that Liam's uncle is a county councillor."

"And that would be enough to make his interview files disappear?"

Ronan shoved a hand up through his hair. "It sounds ridiculous, doesn't it?"

I nodded. It was hard to believe that anyone would compromise an investigation for something so small. Not unless they were ultimately trying to hide something much bigger. If Liam was truly innocent, then why hide his involvement in the case at all?

"Sergeant Mills worked the case then, didn't he?" I said, noting the way Ronan's shoulders stiffened.

"You don't think he'd have anything to do with this?"

"I think it at least warrants another visit to him," I said. "He won't like it but what choice do I have?"

"I can come with you, if you'd like."

I shook my head. "I can handle this. It's time I started getting some answers here. How can I run an investigation if at every turn I get stonewalled."

"Well just watch your back." Ronan paused in the doorway. "Listen, about last night, I just want to say I'm sorry if I made things awkward."

"It's fine," I said. "Don't worry about it. I'm not."

He searched my face before nodding. "Good. Great. I'm glad. I was worried there might be some weirdness between us."

"It's all fine, Ronan," I said. "We're work colleagues. And that's all."

He gave me a tight smile before he turned and left the room. I'd lied. It was awkward. It shouldn't have been and yet it was. I couldn't put my finger on why it was so weird. I'd been telling the truth when I'd said we were nothing more than work colleagues. There was nothing but the case between us.

So then why did I feel like I'd stepped up to my neck in crap?

Pushing up from the table, I sucked in a deep breath. There wasn't time to figure out the intricacies of my relationship with Ronan. The case needed my full attention and right now that attention needed to be fully focused on Sergeant Mills.

He'd dismissed me far too readily yesterday and I'd let him. Well not anymore. This case wasn't going to solve itself, no matter how much I might wish it would. And if Liam Donnelly and his family were somehow involved then I intended to get to the bottom of it.

"I'M NOT QUESTIONING your integrity, Sergeant," I said, fighting to keep my temper under control. The moment I'd entered the room, he had been on the defensive. And no matter how hard I tried to keep things running smoothly his anger was making it almost impossible to get a straight answer from him.

"It certainly sounds like you're questioning it," he said. "Do you know how long I've worked here? Do you know how many years of excellent service I've put in here in this area? The number of cases I've worked? And you to march in here and accuse me of tampering with evidence in an ongoing investigation..."

"I'm not accusing you of anything, sir," I said. "I'm

merely asking you if you know what happened to the files. They're nowhere to be found. The records of their existence are still in the file room but no actual files."

"And you think I should know where every little thing in this station is?"

With a sigh, I tried to let the tension ease out of my shoulders. My body was coiled tighter than a drum and I could feel the beginning of a tension headache starting in the base of my skull. Confrontation was definitely not my strong suit. In fact, I hated it.

"I have a good mind to call your superior and inform him just what you've been doing down here."

"Go ahead," I said, my stomach flipping over. It was the very last thing I wanted to have happen. "Perhaps then you can tell him how evidence from an open case is missing and that you have no idea where it might be."

Sergeant Mills paused with his hand on the telephone. His shrewd grey eyes observed me coolly, as though he were assessing me. And in a way he was. He was looking for a chink in my armour, something that would clue him into my true thoughts on the matter. But I was determined to give him nothing at all.

He withdrew his hand slowly and folded his arms across the front of his chest as he leaned back in his chair.

"You're not worried that they'll think you're the problem in all of this?"

"Honestly," I said. "I just want to get this case solved, no matter the cost."

He looked away, his gaze studying the pictures along the walls. "You don't understand the politics involved in cases like these, now do you?"

"I know there are girls being murdered. The politics don't really factor into my thought process."

He sighed. "The Donnelly's have deep pockets. The files you're looking for just simply don't exist."

I stared at him in shock. "What do you mean, they don't exist? They have to."

"The interviews were all conducted off the record. Liam's uncle and father didn't want his name getting dragged through the mud. Especially in the beginning, when everyone thought it was just a runaway."

"How could you have done that?"

"I didn't," he said sadly. "The Sergeant in charge at the time thought it was the right move. The rest of us had no choice but to go along with it all."

"And the other leads?" I asked. "Did anyone bother running them down?"

He kept his gaze trained on the wall. "I did my job," he said. "If that's what you're asking. I chased up the leads I was asked to. But by the time we realised there was a case it was too late."

"So you did nothing," I said, dropping back into my chair like all the air had been knocked out of me. "She was taken and you lot did nothing at all because you were what? Worried the Donnelly's might not like it?"

"Liam Donnelly had nothing to do with her disappearance," Sergeant Mills said, sounding more than a little irate. "I've told you this because I know you won't leave it alone until you push things too far."

"We're digging girls up out of the ground," I said. "Have you even looked at the pictures? The autopsy results, the suffering they endured... And you lot shut down lines of enquiry without checking to make sure everything was above board?"

"I've told you this for your own good, Detective. The Donnelly's are not involved in this case. And if you can't manoeuvre the political minefield this creates then you'll leave me with no choice but to contact your superior."

Pushing up from my chair, I clenched my hands into fists. "If I find out that Liam Donnelly had anything to do with Clara or the other girl's disappearance, I will hold you personally responsible."

"You're here because I asked for the NBCI's input. Don't push it." His voice was icy and I had the distinct impression that he would do whatever it took to cover his involvement in the cover up they'd so obviously done.

Without another word, I stalked out of the office, leaving him to call after me.

42

October 1st 1996

PART of me wished it wasn't true, that Liam wasn't such a prick. But there's another part of me, a much bigger part, that's glad it's done.

If he wants to be a part of this baby's life then he's going to have to earn it.

Sarah's been off these past few days.

I've seen the bruises and she keeps on down playing it all but she's not as clumsy as she says she is.

Her dad is a mean drunk.

I wish I could help her but I think even if I could, she wouldn't let me.

43

I spent the day keeping my head down. My mother still hadn't spoken to me after her outburst the day before and I wasn't particularly in the mood to forgive her for her behaviour. I thought about calling Detective Geraghty and giving her the meeting she wanted. But I needed some time to think and getting stuck in an interview room would be too much like taking a step backwards.

Since Clara had gone, I'd done my fair share of time in an interview room, sitting across a table from someone who had no real interest in anything I had to say.

The media circus was in full swing and I'd caught a glimpse of the front page of the Independent, which Imelda had tried to hide from my mother. The headlines gave a rundown of the case and its progress. Or lack thereof.

Whoever was doing this, was too good at staying hidden.

Imelda kept giving me pitying glances and in the end I just needed to escape. The atmosphere in the house was suffocating me. Luckily, I had a very willing accomplice in the form of Declan.

"I DIDN'T THINK they'd let you out so soon," he said, his voice heavy with concern.

"You can stop being so worried," I said, touching his arm lightly as he fussed over me as I got into his truck. "I'm not going to break."

He scrubbed the back of his neck with the palm of his hand, looking more than a little disconcerted. "I can't help it. Seeing you hit the deck like that last night."

I started to shrug and cut myself off at the last moment. My arm was still too stiff and sore to go making any kinds of sudden movements. "You've got to know I'm tougher than that," I said. "Remember when we were in fifth year and I really wanted an apple so I decided to climb that tree overhanging the river?"

"Except you'd never successfully climbed a tree in your life and ended up getting dunked." He finished for me. "Of course I remember. I was the one who went in after you."

"But I got my apple," I said. "I hung onto it the whole time."

Declan shook his head but the smile on his face was genuine. "You were so stubborn."

"I don't suppose I've changed a whole lot."

"No," he said. "You've definitely not changed." He reached across me and clipped my seatbelt into place. "What were you thinking last night?" Declan searched my face as though the answer he was seeking was written there, he just needed to look hard enough to find it.

"It's hard to explain," I said. Feeling suddenly foolish. I had behaved like an idiot the night before. In the cold light of day, I'd found it difficult to justify my actions. Sure grief could do a lot of things to the human mind but my behaviour had been utterly irrational.

Even if I had managed to slip past the Guard somehow, just what had I been expecting to find up there?

Deep down, I knew the truth about Clara. I knew she was dead, I'd known it for a long time. I'd watched her get taken and if she'd somehow managed to get away, Clara wasn't the type to stay away from us. She would have come home, if she could. Or at least let us know she was okay.

"Try me," Declan said, climbing into the driver's seat next to me.

"I guess I thought she was up there," I said, refusing to meet his incredulous expression. "Yeah, I know it sounds mad but it is what it is. I know she's out there somewhere, alone."

"Look," he said, "I can't begin to understand the kind of pain and grief you and your family have suffered. But don't you think if she was up there the Guards would have told you by now?"

"I know I'm being irrational," I said, turning in the seat to face him. "I can't explain it."

Declan gave me a small nod. "I know," he said. "Love makes us do crazy things." There was an odd hitch in his voice as he spoke. "Now come on, I owe you a drink and you owe me a story about that arm of yours."

"I thought you'd forgotten," I said grumpily dropping back against the car seat.

"What, forgotten that you'd been shot? Have I hell!" He started the engine and reversed out of the drive.

His enthusiasm brought a smile to my face. It was nice to have someone I didn't feel the need to explain myself to all the time. Someone who would just let me be. It soothed the guilt I felt over the situation with Clara, I'd forgotten how easy it was just to be myself around Declan. And as he pulled out onto the road and I watched him from the corner of my eye, I realised I'd missed the ease of our relationship.

I'd been lonely since Clara was taken, but Declan made me feel a little less alone in the world.

DECLAN PULLED the door to the pub open, gesturing for

me to move in ahead of him. The bar was a lot busier than the first night. Certainly not packed but there was definitely more of an atmosphere.

Reaching the bar Declan dipped his head toward me. "The usual?"

I nodded and jumped as an arm clamped over my elbow. "Alice!" Sarah's familiar voice saw my heart sink.

It wasn't that I didn't like her; I just hadn't planned on spending the evening with her. Plastering a smile on my face, I turned to face her.

"I didn't know you were going to be here," I said, maintaining the pleasant tone in my voice.

"It's so weird, I wasn't supposed to be here but Dick and Rob talked me into it, so I thought why not." She shrugged her thin shoulders and grinned at me. In the low lighting of the bar she looked younger, almost girlish and pretty. And when she smiled it caused her face to light up in a way I hadn't remembered her doing when she'd been friends with Clara.

"Dick is your husband, right?" I asked, surreptitiously scanning the bar.

"You need to come over and say, hi," she said excitedly wrapping her arm through mine. The sleeve of her cardigan rode up exposing a dark ring of bruising around her wrist. Although I couldn't see any higher, I could tell the bruises extended all the way up her arm.

Sarah's gaze met mine, her laughter nervous as she practically ripped the sleeve in her haste to cover the marks. "I'm such a klutz," she said. "I got my arm trapped in the door of the car yesterday when I was bringing in the shopping. Hurt like hell but what can you do?" She shrugged, the expression on her face a poor attempt to mask the panic currently swirling beneath the facade of her smile.

"Sarah, you know you can—"

"And who have we got here?" The booming voice cut me off mid-sentence.

"This is Dick," Sarah said. "My husband." She gestured to the tall man standing in front of us.

He wasn't exactly unattractive, but my mother would have described him as a little rough around the edges. His hair was salt and pepper, his eyes dark and unreadable and despite the ready smile he wore, there was a cruelty in the curl of his lips.

He was definitely older than Sarah and I found myself glancing between the two of them and wondering just what had caused her to fall for him.

As much as I wanted to rid myself of my judgemental thinking, I couldn't. My dislike of Dick was instantaneous. Whatever he saw reflected in my eyes broadened his smile as he wrapped a possessive arm around Sarah's shoulders.

He jerked her in against his side, his hand sliding down past her waist as his eyes locked onto mine.

"Not here, Dick," Sarah said with a giggle that curdled my stomach.

He laughed again and released her but the mirth

from his laughter never reached his eyes as he kept them trained on my face.

"Don't think we've ever met," he said, holding his hand out towards me. I had the sudden urge to deny him a handshake but I forced myself to take his sticky palm in mine. His grip was unrelenting and my eyes drifted down to his dirty fingernails.

"Alice McCarthy," I said. "I knew Sarah from way back."

"It was your sister that disappeared," he said gruffly, his expression shifting. "I was sorry to hear that. She was a good looking girl."

I attempted to jerk my hand back but he held on, his thumb forming small circles on my skin.

"Dick met Clara a few times," Sarah said by way of explanation. "We'd started seeing one another a couple of months before she was taken."

Dick released me almost reluctantly as Declan appeared at my elbow.

"Everything all right?" he asked, giving me a sideways glance.

"Yeah, everything's fine," I said, taking the drink he offered to me. I found myself wishing that there was ice in the glass. The sweating glass would at least give me the excuse I needed to scrub my palm on my jeans without looking like I was completely without manners.

I took a swig of the drink, relishing the sensation of the whiskey as it burned down the back of my throat.

Warmth washed through my chest and I felt the tension in my shoulders slowly releasing.

"You should come and join us," Sarah said suddenly. "Rob would love to see you again, Alice."

I glanced over at the table and caught sight of the serious young man watching from the corner booth. His right eye was ringed with a dark and unsightly bruise. The purple and red mark stood out against his pale face, making it appear fresh but the cut that adorned his bottom lip was beginning to take on the yellowish tinge, suggesting it was an older injury and had started to heal.

Nodding, I followed Sarah as she led me back to the table. Having Dick at my back made the skin covering my spine crawl, the feel of his eyes pressed against me almost as though he'd touched me. But the grip Sarah had on my arm left me with no choice but to traipse after her.

Rob grinned at me, wincing as the movement stretched the cut on his lip.

"Long time no see," he said amicably, pushing up from the booth He reached out toward me awkwardly, dragging me in against his chest in a bear hug.

"You know he's never forgotten you," Sarah blathered on as Rob released me. "I think you were his first love."

Heat marched up over my neck and threatened to crawl onto my cheeks.

"I was eight," Rob said, quickly. "I didn't know what love was."

"Still don't," Sarah quipped back. She gave him a gently shove and Rob's face coloured as he ducked his head.

"Little, Robbie, is getting married," she said, turning back to face me.

"Congratulations." I shot him a smile as he raised his hand and scrubbed it over the back of his neck self-consciously.

"Thanks. Can't believe it myself."

"It's so weird," Sarah said. "It feels like yesterday when I was babysitting the two of you together."

Dick brushed past me, his hand lingering on the small of my back a little longer than was strictly necessary. He climbed into the booth, moving around so there was room for us all.

I let Sarah go next.

Declan raised an eyebrow when I didn't slide in next to Sarah. As though he could read my discomfort he followed her instead, leaving me to sit on the outside. If I needed to I could always make a hasty escape.

"I hope the other guy looks worse," Declan said, gesturing toward Rob with his pint.

"No, I—"

Before Rob could even get the words out, Dick reached over to him and wrapped his thick meaty arm around his neck, jerking his head down toward his lap.

Inwardly I cringed. It looked more than a little uncomfortable.

Rob fought Dick's hold but the other man was a lot bigger, his arms flexing as he held Rob easily pinned in place.

"Little, Robbie, here couldn't fight his way out of a wet paper bag," Dick said with a toothy smile. "The two of us had a little disagreement after a few pints."

"It was harmless really," Sarah said quickly. "Over as soon as it started."

She touched Dick's arm and he released Rob. He bolted upright, his face bright red, the bruises blending with the colour of his humiliation. When Rob stared at Dick, I could have sworn that what I saw reflected in his eyes then was pure hatred.

"Isn't that right, Robbie?" Sarah directed her question toward her brother, steel in her voice.

He jerked as though her words had formed themselves into a hand to strike him and stared at her a moment before answering.

"Yeah," he said softly. "Totally stupid. Meant nothing." Robert pushed up from his chair and gulped down the last of his pint. "I've got to go. Got an early start in the morning." He smiled at me. "It was really good to see you again, Alice."

"Right back atcha." I returned his smile with a warm one of my own. As he walked away, I couldn't shake the feeling that I was missing something. There was definitely no love lost between Robert and his brother in law. But his sister had the same hold on him today that she'd had on him when he was eight years old.

"I'm going to the ladies," I said, hopping to my feet.

"I'll come with you," Sarah said quickly, halting me before I could even take one step away from the table. Climbing out over Dick, she joined me, wrapping her arm through mine. Was I being paranoid or was there a tightness to her grip that hadn't been there before?

"It'll be just like it used to be," she said excitement in her voice.

We crossed the pub together. Sarah leaning in toward me as we walked. "It used to be like this with Clara," she said. "We used to do everything together."

With my free hand I pushed open the bathroom door and smiled at the woman who hurried out.

Sarah slipped out of my grip and headed for the cubicle. "You coming?"

The last time I'd shared a cubicle with another woman, I'd been fifteen. It had made me uncomfortable and I had no intention of repeating the action.

Shaking my head, I turned my back as she disappeared inside.

Pressing my palms to the sink attached to the wall, I dug my fingers in against the unyielding porcelain basin and closed my eyes.

This had been a good idea when it was just Declan and me. With Sarah and her creep of a husband, things had suddenly become overbearing. I supposed I could just leave. It would be easy and I was almost certain Declan would come with me. We could just slip away together...

What was I thinking?

"How are you coping at home?" Sarah's voice drifted over the top of the stall to me and I jolted. She'd been so silent, I'd nearly forgotten she was there.

"Fine." My answer was short. The last thing I wanted to do was go into the problems I was having at home. No matter how close we had once been, Sarah was now a stranger to me. Too much time had passed and we'd both changed. There were some things you couldn't return to, no matter how much you might want to.

"That's not entirely true," she said gently reminding me of the way she would talk to me when I was a kid who had told her a lie.

The flush of the toilet told me she was finished. I twisted the tap, the flow of the water giving me something to concentrate on. Grabbing a palmful of water, I splashed it up onto my face, using the shock of the cold to snap me out the painful reverie I'd been heading into.

As she exited the cubicle, I hit myself with another splash of water. Choosing to blind myself than meet the reproachful look I knew I would find in her eyes.

Blinking away the water from my lashes, I found myself side by side with her as she washed her hands

"You can always talk to me," she said. "You always could."

I nodded and glanced down toward her arms. "It goes both ways, you know?"

She snatched her hands back from beneath the flow of water and adjusted her sleeves. "What do you mean?"

I'd let Rachel down. I'd failed to see the signs. Zoe had very nearly lost her life in the process. I couldn't let that happen again.

"How did you get the bruises?"

"I don't know what you're talking about," Sarah blathered, turning her back to me.

"Yes, you do." I reached out to her and then thought better of it. People who were abused rarely liked to be touched without their consent. "The bruises on your arms, Sarah. I saw them earlier." I paused. There was no doubt in my mind that she would have some story ready to explain them away. It was probably easier for her to pretend than to face the truth.

"Oh those," she said, her relief a little too convenient. "I caught my arm in the car door. Clumsy me." The edge to her words told me to back off but as she stood there with her back to me, all I could see was the terrified look in Rachel's eyes when she'd told me Zoe was gone.

"Does he hurt, Ali?"

If I had hit Sarah her reaction then might have

been understandable. She jerked as though a jolt of electricity had shot through her body.

"Why would you say that?" Her voice was small, meek, and nothing like the woman she had been just moments before.

"Because it stands to reason if he's abusing you, then your daughter is next. If he hasn't started already."

"I wouldn't let him..." her voice choked off. She turned toward me, her face a mask of anguish. Her cheeks were sunken, gaunt. Her eyes were haunted as she searched my face. The circles I'd noticed beneath her eyes earlier had deepened making me think she didn't get a whole lot of sleep.

"You need to speak to the police, Sarah, you need—"

She grabbed my arm, her nails digging into the flesh of my forearm as she clung to me. "Please don't say anything." There was a panic to her voice that I hadn't expected.

"Sarah, you need—"

She shook her head so violently I was concerned she might snap it clean off her neck. Taking her hand in mine, I wrapped my fingers through hers.

"We can do this together," I said. "I can help you get away from him, Sarah. Help you make a clean break. Help you protect, Ali, and—"

Something switched inside her. I saw it the moment it happened, like a light switch had been flicked on inside her head.

Sarah's spine straightened, drawing her shoulders back up. She released her hold on me and took a step backwards. She appraised me with a cool gaze, her eyes shuttered so that I could no longer read the turmoil I'd only glimpsed a moment before.

"I think you're mistaken," she said. "Dick would never lay a finger on us."

"I've seen the bruises, Sarah," I said. "You need to get yourself and your daughter away from him. I know how these things work out and—"

"You're wrong." Her tone was brusque and businesslike.

It was like standing next to a completely different person. How had I misread the situation so badly?

"If I ever hear you spreading such malicious lies again..." She trailed off and dropped her gaze to the floor.

I watched as she sucked in a deep breath and raised her face once more. "I thought you were better than this, Alice." She shook her head. "But you're just like your sister. Both of you jealous, utterly and completely, bitterly jealous." She turned back to the door, leaving me to stand alone in the centre of the bathroom.

Was she delusional, and what the hell did she mean that I was just like Clara. That we were both just jealous of her?

"Sarah, I—"

She paused with her back to me. "I think you

should stay away from me, Alice." I detected the same hint of steel in her voice that there had been when she spoke to her brother. "Just like your sister, your lies are poisonous and I don't need that near my family."

She left, the door swinging shut in her wake.

"What the fuck was that?" I spoke to the empty air and I wasn't surprised when there was no answer.

44

I WAITED A FEW MINUTES. Was I giving her time to get back to the table? Or was I hiding?

I didn't have the answer to either question. The answers were there, somewhere in my head, but I just refused to go digging about for them. It wasn't as though knowing the truth either way would help.

Leaving the bathroom, I practically ran into Declan. He stood, his shoulder leaning against the wall next to the door. Before I could bump into him, he caught me. His strong hands warm against the top of my arms. His heat radiated down through the thin jumper I wore. What would it feel like to have his hands on my bare skin?

I batted the question away as quickly as it entered my head.

"Sorry." I glanced up into his face and found him studying me. "I didn't see you."

"What's up?"

My brain felt like it was swimming in molasses, the inner workings and thought processes slowed to a crawl.

"You look upset," he said. "What's wrong?" As though he could read me as easily as picking up a book and scanning its pages, there was no denying the concern in his eyes.

It would be so easy to tell him. To spill everything to him. Declan was the kind of guy you could talk to, share your darkest secrets without fear of reproach. If there was anyone on this earth who could understand the confused muddle of thoughts in my brain, it was definitely him. And I wanted to tell him. I wanted to spill the truth and feel his arms around me.

My breath caught in the back of my throat.

"I think I'm just tired." The lie tripped off my tongue. It would be too easy to tell him everything. To slip into his arms, take comfort from him however he wanted to give it.

But I couldn't do it. As much as I wanted it, there was no way I could let him in. We didn't belong in each other's lives. Not anymore anyway.

"Sarah said you were upset..."

Her secrets were not mine to tell and as much as I wanted to tell him the truth, there was no way for me to do it while preserving her story.

"I'm fine." He looked unconvinced. "Really, there's

nothing wrong with me, aside from being tired." I found myself wanting to convince him.

Declan's expression relaxed into a smile. "Want me to take you home?"

"Yeah, I think that's wise."

His smile broke down into a grin. "Didn't think I'd ever see the day when you became a lightweight."

"That's not what this is," I said, returning his grin with one of my own. "I—"

Declan dipped his face. His breath hot against my cheeks as his lips brushed mine. The kiss sealed the air in my lungs. The press of his mouth igniting a need inside me I'd long thought dead.

So much time had passed between us. A lifetime.

He pulled back, his eyes searching mine. "I regretted not doing that the night you left."

Shock riveted me to the ground. "That was years ago..."

He shrugged. "I know. Thought I'd take the chance while I've got it."

"Why didn't you say anything?"

"Because you were dealing with so much... I thought if I told you then how I felt you'd feel like I was trying to stop you from going." He sucked in a deep breath and closed his eyes. "And I know you needed to go, Alice. I know it now too..."

I opened my mouth but the words spinning around inside my head refused to form coherent sentences.

How was it possible that he knew more about what

I needed, than I did myself? Because as soon as he'd said it, I knew he was right.

I didn't belong here anymore. All it was doing was tearing old wounds wide open. Ripping wide scar tissue I'd thought long since healed.

"You don't need to say a thing." He cupped my cheek with his hand, the touch of his fingers gentle. "I know this place is painful for you."

"Why are you telling me all this now?"

"Because I didn't want you to go running back to England again without at least knowing how I felt. Because I wanted you to know that not everything here needs to be painful."

He pressed his forehead to mine, drawing me closer into his embrace. I let him hold me. Enjoying the feel of his strong arms around my body. It had been so long since I had felt as safe as I felt in his arms.

Guilt slammed into me. Here I was enjoying myself, enjoying the feel of Declan's arms around me while Clara was...

I'd once sworn I would give up the guilt I felt over my sister. Letting go of her hand was my biggest regret. I had so many regrets over that night but that one in particular was definitely the one that hurt the most.

And for so long after she'd been taken, I'd held onto it.

"I can't do this," I said struggling to free myself from his hold.

"What is it? What's wrong?" The confusion in

Declan's voice was overlain by his hurt over my rejection.

"I just can't, not now..."

"Alice, I—"

I shook my head. "Please, don't. I already feel terrible."

Whatever he was about to say, he bit the words back. His face twisted into a grimace as he swallowed them.

"I'll take you home."

"Declan, I'm sorry."

"There's nothing to be sorry about." His tone was clipped, his face cold and impassive. I'd screwed up royally but how could I explain it to him?

How could I tell him that while I wanted what he was offering, there was a part of me-a very large part—that didn't feel like I deserved what he was willing to give?

How could I take the safety he offered when the guilt over Clara's abduction weighed so heavily on my mind?

I'd thought I could atone for my failures of that night by working with other vulnerable people. Thought I could protect them the way I'd failed to protect Clara. And even at that, I'd failed.

I'd let Rachel and Zoe slip through the cracks. Allowed their husband to wheedle his way back in.

Of course I knew it was stupid to believe I could stop bad things from happening to other people.

Foolish to believe that I could somehow 'make-up' for my past mistakes. The past was just that, past. It couldn't be changed. No matter how many people I tried to help, it wouldn't bring Clara back. Nothing would.

"Thanks." I nodded, biting down on the inside of my mouth to keep from spilling my tumultuous thoughts out at his feet.

The guilt I felt over Clara's abduction was also stupid. I'd been a kid, lucky to escape myself. But knowing this hadn't eased my true feelings. No matter how many times I told myself I wasn't to blame, I still felt it.

We reached his truck and I climbed in. Watching from the corner of my eye as he slid into the driver's seat next to me.

The rumble of the engine as it started vibrated up through the seats before it settled into a familiar purr.

If I told him, he would tell me it wasn't my fault. He would convince me that I wasn't to blame for Clara. And part of me knew that I would believe him. That if I told him, he would help to wash the stain of her abduction from my soul.

As much as I wanted that, I couldn't do it. It felt too much like letting go. By letting Declan's understanding heal me, I would be letting Clara down all over again.

And I couldn't do it to her. Not again. She was mine to carry. I'd let her go once and the feel of her fingers slipping from mine would haunt me for the rest of my life. If I let her go now... Then she would be really gone.

The rational part of me said it wasn't a betrayal. But the emotional side of me just didn't believe it.

Dress it up however you like. At the end of the day, no matter the shape it came in, it was still a betrayal.

45

"SIOBHAN," Claire said before she corrected herself. "I mean, Detective Geraghty. I think I've got something here." The excitement in her voice got me out of my chair and halfway across the small room before she'd finished speaking.

"What is it?"

"I went back through the records for vans at the time."

"I thought the list was too big to throw up anything valuable?"

"It is," she said. "If we have no idea what we're looking for. But when I input the name Barry Donnelly, there was a hit."

My brain felt as though it had been turned to mush and I stared at her in confusion. "Barry Donnelly?"

"Liam Donnelly's father," she said, unable to contain her elation. "He had a white van at the time of

Clara's disappearance that matches the description Alice McCarthy gave at the time."

I stared at the blinking cursor next to the entry on the screen.

"And where's the van now?"

"That's the not so great news," she said. "Two weeks after Clara's disappearance the van was involved in an accident and was written off. It was taken for scrap."

"Son of a bitch." The words tripped out of my mouth before I could stop them. "I asked him in the interview room whether he knew anyone at the time that was driving a white van that matched the description we had and he swore he knew nothing."

"He was lying."

"It's enough to drag him back in here," I said.

"This is good work, Claire," I said. "Really good work."

I turned away from her as her face split into a wide smile. It wasn't going to be easy to get Sergeant Mills to agree to us picking Liam up once more. But there was no denying the evidence. He'd lied. And, politics or not, it deserved further investigation.

46

"THANKS FOR DRIVING ME HOME," I said, twisting in my seat as Declan pulled into the driveway.

"You don't have to sound so formal about it," he said, keeping his hands firmly planted on the steering wheel.

In the darkness of the car, I could only just make out his profile against the window; the rest of his features were hidden in shadow. How was I supposed to read his expression when I couldn't even see it?

"I'm sorry about earlier, I—"

"Don't."

"You won't let me explain." I'd been mulling it over during the drive. He deserved what little of the truth I could share with him.

"I don't need to hear it," he said, finally turning to face me. Not that it made a difference. I couldn't make his features out any better with him facing me.

At least this way, I knew he couldn't read my face either.

"It's not the way you think it is."

Declan sighed and reached out in the darkness, his fingers brushing my cheek before letting me go. "It doesn't matter, Alice. It's not going to change anything, is it?"

I hesitated long enough to make his shoulders droop.

"I didn't think so."

"What's made you so understanding all of a sudden?" I snapped.

"I saw it then and I can see it now," he said softly. "You're too busy trying to save everyone around you that you can't see what it's doing to you."

His words stunned me into silence. I sat there and not even the heated seat could stop a chill from creeping over my skin.

"I'm not trying to save anyone," I said.

Rather than see his smile, I could hear it in his voice. "It's all right, Alice. I get it. This is probably some misguided attempt at ridding yourself of the demons that came as a result of Clara's abduction."

My continued silence seemed to be all the confirmation he needed.

"I know because I've done it myself."

His quiet confession filled the car faster than if we'd been submerged underwater.

"You remember Geoff?" he said softly.

"Your brother?"

Declan nodded. "A year or so after you left, Geoff died."

"Shit," I swore emphatically.

"Yeah, shit," Declan echoed me sardonically.

"I didn't know. I'm sorry to hear that."

"So am I," he said. "I say he died but that makes it sound like he just dropped dead. What I really mean to say is Geoff killed himself."

The tension thickened in the car and my hand crept toward the handle on the door. The urge to dive out into the crystal clear night air was almost overwhelming.

It wasn't the topic of conversation that got to me. It was terrible and tragic and all those other words you insert into the platitudes that come after the death of someone, especially one so young. But that wasn't the reason I was feeling claustrophobic.

No. It was the note of bitterness in Declan's voice, the rough edge of guilt that peeked through his words despite his best attempts to keep his voice flat and void of emotion. I heard it because I knew what to listen for. I heard it because it was the same tone of voice I heard inside my own head every time I thought of Clara and the night she was taken.

"Why?" It sounded like a stupid question as soon as it left my mouth but I knew Declan would understand.

"Geoff got himself caught up with the wrong crowd. Ended up getting into drugs and some other things he wasn't proud of." Declan trailed off and peered out the window.

As I sat and waited for him to continue, I became acutely aware of the second hand on the dashboard clock as it moved steadily around. For such a new truck, it seemed like such an old-fashioned addition. Most of the newer trucks had digital displays and I would have expected Declan to want only the very best and most up to date mod cons.

"That's a lie," he said finally.

"Geoff was a good guy. He didn't just get in with the wrong crowd, that makes him sound like an idiot and he definitely wasn't the idiot of the family."

He fell silent again and I waited patiently for him to continue.

"I got involved with a bad crowd. I wasn't doing drugs or anything but it would have gone that route if I'd stayed." He sighed as though simply getting the words out had cost him something.

"Geoff was the reason I got out."

"He saved you," I said quietly and watched Declan turn his head in my direction. Even though I couldn't see his eyes, I could feel the weight of his gaze on my face.

"You could say that," he said. "Yeah."

"But he got sucked in instead?"

"There was a job, I was supposed to do." Declan turned his attention back to the windscreen. Perhaps it was easier to tell me, when he didn't have to look me in the face.

"Geoff told them, he would do it in my stead. They weren't best pleased, of course, but they agreed. I was pissed as hell. I thought I was the big man and that he was deliberately trying to steal my thunder. I was pretty dumb back then."

"You definitely had your moments."

Declan ducked his head, a small chuckle escaping him. "Geoff reckoned I was an eejit." He fell silent once more and I fought the urge to prompt him. One misstep and whatever he was going to say next would be lost. This was definitely a one and done story. I had a feeling that there would never be another time when Declan was willing to make himself as vulnerable as he was right now.

"I didn't want to listen to him, I thought I knew better. But the bastard wouldn't tell me what the job was. Even afterwards, he still wouldn't tell me."

"So he did it for you?"

Declan nodded. "It was bad," he said. "I know it was. Geoff wouldn't talk about it but when he got back that night. I'd never seen him so pale in all my life. It was like he'd seen a ghost. He locked himself in his room and wouldn't come out."

"Did he ever tell you?"

Declan shook his head and gripped the steering wheel in both hands. "He wouldn't talk about it, but I knew it was bad." He sucked in a deep breath and let it out in one long whoosh of air. "He hung himself two weeks later."

I felt the shock of his words settle over me like a cold blanket. It took me a second to realise he was still talking to me.

"You remember the shed out back where we used to meet up?"

His question brought back a flood of memories. Mostly ones I would rather have left buried.

"Yeah."

"He hung himself in there. I found him. His note said I wasn't to blame myself but..." he trailed off. Without pausing to think about it, I reached out to him and pressed my hand to his arm.

"I'm so sorry," I said, my words falling so far short of my true feelings. That was the problem with telling someone you were sorry for their loss. The words were never really enough. But it was all I had to offer.

"If I hadn't gotten so wrapped up with the lads, he wouldn't have needed to step in like he did. And he'd still be alive."

"You can't know that for certain," I said, regretting the words the instant they left my mouth. No matter how true it might be, it wasn't what Declan needed to hear.

"I do know for certain. He hung himself because I was a fool. Because he had to save my ass and do something he couldn't handle." His voice cracked over the words.

"So when I say I know what it's like to carry shit like that, I'm not kidding."

"Geoff knew what he was doing," I said. "He loved you. He wanted to help you."

"And it got him killed." There was no mistaking the bitterness in Declan's voice now. "I'm the reason my brother is gone."

"And Clara is gone because I couldn't hold onto her," I said.

"You know that's not really how it was."

"Just like you know, you're not the reason your brother killed himself?"

Declan's laughter was short. "Touché."

"I know neither of us are responsible," I said. "But I know it doesn't feel that way."

"It definitely doesn't feel that way."

"How are your parents coping?" The question made me think of my own parents and my mother's inability to deal with the idea that Clara was really gone.

What would she do if they ever found a body? Would she find a way to blame me for that too?

"About as well as you could expect," he said. "They don't understand and I think that's what eats them up inside. He'd always gone to them in the past and then this time..."

"It's normal to look for a way to understand such a senseless tragedy," I said. It made me sound like some sort of useless self-help book.

"It is," he said. "Doesn't mean you'll find one

though." He hesitated and then leaned across the divide between us. His hand cupped my cheek before he drew me in for the second kiss of the evening.

I was too shocked to move away. Not that I really wanted to. Being with Declan made me feel alive in ways, I hadn't felt for far too long.

Perhaps, there would be a day when I was ready to let go the suffocating grief and guilt that had kept me stuck all these years.

Slowly extricating myself from his kiss, I pressed my hand to his chest. "Thanks for driving me home."

He nodded. "Don't be a stranger, Alice."

There was an unspoken promise in his words. He wouldn't wait forever for me. And I could understand that.

Pushing open the car door I stepped out. The wind had picked up since we'd left the pub and it whipped my hair about my face, making it difficult to see. It took me a moment to get it under control enough to see where I was going. I turned and watched as Declan reversed back out onto the road, leaving me alone in the driveway.

The house behind me was dark as I trotted up to the front door.

From the corner of my eye, the flicker of something white caught my attention and I turned toward the side garden.

White papers were strewn through the hedgerow,

the wind catching them and ripping them into the air in some sort of complicated dance.

Hurrying up the path at the side of the house, I scooped up the nearest piece of paper and stared down at the picture of Clara. Her smiling face peering back up at me from the page, eyes crinkled, head thrown back in a full abandon as she laughed at something only she knew. Except there was something wrong with her eyes. They were black, as though the printer had screwed up somehow.

And that wasn't the only thing.

My heart came to a stuttering halt in my chest as I stared at the image. I knew this picture from my old photo album.

Just like the rabbit, it had disappeared all those years ago. I'd assumed Mam had tossed it out during one of her cleaning bursts. I'd asked her and Clara at the time but they'd both denied seeing it...

Grabbing another page, I found myself staring down at a picture of Clara and me. She was chasing me across the sand. Dad had taken the picture during one of our trips down to TráMór one summer when we'd both still been kids. But instead of Clara's smiling face as I remembered it, someone had taken a black marker to her face and blacked it out. Making her a faceless void that chased me.

I glanced back at the other one still clutched in my hands and realised that was why her eyes had appeared black. Someone had erased them.

And whoever they were had printed the pictures in black and white and dumped them in the garden. Turning the page over, my eyes raced over the words printed there.

My heart stuttered back to life as it picked up the pace and hammered against my ribcage. Almost as though it could escape if it just beat hard enough.

—*for this curious child was very good at pretending to be two people.*

"But it's no use now," thought poor Alice, "to pretend to be two people! Why, there's hardly enough of me left to make one respectable person!"

I knew the words almost by heart. Alice in Wonderland had been my favourite story as a child and whoever had printed off the pictures must know it. I flipped over another picture and the same quote glared up at me.

Fanning the images out in my hand, I stared at the printed words each one bore.

Fear clawed its way up the back of my throat like a living creature bent on escape.

First the white rabbit alarm clock on the doorstep and now this. These were no mere coincidences, that much was certain.

Whatever was going on, I was in over my head.

47

"What's this about, Siobhan?" Ronan asked, his groggy voice making me think I'd woken him up.

"I got a phone call from, Alice McCarthy." I handed him a paper cup filled with black coffee. Luckily for us, the hotel had very graciously given us two take-away coffees despite the lateness of the hour.

"Thanks." His gruff acceptance of the coffee made me smile. And I felt my smile stretch wider when he gulped the bitter drink and grimaced with distaste. "Would a bit of sugar have killed you?"

"Won't kill me," I said. "It might kill you though."

He grimaced and took another deep swallow. "What did she call you for?"

"She wouldn't say on the phone," I said. "But something has definitely spooked her."

"What makes you say that?"

I climbed carefully into the passenger seat before answering him.

"I could hear it in her voice."

Ronan raised a skeptical eyebrow in my direction as he started the engine and put the car in gear.

"I don't know how you do that," he said. "I've never been very good at reading emotions."

"I've always been able to do it."

Setting my coffee down in the cup holder, I grabbed the overhead handle on the door, my grip punishing as he spun out of the car space.

"You don't like cars, do you?" The screech of the tyres as he tore out of the car park made me cringe.

"Can't say I'm a big fan, no."

"Why is that?"

"Car accident when I was younger." I kept it deliberately vague. Talking about a car accident while I was currently the passenger in another car seemed too much like tempting fate. That didn't stop the memory from replaying inside my head though. The high-pitched crunch of metal as the cars collided. The wash of glass across my face as the window next to me exploded inwards like the hand of some great monster had punched it. The sound of my mother's scream cutting off abruptly.

Opening my eyes once more, I stared out the window, watching the flash of the white lines disappear beneath the car.

"Must have been a bad one," Ronan said, glancing over in my direction. "You're as white as a sheet."

"I'm tired," I said. "That's all."

Ronan indicated and we turned off the main road and onto the smaller one that led to the McCarthy's house.

The house was in darkness when we finally arrived and I could feel Ronan's confusion when he glanced over at me.

"I thought you said you got a call from, Alice?"

"I did." Without waiting for him, I pushed the door open and stepped out, the crunch of the gravel ringing in the night air.

From the corner of my eye, I spotted a loose paper sitting in the rose bush next to the driveway. Curiosity drove me across the gravel and I reached tentatively through the thorny branches, only snagging my coat on the wickedly sharp points once as I withdrew my arm.

There wasn't enough light to see the image clearly. And I carried it back towards the car, studying it once I was bathed in the brilliance of the headlights.

"What is it?" Ronan moved around the front of the car and joined me in the glow of the high beams.

"A communion picture," I said. There was nothing about the photograph that recognisably stood out to me. One little girl stood in the picture, her hands clasped in front of her in prayer. The curve of her smile told me that prayer couldn't have been further from her mind as the picture was taken. An older girl stood next to her, her face completely blacked out. Although the picture I held in my hands was nothing more than a copy of the original, I could tell that whoever had used the marker on the other girl's face had done so savagely.

The edges where her face should have been were frayed as though the pen used had gone through the page.

"Well that's creepy," Ronan said. The porch light over the front door flicked on and Alice appeared in the doorway.

"You want to tell us what this is all about?" I raised the picture so that it caught the edge of the light. The paper became opaque and it was then I noticed the writing on the other side.

Flipping it over, I stared at the quote.

"Alice in Wonderland," Alice said softly.

"Just like the locket..." I met her gaze head on.

"Shit." Ronan scrubbed his hand over his face. "I'm going to need more coffee. I'm not awake enough to deal with this freaky level of crap."

"Come in," Alice said, directing us into the house. "The kettle is just boiled."

STANDING IN THE SILENT KITCHEN, I surreptitiously took in my surroundings. The bright yellow walls were covered in pine shelves. Small knick-knacks were cluttered together. Mostly rabbits. Some wearing clothes, some holding carrots. There was even one smoking a pipe. Despite the number of them, there wasn't a spec of dust in sight.

"My mother collects them," Alice said, catching me eyeing the ornaments.

"It's..." I fumbled for the right word. "Cute."

Alice grimaced. "Clara bought her that one for her birthday before she disappeared." She gestured to the rabbit wearing a waistcoat. "Mam has collected them ever since. Every time she goes out, she comes home with another one to add to the set."

"And where is your mother now?"

"Mam and dad are in bed. I didn't want to wake them..."

I nodded. "We will need to talk to them about this," I said, setting the picture down on the table with the others. "We need to know if they saw anyone. The pictures, is that you and Clara?"

It was a guess but it was the only thing that made any kind of sense. For some reason, the killer was using Clara and Alice to communicate with us. First through the use of Clara's clothes and the inscription on her locket and now this. There was no denying that Clara McCarthy's disappearance was the key to unravelling the mystery.

Unless the killer was jerking our chain...

Why would they? It's not as though drawing particular attention to the McCarthy case was going to throw us off course. We had no other leads. I'd gone through the interviews with the other missing girl's family members. There was nothing.

No one had seen anything. No one except Alice.

"Yeah," Alice said. "I was getting my first communion. Really thought I looked like a princess."

"Doesn't every little girl?" I gave her a small smile.

"Do you want coffee?" Her gaze was flat as she turned away to the kettle.

"Four sugars," Ronan quipped up, unzipping his jacket and dropping onto one of the wooden kitchen chairs.

He tugged on a pair of gloves carefully. From the corner of my eye, I watched as he began to sift through the images stacked on the table. The pages were a little damp, the edges of the pages ragged.

"Where did the pictures come from?" I asked, turning my attention back to Alice. She stood with her back to the kitchen, her gaze trained on the window.

In the harsh light from the overhead lights, the glass had become a mirror, throwing back her reflection. Yet she kept staring. Was she hoping for some inspiration?

"Alice?" I kept my voice deliberately soft, mindful of the fact she'd said her parents were asleep upstairs. The last thing I wanted was a repeat of the other day's events.

I needed to speak with Alice and something told me she would be far more comfortable, willing even, to talk with us in familiar surroundings. Bringing people down the station often had the opposite effect on them, making it so they clammed up entirely.

I needed her to open up to me. I needed the truth.

"I came home and found them in the garden," she said. "The wind had blown them all around the place. It took me ages to pick them all up."

She turned back to face me once more with a rueful smile. "I must have missed one."

"When you got home, did you see anyone else in the garden?"

She shook her head. "There was no one..." Her hesitation told me there was something she holding back.

"There's something you're not telling me?"

"Sorry," she said. "You asked was there anyone there and I said no but if I'm honest I was too shocked by the pictures to think of looking for anyone."

It was an honest answer at least. Most people would forget to check their surroundings when suffering a shock.

I nodded. "That's understandable." Sucking in a deep breath, I decided to plunge in headfirst.

"When we got here and I asked you what this was all about, you said, 'Alice in Wonderland,' can you tell me what made you say that?"

"The quote, it's from Alice in Wonderland. I recognised it."

"And that's it?"

She swallowed hard and moved over to the fridge.

The door hid her from view and when she emerged a moment later, her eyes were red rimmed.

"Alice, you need to tell us what you know. No matter how small or unimportant it might seem to you."

"Alice in Wonderland was my favourite story when I was a kid. Clara knew it. I used to make her watch the Disney movie with me over and over."

"Does anyone else know this?"

She shrugged. "Everybody knew. I wasn't exactly discreet about my interests."

I opened my mouth to ask another question but she silenced me with a shake of her head. "That's not all. There's this."

From the counter next to the kettle, she picked up a small white rabbit. He held a pocket watch aloft. I remembered the same rabbit being on the table in the living room when we'd come to speak to Alice and her parents. The tick had been out of sync with the other clocks in the house. I remembered because the sound had jarred me.

Now, it was silent.

"It's the white rabbit," she said.

"Excuse me?"

Ronan had set the pictures down and had turned his full attention to the two of us.

"The white rabbit from Alice in Wonderland. She follows it down the rabbit hole and ends up in

Wonderland." Alice carried the rabbit over to the table and set it down between us.

"It's mine," she said before I could ask her. "It went missing years ago and then the day after I got home, it turned up on the doorstep..."

"What?" Ronan didn't bother to hide the note of irritation from his voice.

"Clara bought it for me, when she was going away to camp one year. I kept it in my bedroom and before Clara disappeared. The white rabbit went missing from my room."

"And you didn't think you should bring this to our attention when it turned up on your doorstep?" Ronan asked, picking the rabbit up and turning it over carefully in his hands.

"I didn't think it was important."

"But now you do?" I kept my voice even. There was no point in losing my temper. What was done was done. Getting angry wasn't going to change anything.

"It's too weird," she said, gesturing between the rabbit and the pictures. "The photos come from my old album."

"Let me guess, that went missing too?"

She nodded, her face pale. "It's like they tried to erase Clara from the pictures completely."

I snapped on a pair of gloves myself and began to go through the photographs one by one. They were all the same. Each time Clara appeared in one with her sister, her face was missing. Of the few pictures where she appeared alone, her eyes were gone.

It was definitely a message of some sort but it was beyond my understanding.

"You don't know anyone who would want to send you something like this?"

Alice looked at me in horror. "You're asking if I know a sick fuck capable of this? Whatever in hell this is?" Her voice rose.

"I have to ask, Alice."

She shook her head.

"Who would have access to the pictures?"

She shrugged. "I guess anyone who came to the house. My friends, Clara's friends, Liam..." she trailed off.

"Was Clara seeing anyone else at the time of her disappearance?"

Alice's head snapped up so fast, I worried she would give herself whiplash.

"What has he told you?"

"Who?" Ronan prompted.

"Liam of course," she said. "Who else? Nobody else would suggest Clara was dating another guy. She loved him and he treated her like shit."

"What exactly do you mean, he treated her badly?"

"The night she disappeared when she came to pick me up from the disco she was upset and her shirt was ripped."

"You think he laid hands on her?" It was dangerous

territory. I couldn't put words in her mouth but I needed her to be as specific as she could about the situation. If Liam had assaulted his pregnant girlfriend and he hadn't told us, then what else hadn't he told us?

"It wouldn't have been the first time. Clara came home a couple of times with bruises. I saw them and tried to ask her about them but she never wanted to talk about it. She would always brush it off like it meant nothing."

"Did you tell anyone else at the time?"

"I threatened to tell Mam and Dad but Clara nearly lost her mind. Screamed at me to mind my own business and to stay out of hers. That I didn't know what the hell I was talking about."

"Is it possible that she could have been seeing someone else at the time? Someone she didn't tell you about?"

Alice buried her face in her hands and silence flowed into the kitchen. I waited for her for what felt like forever and when she finally raised her face once more, her expression was grim.

"She could have been seeing someone else. I can't say she wasn't. There's one person who would have known for sure though."

"Who?"

"Sarah Coughlan, her best friend. They were always together. Clara told her everything. If there was someone else, it would be Sarah she told about it."

I nodded and pulled my notepad from inside my

jacket. "We'll be talking to Sarah about this. See if she has anything to add."

As I sat at the edge of the table, I could tell there was something she wanted to say, something she was holding back.

Ronan pulled a couple of plastic evidence bags from his back pocket and proceeded to slide the pictures inside carefully. They were still damp, the least thing would tear them and a misstep like that could cost us evidence. Not that I really thought we were going to get anything from the images. The killer had been clever. Too clever to leave us anything.

But it was still something to go on. For some reason the killer felt an affinity with Alice.

"The night Clara was taken, you said in your original statement that you barely got away. How did you get away?"

Alice swallowed hard and turned her face back to the kitchen window, as though the answers she was seeking would somehow appear on the glass.

"He tried to bundle Clara into the van and then he came looking for me. He grabbed me by the hair," she said, gesturing to the front of her scalp. "He was behind me and I couldn't see him. I thought he was going to rip my head clean off. And then he was dragging me." She sucked in a deep breath and squared her shoulders. "I tried to fight him. I could feel his fingernails digging into my scalp and—"

"Did anyone ever look at your scalp?" I asked, interrupting her. "You know, did a doctor look you over?"

She shook her head. "They didn't believe me. Said I was drunk, that I was making it up." There was no denying the bitterness in her voice. I couldn't begin to imagine the anger she felt. To have something so traumatic happen and for those around you—the people you were supposed to turn to for protection—just dismiss you and think you made it up.

"Clara got out of the van, I don't know how and she kicked him in the nuts." The ghost of a smile played on Alice's face. "She'd taken some self-defence classes the year before as part of transition year in school. Clara loved all that kind of stuff."

"When she kicked him, what happened then?"

"He let me go and we ran. I was holding her hand when we went down the embankment at the side of the road and I let her go." Alice closed her eyes. "I thought she was right behind me. I could hear her running. Or at least I thought I could. I found out later when I looked it up that trauma can do that to you; make you imagine things that weren't real. The fight or flight response kicks in. It kicked in with me and I couldn't hear shit over the sound of my own heartbeat."

"When did you realise Clara wasn't behind you?"

"I fell in the river," Alice said. "I nearly drowned. I don't know how I managed to drag myself out. I don't remember it. I just remember waking up on the bank and I couldn't find Clara."

"What time was this?"

She shrugged. "I don't remember. I fell asleep for a while and when I woke up it was getting light out."

"And that's when you headed back toward the road?" Ronan prompted.

Alice closed her eyes. "I was so cold. I thought I was going to die out there, freeze to death or something. I thought Clara was getting help..."

"Did you see or hear anything else, Alice?" I halted my pen, afraid the scratching of the ballpoint on the surface of the paper would disturb her.

"There was something," she said finally. "I heard someone call my name, I thought it was Clara. That was why I thought she'd gone for help."

"Could it have been Clara?" I leaned a little closer.

Alice shrugged and opened her eyes. "I don't know. I wasn't even thinking straight. I couldn't feel my hands or my feet. They were so numb with the cold. I'm not even sure now if I heard something or not."

"Try," I said gently. "Even if you think it's not important. It might be important to the case..."

Alice's brow furrowed in consternation. "I told you, I can't remember." Every word was tipped with frustration. Not that I could blame her. I knew what it was like to have elusive memories. So close you could almost taste them but still so utterly and completely out of reach so as to be useless.

"If anything comes to you," I said, pushing up onto my feet. There was no use pushing her further. The harder she tried, the less she would remember. "Give us a ring. I'll send Ronan around in the morning to have a chat with your parents about the pictures and—"

"Please don't," Alice said softly. "Things are hard enough around here already."

"We have to," I said firmly. "We need to know if they heard anyone, or saw anything unusual."

She nodded and buried her face in her hands once more. "I'm sorry, it's just with everything..."

I touched her shoulder briefly and she looked up at me. The dark circles beneath her eyes were getting deeper. Clearly, I wasn't the only one around here that sleep was eluding.

"Will she ever be found, do you think?" There was a vulnerability in Alice's voice as she spoke.

"I hope so," I said. "I know I'm going to do my best to bring her home to you."

She nodded. "I know you will."

"We'll take these with us and get them analysed," Ronan said, breaking the moment. "I'll need to take some fingerprints when I come round tomorrow. You know, to eliminate everyone here."

Alice nodded again. "I'm familiar with procedure."

We moved toward the door and I paused. "I heard about what you did over in England."

Alice's eyes darted to the side as he lips twisted up into a grimace.

"I just did my job," she said.

"No. It was more than your job. You saved that kid. Not everyone would put themselves between a gun and an innocent like that. Your parents must be very proud of you."

"I haven't told them." Her voice was flat, as though she were telling me the weather.

"How come?"

"I don't want to worry them unnecessarily."

I bit down on my tongue. There was more to it but she clearly wasn't willing to tell me.

The creak of a floorboard told me we weren't alone anymore. The kitchen door slapped open to reveal Ita McCarthy standing there in her dressing gown.

"What's going on here?" Her voice was strained, her face pale as she took in the scene in the kitchen.

"We were just leaving," I said, moving out into the hall past her.

"Alice, what is this? Is there news on Clara? Have you found my daughter?"

"No." I slipped my jacket back on. "We don't have any new information on Clara. I'm sorry. Alice needed to speak with us."

"Mam, I—" She was floundering. I could see it in her face, the panic reflected in her eyes as she glanced from her mother and back to us.

"Speak to you? Whatever for. Alice, what is this?"

There was an edge to Mrs McCarthy's voice. I recognised it as the same edge she'd had in her voice the last time we'd paid a visit.

"We'll go now." I gestured for Ronan to follow me. Perhaps if I gave Alice space, she would find a way to explain the new developments to her mother without further upset.

"I'll be around in the morning," Ronan said gently, keeping the pictures out of sight as he followed me to the front door.

"How could you bring them into the house again, after everything? How could you bring them back here? How does this help your sister?"

I slipped out the front door, unwilling to listen to the burgeoning argument.

Standing out on the drive, I listened to the voices as they rose on the other side of the door and closed my eyes. The soft mist that had started to fall while we were inside quickly covered my face and hair.

"Should we have just left like that?" Ronan asked, standing next to the car, uncertainty visible in every line of his body.

"Strictly speaking, no," I said. "But staying would only have made it worse. They need time together. Time to pull themselves into some kind of unit and we'd just get in the way right now. There'll be time enough in the morning for the practical things like fingerprints and statements."

He nodded but his expression suggested he was still somewhat unconvinced.

"I feel bad too, you know." I gestured back toward the house as I joined him at the car and climbed into the passenger seat. "But we can't fix this."

"Is there anything we can fix?" He raised an eyebrow at me as he gave me a wilted smile.

I shook my head. "In these kinds of cases," I said. "The best we can hope for is some closure."

"And if we fail at that?"

"Then we keep trying until we stop failing."

I took the packet of photographs from where Ronan had thrown it onto the dashboard. The plastic was dotted with droplets of water and the gloom of the car somewhat obscured the images inside. But that didn't stop me from feeling the oddly penetrating gaze of the young women in the photographs. It was strange. Whoever had defaced the images, it was as though they were trying to steal something from Clara. As though her eyes staring up at them from the photograph could condemn them somehow.

Did they feel guilt?

Or was it simply the case that kidnapping her wasn't enough? That whatever they had done to her, whatever horror they had visited upon her, hadn't been enough to satisfy them? And now they needed more?

There were far too many questions and not enough

answers. And the more I delved into the case, the more questions I found myself faced with.

But I had the sinking feeling that I was never going to have all the answers I needed. That whoever was doing this would do everything in their power to keep me at arms length, leaving them free to go on killing.

48

BEING that close to her was thrilling. I could still smell the tantalising scent of her strawberry shampoo, even now, hours later. Was it the same shampoo she had used back then? It certainly smelled similar.

It had been so long since I'd been within touching distance of her. And the urges rising inside me had almost been my undoing.

It had taken every ounce of my willpower not to take her there and then.

But with him there, that was impossible. I knew what he would do if he caught me with her. He would destroy everything I've been working toward. Spoil it all.

Spoil my fun.

With her I could create a life. The life I'd always dreamed of having. The one I'd been denied.

She was my ray of sunshine, delivered back to me.

I'd always known Clara could bring her back, that she wouldn't fail me. She was the only one who understood, the only one who wanted Alice as much as I did.

She would make everything right...

He was the problem. He would insist on taking his carnal pleasures out on her. His perverse anger would tear at her. Destroy her innocence.

And she was innocent. I could see it in her eyes when she looked at me.

With Alice, everything needed to be different. Special. We would be together and she would be safe with me. Loved and cherished, as she deserved.

My little princess.

I would protect her from him, no matter the cost.

I would save her.

49

"Why were they here, Alice?" Mam's voice was shrill and made my head ache.

"I told you. They needed to go over my statement."

"You're lying."

"It doesn't matter."

"The hell it doesn't. What did that Guard mean when she said your parents should be proud of you?"

"Nothing..."

"Don't 'nothing' me. I know when you're lying to me, Alice McCarthy. What was she talking about?"

There was a desperation in my mother's face that I hadn't seen before.

"I was shot," I said, letting the words drop into the air before I could talk myself out of it. "I was working a case involving a young girl and her mother. The father got his hands on a gun and I got shot."

She went white around the lips and I could see a

tremor start in her hands. I darted forward as she sank into the kitchen chair the male detective had vacated only moments before. Before I could touch her, she slapped my hands away, her eyes two black pits of accusation as she stared up at me.

"You were shot and you didn't tell me?"

"I didn't want to worry you, I—"

"You didn't want to worry me?" A bark of a laugh escaped her. The sound far more worrying than the hysterical note I'd detected in her voice when the detectives had been here. "That's all I ever do. You don't talk to me and I worry."

"I'm sorry. It's just with everything going on here, I didn't want to add to it all."

"You could have been killed and I wouldn't even have known. Do you know how much that hurts, Alice? Do you know how much it hurts not to know what has happened to your children? To know they're out there somewhere but you can't find them. Can't bring them home where they belong."

We weren't really talking about me anymore, which was a small relief. The Clara conversation was a minefield I had navigated before but I'd never had to do it in relation to my own choices.

"We're going to find her," I said. "With all the new evidence the detectives are—"

"She's never coming home is she?" There was a stark vulnerability to the question I'd never seen my mother expose before. "I keep praying she'll walk through that door and everyday she doesn't it hits me all over again."

What was I supposed to say to her? Everything I could think up sounded contrived and pathetic.

"I do the same thing," I said softly. Perhaps, this was the way for us to build a bridge back to each other. "I keep thinking I'll wake up and it'll all have been a nightmare."

"It's not though."

I shook my head. "No. It's not."

"She was my first baby... I can remember when I held her in my arms for the first time. I'd thought all that talk about falling in love with your children was just nonsense. That they just made it up. But when I held her in my arms and looked into her face, into her eyes, I knew it was true. She was my first big love." She smiled at me. "Don't get me wrong. I love your father, always have. But holding your child is something different. Something purer. I thought I could teach her that with her child. That I would get the chance to explain it to her before..."

She sucked in a deep breath. "And even when you came along. I thought I would have to give up some of that love for her, so I could let you in. I think part of me resented you for that. I worried before you arrived that I wouldn't be able to love you both equally. That you would feel like I loved you less."

Despite not wanting to feel hurt over her confession, I couldn't help a small sliver of pain that pierced me.

"I was wrong. Loving you both was so easy."

I let my shoulders drop.

"But you keep making it harder," she said, quietly.

I felt my breath hitch in my chest as my world came crashing down around my ears.

"We keep trying with you but you're always so distant, as though you don't want to be a part of this family anymore."

"I'm distant?" I couldn't keep the anger from my voice. "I'm not the one who's distant. I don't blame you for Clara's disappearance," I said. "Not the way you blame me."

She drummed her fingers against the tabletop and frowned, her gaze trained on her hands. "I don't blame you."

"Yes you do," I said, my voice rising. "You always have. I came back that night and Clara didn't but with the way you carry on, you'd swear I was responsible for her going missing. Sometimes I think you wish we were both taken."

"That's not fair." Her face was pale, her lower lip trembling. "You don't know what it's been like."

"And whose fault is that? Did you ever stop to think how I might have felt? I was a kid and you treated me like a criminal."

"We were struggling to come to terms with it, we—"

Hopping to my feet, I started for the door. "I'm going to bed. I don't want to hear this anymore."

"You're so good at running away, Alice. You always were." Her unspoken accusation hung in the air between us. I left her there and started up the stairs.

"If you walk away this time," she followed me out into the hall, "we're done. For good this time."

"Then I guess we're done." I carried on climbing the stairs, leaving her to stare after me.

Pushing open the bedroom door, I stepped inside and flopped down onto the edge of the bed. Guilt gnawed at me. I'd been too hard. I wasn't giving her enough credit for all that she'd been through.

But as much as I wanted to sympathise with her, I couldn't bring myself to do it. I'd been a child—a thirteen year old definitely wasn't an adult—and yet she'd cut me loose that day. When I'd come home and told my story. When I'd told them what had happened, she hadn't believed me. And it had been in that moment I'd known that whatever childhood I'd had was over. With Clara gone and nobody to believe me, I had to grow up. I had to grow up and make them understand what had been lost.

Lying back on the bed, I closed my eyes and let the exhaustion overcome me. Falling to sleep was as easy as falling into a river.

THE COLD WATER froze my airways, making it impossible to draw breath. I spluttered, my arms windmilling as I half swam half-doggy paddled to the riverbank.

My body was a leaden weight as I dragged myself up onto the mud. Retching cleared at least the worst of the water.

The alcohol in my system had burned away, leaving me fuzzy headed. Lying in the mud, I stared up at the dark sky overhead.

At least the world wasn't spinning anymore.

Rolling onto my side, pain lanced through my head and I raised my hand to the bump on my forehead.

When had that happened?

I closed my eyes and dizzying images of running through the woods flitted through my mind. The metallic tang of blood filled my mouth and I brushed my fingers against my lips. It was too dark to make out the colour smeared on my fingers but I already knew.

"Clara?" My voice was a croak and barely above a whisper.

Panic gripped me. What if she had fallen into the water after me? She'd been right behind me and I hadn't seen the riverbank.

Pushing onto my knees, I tried to peer into the murky water but while I could hear it rushing past, I couldn't see anything beyond the dark glint of the water's surface.

Clara wouldn't have fallen in the water. She was slower than I was. She'd have seen me fall and that would have stopped her.

Right?

"Clara?" I called again but my voice barely lifted above the rush of the river water.

Exhaustion clung to me, making my eyelids heavy. Every time I sucked in a breath, my chest burned and the wheeze in my lungs reminded me of the bout of pneumonia I'd suffered last winter. I'd been stuck in bed for two weeks, too sick to truly enjoy my time away from school.

When I opened my eyes again it was to the patter of raindrops on the leaves above my head. The sky was grey with the beginnings of the dawn light struggling to peek through.

Rolling over onto my side, I made it to my feet. My knees were jelly and every step was a lesson in self-control. I glanced down at my legs to make sure I still had them. Every time I lifted my foot, it felt like it belonged to someone else. As though I was somehow disconnected from my body.

My teeth had stopped chattering but I was still cold. The kind of cold that seeped inside you and never stirred out.

Making my way back through the trees, I tried to imagine the direction the road lay in. If I could just find it then maybe I would find my way home.

Was Clara waiting for me there?

Mam and Dad were going to kill me when I got in. I was definitely going to be grounded. As I trudged through the trees, I realised I'd have given anything to hear them scold me.

"Clara!" My voice was a little stronger but not by much. My throat was rough, as though I'd swallowed a bunch of wire wool.

The trees continued their silent appraisal of me as I trudged on. Breaking through the last of them, I found myself on the side of the road. Scrambling over the embankment wasn't as difficult in the light as it had been in the dark.

It was empty. No sign of the van from the night before. No glaring headlights to blind me. No gruff voice whispering in my ear. No hand clutching my hair, fingernails tearing at my scalp.

Had I imagined it?

No. Clara had been with me. I hadn't imagined it.

"Alice!" The voice called to me from the direction I'd come from. Clara? Had I left her behind? Was she trapped, hurt or worse?

"Clara!" My voice cracked over her name painfully before it cut out.

Panic constricted my chest, like a too tight hug as the sound of a car approached from behind.

The urge to turn and race back into the trees gripped me.

Close.

Closer.

If I was going to run, I needed to go now.

He's coming back.

"Run..." Clara's last whispered word to me burned inside my mind.

My legs seized up.

I tried to move them but they refused to budge. They buckled beneath me and I hit the road with a dull thud.

Tyres crunched on the gravel next to me.

"Alice McCarthy?" The unfamiliar voice sent me into a tailspin.

If I couldn't run, at least I could crawl.

"Wait, where are you going?"

The sharp stones dug into my hands as I tried to scramble away. Strong arms lifted me from the ground and I found myself staring into the red face of a Guard, his hair flattened on his head where his hat should have sat.

His navy uniform was immaculate, the buttons shining in the glow of the headlights.

"Your parents are worried sick about you," he said.

Bile rushed up my throat and I had enough time to close my eyes and wish for the ground to swallow me whole before I vomited onto the front of his jacket.

50

October 7th 1996

SARAH and her boyfriend picked me up today after my doctor's appointment. He's kind of creepy. I tried to tell her that but Sarah seems besotted with him.

She wouldn't let me near him before this and all of a sudden she's like, 'Oh, Dick will pick you up if you want.' Or, 'Dick can drop you off.'

Personally, I'd much rather walk than sit alone in the van with him.

Baby boy nearly kicked my bladder to bits today. I've been playing him my favourite Boyzone song through my headphones because I read in a magazine that babies can hear things even in the womb.

Mam said we'll go shopping come the end of the month for some baby bits and I'm so excited. It's all starting to get real.

I can't wait to meet him.

51

"My name is Detective Siobhan Geraghty," I said, extending my hand to the young woman in front of me. Her grip was timid and she took her hand back quickly, placing it in her lap.

Sarah Coughlan sat in the same place Liam Donnelly had been sitting less than twenty-four hours previously. From my reading of the interview files, she hadn't changed a bit in the twenty-two years since her friend's disappearance.

I kept my gaze trained on the file in front of me and watched surreptitiously as she tucked a phantom strand of mousy brown hair behind her ear.

Her too-wide eyes darted around the room, making me think she was uncomfortable in confined spaces. That wasn't unusual; plenty of people were claustrophobic and the interrogation rooms weren't exactly roomy.

"What am I doing here?" Despite her obvious discomfort and timidity, there was nothing to suggest shyness in her question.

Her voice though soft, was direct, almost confrontational.

"I wanted to ask you a few questions about your friend," I said. "Clara McCarthy. And go over the statement you made during the initial inquiry."

"I'm not sure I can be of much help," she said. "And I won't be able to stay long. I've got to pick my daughter up after school."

"It says here that you're married, Mrs Coughlan."

"What does that have to do with anything?"

"Any chance your husband could pick your daughter up? I wouldn't want to pause the interview and take up more of your time another day by revisiting old ground."

"He's out. Fishing I think he said."

"Alone?"

"No. My brother is gone with him. They get along well, which I suppose is a blessing."

"It doesn't sound like you really believe that."

"Well it's not easy when he spends more time with him, than he does with me."

I shot her a sympathetic smile.

"Well, I'll try to keep this short then, so you can pick your daughter up on time."

She nodded and shot another nervous glance around the room.

"Can I get you something to drink?"

"No." She shook her head. "I'd just like to get this over with." She smiled, but the warmth never reached her eyes.

"In your initial statement you stated your belief that Clara McCarthy had fled to England for an abortion. Is that correct?"

Her hands fell still in her lap and I noted the ragged fingernails. Was it hard work, or just nervous habit that left them in that state?

"I said that." She shrugged. "We'd spoken about the possibility. Clara didn't think she was ready to be a mother. She wanted a life, said there was too much she wanted to do still and..." Sarah glanced away and gazed at the floor.

"And what?"

"She wanted to punish Liam."

"Why would she do that?"

"He'd been cheating on her. His father told Clara that Liam needed to sow his wild oats, that she shouldn't tie him down." Sarah dug her fingers into the sleeve of her cardigan. "You know he offered her money to get rid of it. Who does that? What kind of monster offers another human being money to be rid of their child?" She sucked in a deep breath and I noted the slight tremor in her hands as she plucked at her cardigan.

I hadn't been expecting the level of vitriol she'd expressed and I tried to keep my expression neutral.

However, there was no mention of bribery in the files. Not that it was unsurprising. How could there be a mention of bribery when all the files pertaining to Liam Donnelly didn't even exist.

"And you knew this how?"

"Clara told me," she said. "She was so upset, I thought she was going to do something stupid."

"Why didn't you mention any of this at the time?"

"Because Liam frightened me. I thought if I said something about him, that his family would come after mine."

"You mean he threatened you?"

She shook her head. "Nothing like that. But everyone knew not to cross them. My parents were already struggling with their benefits. And there are certain people in this world that you don't mess with. Everyone knows it. And in a small town like this, well..." She shrugged.

"I don't think I'm following."

"If I said something, the social would have found a reason for my parents not to get their money every week."

"You think Liam's family had that much power?"

"His uncle was a TD, and some of his family worked in the social welfare office in town. What do you think?"

"I think intervening in the way you suggest would have been a crime."

She laughed, the sound high and brittle. "Clearly, your experiences aren't mine."

Tenting my fingers in front of me, I leaned my elbows on the table. "So what changed?"

"Excuse me?"

"What changed that you can sit here today and tell me all this?"

Her smile was hesitant. "I'm not afraid of bullies anymore, Detective. I left those fears behind me when I became a mother."

I returned her smile but it wasn't entirely honest. There was something about the whole thing that seemed just a little off.

"So where do you think Clara McCarthy is?"

"I don't know," she said. "I'm not the detective. I wouldn't know the first place to begin speculating about it all. And anyway, from what I've heard from Alice you lot believe Clara is dead."

"You're still in contact with Alice McCarthy?"

"I used to babysit her when she was younger. We've always been very close. I tried to be there for her when Clara disappeared."

"Do you know if Clara knew a Evie Ryan?"

Sarah paused. "No, I don't think so... She's one of the other missing girls, right?"

I gave her a tight smile. "Yes."

"Should Clara have known her?"

"It's just another line of enquiry, we're exploring all avenues."

"You really don't know what happened, do you?"

"What makes you say that?"

"This," she gestured to the air, "it all feels like you're clutching at straws. If you had something concrete you'd have made a move already. And if you're planning on pinning this on the Donnelly's I think you'll find yourself up against a brick wall."

"Why would I pin this on the Donnelly's?"

My question seemed to catch her off guard. "Well, it just seems like you're terribly interested in what happened between Clara and Liam. It makes sense you'd look at him."

"He was very young."

Sarah's gaze fell into her lap. "It's amazing the things you can do when you're young. Most believe themselves infallible, that no matter what they do, the consequences will never catch up to them."

She glanced at her watch and pursed her lips. "I'm going to have to go if I'm going to get across to the school on time to pick Ali up."

"One last question," I said, halting her before she could climb to her feet.

Sarah quirked an eyebrow at me.

"Do you know anyone who drove a white van at the time of Clara's disappearance?"

She pursed her lips and a line appeared in the middle of her brow. "I think Liam's father had a white van. I can't swear to it but I'm sure I saw him driving it around a couple of times. Why?"

"Thanks for your time, Sarah," I said, dismissing her last question without an answer.

She nodded as she grabbed her bag from the floor and stood. I directed her to the door and she paused, half way out.

"Do you think you'll find her?"

"We're going to do our best."

"She's dead though, isn't she?"

"I'm not willing to speculate." Even though everyone knew it was a murder enquiry and not a missing persons investigation, I found myself unwilling to share any information with Sarah.

"Well I've got faith that she'll be found. One way or another."

My smile was polite, without the slightest hint of warmth.

Following her out into the foyer, I watched her leave.

"Detective Geraghty," the sergeant's voice cut through my contemplation and I turned to find him waving me over from the door to his office.

He held the door for me as I stepped inside. I stopped dead on the threshold.

"Hello, Detective Geraghty." Paul pushed up from his chair and my heart stalled out in my chest.

"What are you doing here?"

"I called them down," Sergeant Mills said briskly.

"Them?" My voice was cold.

"Sergeant Mills thought you could do with a little

back-up, that's all," Paul said, smoothing over the situation with his well-practiced charm. "He thought it prudent considering the sudden growth of the case and the renewed media interest what with the body of the newest girl turning up."

"Who else is here?" I clenched my fists, driving my fingernails up into my palms. As much as Paul tried to paint this as nothing more than them stepping in to help out a fellow officer, I knew what it really meant. Sergeant Mills had made the call and they'd all come running because they didn't think I was capable of handling the case on my own.

"Now is not the time to discuss it," Paul said, turning his attention back to Sergeant Mills. "If you wouldn't mind giving us a few moments alone, so that Detective Geraghty can get me up to speed on everything here?"

Sergeant Mills smiled broadly and shook Paul's extended hand enthusiastically.

"Of course," he said. "Good to know things are finally in hand."

He turned his smile on me and it took every ounce of my strength not to lash out at him and wipe the smug grin from his lips. Instead, I turned away and moved over to the window, staring out at the street beyond the window blinds.

The soft click of the door signalled he'd left and I turned in time for Paul to drag me into his arms. His mouth came down over mine, a possessive, hungry kiss that under other circumstances would have pleased me.

Planting my hands against his chest, I shoved hard. Managing to send him backwards a couple of steps.

"What the hell is this?" I whispered, fury carved into each word.

"Well I thought it was my saying hello," Paul said, managing to sound both hurt and confused. "Obviously I've misread the situation."

"Damn right you have." I sucked in a deep breath and tried to let go the worst of the anger constricting my chest like a vice. "Who else is here?"

"Brady's coming. He'll be here tomorrow, he sent me ahead."

"Shit."

Paul tried to draw me in against his chest once more but I held him at arm's length.

"And why are you here? I thought you were working your drug case."

"I volunteered. Thought you might appreciate a friendly face in all of this."

"What's that supposed to mean?"

"It means your mate Mills there really has it in for you, Siobhan. He wants your ass in a sling. Says you've been upsetting some important people around here. Brady's not happy about it, he got a phone call from a pissed off TD right after he spoke to Mills."

It was going from bad to worse. How the hell was I

supposed to do my job when people were far more interested in covering everything up?

"They've screwed up here," I said. "Interviews that were supposed to have taken place never did. Everything was kept off the record."

"Mills seems to think you're hung up on one aspect of the case," Paul said. He shoved his hands into his pockets and slowly began to pace the room. "Says you won't investigate any of the other girls involved, just this one McCarthy case."

"I'm doing my job," I said. "I know how to conduct an investigation but so far I've been chasing my own tail trying to navigate the mess they made of this in the first place."

"So you agree then that you're hung up on one particular avenue?"

"No." I shook my head. "That's not what I'm saying. I'm following the evidence where it leads."

Paul rocked back on his heels and watched me, his gaze travelling down my body and then back up once more.

"Look, we both know you're not the most diplomatic detective around."

"What's that supposed to mean?"

"You see," he said. "You can't even take a little criticism. You should have played ball with Mills, listened to his concerns, nodded and then got on the phone to Brady so he could sort it out if it was really that much of a problem."

With a sigh, I dropped back against the wall. "You and I both know if I'd called Brady in he'd have kicked me back to Dublin and put someone else on this."

Paul grimaced. "Maybe you're just not cut out for leading cases, Siobhan."

I opened my mouth to answer him but he raised his hands in mock surrender. "Look, don't shoot the messenger. I'm just here to get things back on track until Brady can make a decision about how he wants things to progress."

I bit back my anger. There was no point in lashing out at Paul. He was only here to do his job. And taking my fury out on him would only make things worse. Especially if he really believed that I wasn't cut out for leading cases. A poor report from him would be dire for my career. He was a senior officer and too well respected to ignore.

"Fine, what do you suggest?"

"Well for starters," he said, his voice low. "I think maybe we should start over with a proper hello?" He took a step forward.

"How about I take you to meet the team and get you caught up on where we are?"

His smile faltered. "I'm really sorry about this, Siobhan. I'm not trying to step on your toes here, I'm just trying to help."

Shit. How was it he could always managed to make me feel like a complete asshole when I was just trying to do my job?

"But you're right. We should get straight down to brass tacks." His voice was cold and business like. His smile nothing more than polite.

Paul pulled the door open next to him and with a flourish, gestured for me to leave. Normally, I would have looked at his behaviour as being endearing but there was no mistaking the edge to it now. He was pissed at me, that much was obvious. But there wasn't much I could do about it.

We had a killer to catch. For all I knew, he already had his next victim and if we didn't get ahead of him, before too long we'd been digging another mutilated girl up out of the soft dirt.

52

It's all beginning to come together.

Soon she'll come home. I can feel it deep down inside. Warm butterflies flutter around in the pit of my stomach. The anticipation is so sweet, I can practically taste it on my tongue.

Soon, we will all be together. Happy. Secure. Loved.

And nothing will stop me from having her.

Not even him.

53

PAUSING at the top of the stairs, I strained to decipher the hushed voices coming from the kitchen. My bag was packed and I'd looked up the flight times but I couldn't bring myself to just leave.

It would easier to just walk out the door, to walk away and leave them all behind. Never look back.

As much as I wanted to do that, there was still a part of me that refused to give up. It was childish to believe I could ever have the kind of relationship I dreamed of with my parents. There was too much water under the bridge, too many accusations, and emotional wounds to contend with.

Yet, I still couldn't bring myself to just go.

It hadn't stopped me from booking a taxi though, just in case. I pulled the sling off and shoved it into my pocket, letting my arm hang loose at my side. It ached but no worse than a niggling headache and I could manage that.

Clattering down the stairs, I set my bag in the hall, giving them the time they needed to compose themselves before I pushed open the kitchen door.

Mam's icy stare was enough to tell me it was a huge mistake.

Dad kept his gaze trained on the paper in his hands but I could tell from the way his eyes darted back and forth in the one spot that he wasn't actually reading anything on the page. They were going to ignore it.

Imelda leaned against the sink, her gaze sympathetic but not even she said anything.

"When are you leaving?" Mam's voice cut through the tension.

"Do you want me gone?" I held my breath.

"I think it's for the best." She slid her glasses off and placed them on the table. "We've got a lot to do here and we don't need people around who don't actually want to be a part of this family."

Coming down had been a huge mistake.

Tears pricked at the back of my eyes and it took all of my willpower to keep them at bay.

"Fine." I turned back to the sink and grabbed a glass, filling it with water gave me the time I needed to compose myself. "I'll get my flights sorted and then I'll be out of your hair."

I turned back to face her but she climbed to her feet and with one last icy look, left the room.

"Your mother is under a lot of stress," Dad said finally. He raised his face and met my gaze head on. "Just give her some time."

"You know what she's doing," I said. "Why not stop her. It doesn't have to be like this, I..."

He shook his head and set his paper aside. "You've got your life in England now, love. It's better this way. You two were always too much alike. Too stubborn by half. When they find Clara and bring her home, maybe then it'll be different."

"Dad, I—"

He cut me off with a shake of his head. "Just go, love. Don't make it harder."

I set the glass down on the table. My hands shaking so hard I thought if I kept a hold of it I would spill the contents across the floor. This was it. They had both washed their hands of me.

I wasn't sure what I'd been expecting but it wasn't this.

Naive to the end.

Imelda caught me on the way out the front door.

"Where are you going to go?"

I shrugged. "You heard them, they want me gone. I need to book my flights and get back."

"You can call 'round mine and use the laptop."

I shook my head. "I'm fine, Imelda." Seeing her crushed expression. "Thanks though. Means a lot but I've got a taxi booked.

"You were going to leave anyway?" There was no accusation in her voice, just quiet resignation.

"I have to."

"It's not right." She scrubbed her hand beneath her eyes. "I'll talk to her, see if I can make her see sense. She's just angry."

"Thanks." I grabbed my jacket from the bottom of the stairs and slipped both arms through, cringing slightly at the angle I had to manuoever my arm before I could get it into place.

She walked me out as the taxi pulled up outside and I loaded my stuff into the backseat.

Imelda dragged me into a tight hug. "You look after yourself, kid," she whispered against my hair. The cold damp air soaked in through my clothes and I pushed her gently away.

"Go in before you get wet, the last thing Mam and Dad need is you getting sick in the middle of all this."

Her smile was watery but at least it was genuine.

"I'm supposed to say things like that," she said. "I'm the adult here."

I grinned at her and climbed into the taxi.

"Message me when you get back safe."

"I will."

She shut the door, sealing me into the backseat and the heat that swirled around me.

"Where are we going then?" The friendly-faced taxi driver settled himself behind the wheel.

I gave him Sarah's address. The thought of just leaving without at least saying goodbye to her, especially after everything that had happened just didn't feel right.

We pulled out of the drive and I stared at the house as we left it behind, my vision blurred.

"Did you have a good holiday then?" the driver asked.

When I didn't answer him, he took one look in the rearview mirror and fell silent, his smile sliding from his face. I could feel the weight of his pity pressing me down into the seat like the hand of some great monster.

It FELT weird dragging my suitcase out of the taxi outside Sarah's house. As I made my way up the narrow path the sound of raised voices reached me and my heart stalled out in my chest.

The smash of glass breaking caused me to pick up my pace and as I reached the side of the house I could hear Sarah's voice, the pleading in her voice stirring my anger.

"I said I was sorry," she said.

The memory of her trying to hide the bruises on her arms flooded back into my head.

The sound of a flesh meeting flesh turned my stomach and I peered through the kitchen window.

There was no sign of Sarah but I could see Dick.

With his back to me, he looked much larger than he had the night before.

He drew back and kicked something at his feet.

My gaze dropped to the floor and my stomach followed suit.

Sarah.

She lay on her side, curled around his thick legs.

"Stupid bitch!" He drew back and kicked her again.

My hand hit the window, the slap of my palm shaking the glass in its frame.

I'd let Rachel down. Failed to see what was going on, failed to recognise the signs. I wouldn't do it again.

Dick turned, surprise on his face as I pressed my phone to my ear.

"Gardaí please," I raised my voice, keeping the words crisp despite the tremor running through my body.

54

October 16th 1996

SARAH'S BOYFRIEND is definitely a creep. He tried to put his hand up my skirt in the van today and Sarah just brushed it off.

She said I was making a big deal out of it all. And then she had the nerve to tell me Dick wouldn't touch a whale like me anyway.

She's different since they met. I can't put my finger on it exactly but she seems crueler somehow.

I just wish I had my friend back...

Liam is trying harder these days ever since he felt the baby kick. I want to believe he's changing but I'm not willing to risk it just yet.

Mam says we'll go shopping this weekend. I've been saving up all month. I don't think I've been this excited since I got pregnant.

Alice says she wants to come too. I told her about the baby hearing stuff too and she spent all last night whispering to him. She'll be a great aunt, I know she's going to spoil him rotten and I'll have to watch for that. I don't want him getting too spoiled.

Roll on the weekend!!!

55

TWO HOURS LATER, I was sitting at the kitchen table with Sarah, my shoulder shooting achy cramps up into my neck and jaw.

The moment Dick had realised what I'd done, he'd fled. Closing my eyes, I could still remember the violence as he'd ripped open the back door and come after me. I'd run but I wasn't fast enough and his hand had found my hair, jerking my head back before he'd thrown me into the grass.

My phone had crunched beneath his boot as he'd stamped on it.

"Silly cow, you don't know what you've done."

There had been a moment when I'd looked into his eyes but the emotion I'd seen there, I couldn't name. He wanted to hurt me, that much was obvious. Given half a chance, he would probably kill me.

Instead, he'd run, jumping the back fence as the sirens from the Garda cars had split the air.

And now, Gardaí were out there looking for him.

Silence drifted in around us in the kitchen, broken only by the sound of Sarah's unsteady breaths and my own unsettled heartbeat.

Something nagged at me. I touched my hand to my hair, running my fingers through it. A memory niggling in the back of my mind that refused to surface. Was it something Dick had done?

Sarah raised her tear-streaked face. "If you hadn't come along when you did, I don't know what he would have done."

Even though Dick was long gone, there was still an atmosphere of fear in the kitchen. But that was the way with bullies. They inflicted their damage before running, never sticking around to face the consequences of their actions.

Sarah on the other hand was a different matter.

"Are you sure you don't want to go to the hospital and get checked over?"

She shook her head again. "I'm fine, really. They're just bruises."

"Do you know where he might have gone?"

Sarah started to shake her head and then paused. "He spends a lot of time with Robbie. They go out fishing and hunting. They're often gone for hours. That's where he was supposed to be today..." She trailed off her tears starting afresh.

"They'll find him," I said decisively. "You don't have to worry about him anymore." I pushed up onto my feet and Sarah's hand found mine, her grip painful as she crushed my fingers beneath hers.

"What would I do without you?"

"You'd figure it out," I said, slowly extricating myself from her. "Sarah, has Dick ever beaten Ali?"

The colour drained from Sarah's face. "Never." The word was nothing more than a whisper of sound. "I wouldn't let him touch a hair on her head. I would kill him if he touched her."

"Where is she now?"

"I dropped her off at her grandparents after school. It's her birthday on Saturday and I wanted to get some things organised without her knowing."

Relief flooded through me. At least she wouldn't have to see her mother in the current state she was in. There were some things in this life that children should never have to see. This was definitely one of them.

"I'll get the kettle on," I said, crossing to the sink. Sarah was on her feet in a flash.

"Let me. You're my guest."

"Really, it's fine, I—" Sarah cut me off with a determined shake of her head as she grabbed the kettle from my hands.

"Sarah, you need to rest. You've been through something traumatic."

"I'm fine, I wish people would stop thinking I'm this

delicate little thing that needs protecting all the time. I'm capable of taking care of myself." Her curt tone told me I'd touched a nerve and short of wrestling her for the kettle, she wasn't going to give it up.

With a smile, I backed off. Watching as she filled the kettle and set it back on the stand.

"Do you want some—" she halted, her eyes settling on my suitcase in the corner where I'd dumped it after Dick had fled.

"You're leaving?" Her voice was flat.

"It's time," I said. "They don't have news on Clara and things aren't great at home. That's why I came by, to say goodbye."

"Oh." She turned her back to me.

"You know what it's like," I said. "I don't belong here anymore, I—"

"Why don't you stay here?" There was no mistaking the note of hope in her voice. "I could make you up a room and—"

"I really can't. There are too many things I need to get sorted at home." Her shoulders drooped.

"I just thought what with everything, this would give us a little time to reconnect. You know, for Clara."

"It's because of her, I have to go."

With her back to me, she nodded. "I get it. It's too painful." The sound of the kettle beginning to boil saw her move back into action once more.

I dropped back onto my chair and stared at the broken screen of my phone. I wasn't going to be able to call Declan and let him know what had happened. I wasn't even going to get to say goodbye to him.

Regret swilled around in my stomach. Maybe, if I was lucky, he would understand.

"What's wrong?" Sarah said, pausing on her way back to the table.

"Nothing," I said. "Well not really nothing. Phone is bust." I held it up so she could see the crushed screen.

"Do you need to call someone?"

"Not really," I said. "I was just regretting not telling Declan that I was leaving."

"You two really seemed to be cozying up last night." Sarah smiled but there was no warmth in her eyes. "Looked like you were going back to old mistakes."

"Excuse me?" I couldn't keep the surprise from my voice.

Sarah sighed and set the teacup down in front of me. The fine bone china so delicate I could see through it. I had sudden visions of myself behaving like Mrs Bucket's friend off the television and spilling the tea all over the table and myself.

"I'm sorry," she said. "I shouldn't have said that. It's just with everything you're going through, I don't see how re-treading old ground is healthy right now. I mean you and Declan didn't work out the first time 'round, what makes you think this would be any different?"

"I don't know." I sighed and picked up the cup, taking a sip of the sweet hot drink before I answered.

"You're probably right. I was having doubts last night and then today, after everything here... I don't know. Just part of me wants to maybe at least give it a shot."

Sarah sighed and reached across the table to touch her hand to mine. "There's something amazing waiting for you, I just know it."

With a small smile, I finished the last of the tea and set the cup down on the table.

"Can I use your bathroom?"

"Of course," she said. "Upstairs, second door on the right."

Pushing up from the table, my head swam and I blinked away the dizziness and gripped the table to steady myself.

"Are you all right?" Sarah stared up at me with concern.

"Fine," I said. "I just got up too fast."

Moving away from the table, I made it up the stairs without another incident. The first door at the top of the stairs stood ajar and I caught sight of a pink frill.

Pushing the door open, I stepped inside and my heart stalled out.

Alice in Wonderland paraded across the walls. The Mad-Hatter's tea party depicted on one wall, while the other was dedicated to the Queen of Hearts.

The wall over the bed showed Alice speaking to the white rabbit. The crudely drawn speech bubble from Alice's mouth and the rabbit's contained some scribbled words.

I took another wobbly step into the room and focused on the words.

"Alice: How long is forever?"

"White Rabbit: Sometimes just one second."

The small single bed against the wall was neatly made, the stuffed animals arranged carefully across the duvet. The large white rabbit sitting pride of place among the others.

With hands that shook, I picked up the framed picture from the dresser top and stared down at the smiling child that beamed out of the photograph. The little plaque on the bottom of the frame read: Ali. November '17, Aged 9.

Something nagged at me but the more I tried to grab onto the memory, the more it eluded me.

My gaze snagged on a small picture album sitting on top of the white bedside table.

The edges were frayed from use, the sunflowers on the front faded from sitting too long in the sun. My hands shook as I reached out and flipped the album open.

Clara stared up at me, the same picture from last night. The one I'd found in the garden... My heart stalled out in my chest as I noticed the black marker concealing her eyes.

"Do you like it?" Sarah's voice cut through the fog slowly taking over my mind.

She stood in the doorway and I took a step back, my legs bumped the edge of the single bed and I dropped onto the duvet.

What was wrong with me? Why couldn't I think straight?

"I named her for you, you know." Sarah smiled and crossed the faded pink carpet. She took the framed picture from my hands and set it back on the dresser before flipping the picture album shut. "Well almost. Alison is pretty close to Alice I think."

"Sarah," I said, managing to get her name out despite the slurring of my words. "I think there's something wrong with me. You need to call someone..."

She shook her head, the movement jagged as I tried to blink away the greying of my vision. My limbs were leaden and as hard as I tried to draw a deep breath, I couldn't.

"You're just tired, Alice," she said. "You need to sleep, then everything will be better. Things will be better."

"Pleas—"

Gently, she pushed me back on the bed, cradling my head onto the soft pillow. "I don't want you to hurt yourself," she said. "Until you understand, we need to do things this way." She crouched next to the bed, her face level with mine. "But I swear, I won't let him hurt you. I won't ever let him touch you like the others so you don't need to be afraid. I'll keep you safe. Keep you both safe."

I struggled against her touch. In my mind I was stronger, strong enough to fight her off and flee from the room. But when I opened my heavy lids, I hadn't moved. She was still poised next to me, her smile beatific as she brushed my hair back from my face.

"Sleep, Alice. And when you wake, we'll all be together."

I tried to raise my arms, willed my body to respond as the darkness crept closer.

But nothing happened. I felt my tears slid from my eye, felt it track over my cheek and run down into my hair. And still I tried to move, until there was nothing but the feel of her hand on my face and the twisted whisperings of her endearments in my ear.

And then, blissfully... nothing.

56

SOMETIMES, finding yourself demoted isn't always such a bad thing. As I searched through the files Claire had compiled involving young offenders with crimes that potentially fit our man, and those who owned white vans around the same time, I found myself relaxing into the task at hand.

The direct order to stay put grated on me, though. I wasn't a child who needed instructions. But there was definitely something to be said for not having to constantly organise and rally the troops, especially now that everyone was beginning to flag as the weekend drew in.

"There are too many variables," Ronan said, dropping down into the chair next to me. "We need something to narrow it down."

I nodded. It was too much.

"Where's his royal pain in the ass?" Ronan asked,

scanning the office. The tension between the two men was enough to cause the station to combust and I'd been glad when Paul had said he was taking Claire out to have a look at the most recent crime scene. He wanted a feel for it. I couldn't blame him; it was definitely the kind of case that benefited from a hands-on approach.

"Out," I said, keeping my gaze trained on the pages in front of me.

The sound of a commotion from the other room drew me out of my concentrated study. Ronan hopped to his feet and I followed him, pausing in the doorway as a couple of uniformed Guards hurried past.

Ronan was deep in conversation with one of the Guards and when he finished I jerked my head back toward the office.

"What is it?"

"They're setting up a hunt for Dick Coughlan. Got a call today from Alice McCarthy, she was down at the Coughlan's and she reported a domestic. By the time the nearest car responded he'd already legged it."

"Anyone hurt?"

"No one hurt enough to go to a hospital. Although, Mike said Mrs Coughlan had some nasty looking bruises that weren't new."

"He's been abusing her?" I ran back over my memory of the interview with Sarah Coughlan, searching for any hint that what Ronan was telling me was true. Not that you could tell who might be a victim of abuse. The abuser relied on secrecy, on keeping the victim silent. Most of it was a gradual progression, an upward spiral of abuse both mental and physical, which led to the victim feeling that they were to blame for the abuse they suffered.

"Looks that way."

"Jesus," I said. "How long have they been married?"

Ronan shrugged. "Don't rightly know. Mike knows them." He turned his attention back to the main room. "Hey Mike!"

The man he'd been speaking to a few minutes before crossed the room, his stride lazy. "Need me to come in there and solve it for you?" There was a wide grin on his face as he leaned against the doorframe.

"You wish," Ronan said. "You know the Coughlan's right?

"Well, I know them in passing."

"How long would you say they've been married?"

"Jeez," he said, scrubbing his hand back through his hair, the sudden discomfort he felt obvious in the tensing of his shoulders. "A long time. Twenty years I think. They got married when she was young. He's a bit older than her, not that there's anything wrong with that but he got her when she wasn't even out of school. Seems a bit weird to me."

"Is the kid all right?"

"Kid?" Mike repeated the word back to me as though I'd just asked him the state of affairs on an alien planet.

"The daughter," I said. "Is she all right, was she at home?"

"I'd nearly forgot you're not from 'round here." Mike gave me a friendly smile. "Their daughter is dead. Been dead for a year, maybe more. Sad state of affairs it was too."

"That's not possible," I said, feeling the bottom drop out of my stomach. "I..." I cut myself off before I finished the sentence and plastered a smile on my face. "You know, you're right. I must have forgot."

"You're working too hard," he said. "You should come out with us tonight. Now that the big-bad wolf is down from Dublin, you're just one of us."

"Maybe." I returned his warm smile. "Ronan can I have a word?"

I left the two men as I turned back into the office and hurried back over to the pile of files on the desk.

Ronan joined me a second later.

"What is it?"

"She lied," I said. "Sarah Coughlan lied to me."

"About what?"

"She said she needed to get out of the interview early because her daughter Ali was finishing school."

"I don't understand," he said. "Why would she lie?"

"I don't know," I said, "but I think we should find out, don't you?"

"And how are we supposed to do that?"

"The husband's name," I said. "I'm going to cross

reference him with the files Claire pulled for previous offenders."

"Look, the guy is obviously an asshole but it doesn't make him a killer."

"No. But what reason would Sarah have for lying to me? It doesn't make any sense. Not to mention, she knew Clara. I don't believe in coincidences."

Ronan nodded. "Fine, what's the husband's name?"

"Dick Coughlan," I said, typing the name in the computer. The wheel crawled around the screen before a big fat zero appeared.

"There's nothing," I said. "In all the files Claire pulled there's nothing on a Dick Coughlan."

"What about Richard?" Ronan asked, his fingers flying over the keyboard of his own computer. I held my breath, waiting for his answer and when he shook his head, I felt my heart drop.

It was a dead end. I'd been so sure.

"Maybe the guy we're looking for doesn't have any priors?"

Closing my eyes, I leaned back in my chair. "That doesn't make any sense. This isn't the kind of thing you just wake up one morning and start doing. The savagery involved, it's too much. If Clara McCarthy was his first offence then something serious must have happened to tip him over the edge."

"That's assuming she was murdered with the same level of rage involved."

Scooting the chair across the floor to Claire's desk, I

grabbed the files she'd been compiling on Sarah Coughlan. There was a birth certificate, driver's license entry, marriage license, and birth and death certificates inside the beige folder.

"Why are you searching her name now, you don't think she has anything to do with this, do you?"

"No, but we're definitely missing something."

I paused over the death certificate. My eyes scanning over the cause of death, Alison had died from internal bleeding.

"Shit," Ronan said, reading over my shoulder. "She was hit by a car."

I nodded. "Can you find anything about it in the files. Was anyone charged?"

Ronan moved away and only the sound of his fingers hitting the keys told me he was still in the room.

We were so close I could taste it. There had been something off about Sarah when I'd interviewed her but I hadn't been able to pinpoint just what it might be. However, knowing I'd caught her in a lie.

My breath caught in the back of my throat as I scanned the marriage certificate.

"I know why we haven't been able to find anything on Dick Coughlan," I said, my voice strained. "He wasn't always Dick Coughlan. Coughlan is Sarah's maiden name. He took it when he married her. According to the file here, his name was Keith Richard Reardon before he got married."

"Shit..." Ronan mumbled and my head snapped up.

"What?"

"The car that hit Alison," Ronan said, "was registered to her father but the name on this says Richard Coughlan. They determined it an accidental death, nothing more than a tragic accident. According to the statements from both parents, Alison was playing in the driveway and Dick didn't see her." Ronan hesitated and lifted his gaze to me. "He reversed out on top of her."

Typing the new name into the computer, I widened the parameters to a country-wide search. This time the computer gave me a very different set of entries.

"It's him," I said, scanning the list of prior offences.

"Why didn't we know this before?" Ronan asked, coming to stand behind me.

"He grew up in Galway so he wasn't local to this area. When he got down here, he was probably already going by the name Dick and not Keith."

"That still doesn't make sense though, why didn't we know about these files, why hasn't someone linked his names together? The man is a bloody criminal?" I could hear the frustration in Ronan's voice and I couldn't blame him.

Leaning back in my chair, I turned so I could see his face.

"They had a push a couple of years ago to start computerising the older case files. There's only a fraction of the files actually logged. We're lucky we found this. There's probably a lot of other things that haven't made it onto the system yet."

Ronan shook his head and scrubbed his hands over his face.

"When the cases were initially investigated the files probably weren't computerized. Nobody knew what they were looking for anyway because of a lack of inter-county cooperation. Christ, if the domestic hadn't been called in earlier today, we wouldn't yet know his real name."

"Petty theft. Indecent assault but the charges were dropped. There's even a caution listed because he was picked up outside a neighbours house in the middle of the night." I shook my head. How could they let so much slip through the cracks?

Of course, I knew how. Understaffed and over-worked in the more rural parts of Ireland meant there were holes in the net for offenders like Dick Coughlan to slip through.

I turned back to the screen and clicked to the next page, my heart climbing into my mouth as I scanned the records.

"Guess who was the proud owner of a white Ford Transit van at the time of Clara's disappearance." I couldn't keep the glee from my voice. It wasn't proof of wrongdoing but it was a thread and if I just kept pulling at it, I knew the whole story would unravel.

"What does all of this mean?" Ronan asked, straightening up.

"It means we go and have a little chat with Sarah Coughlan because I think she knows more than she's been telling us."

"Do you think she's in on it?"

"At the very least I think she's covering for him," I said, climbing to my feet. "I just hope to God I'm wrong though."

Ronan grabbed his jacket from the back of his chair and the keys from his desk.

"Are we going to tell the others?"

I shook my head. "We're only going to check it out. If we find something, we'll call in the cavalry."

Ronan's grin was infectious. "Suits me."

57

October 17th 1996

I THINK Dick is following me. I can't be sure but I'm almost certain I saw his van earlier, sitting outside the house.

I asked Sarah and she said I was mistaken. He's gone to Waterford with some job or other. She asked if maybe it was Liam but I know it's not. He wouldn't just sit outside the house like that. He'd have come in.

Alice is doing my head in at the moment. Banging on about the disco she's going to. It's going to be the 'event of the year', apparently. Her words not mine. I can't blame her for being excited though. I was probably the same going to my first disco but baby boy has put paid to all of that.

I can't believe how much my belly is starting to show. I used to be able to hide it a little bit with my baggy jumpers but now every time I look in the mirror I'm even bigger.

And soon he'll be here. I can feel him squirming around in there and I think I'm starting to get nervous.

What if I'm not a good mother? What if I do something wrong?

I want to get it right, give him the best life I can and love him. Is that enough?

I suppose I have to hope it is.

I'm a little excited too though at the thought of holding him in my arms, my own little boy.

He's kicking now, it's like he knows I'm thinking about him.

I love you, baby boy. Mommy can't wait to meet you!

58

My eyes felt like someone had attached tiny lead weights to them while I'd been asleep. The mattress beneath my back was lumpy. Was I back in the hospital?

My memory was foggy and refused to cooperate as I struggled to remember just what had happened.

The sound of someone humming drew my attention and I focused in on the noise.

The room in Sarah's house. Her daughter Alison. The pictures...

Sarah drugged me.

The memories came back in fragments and as soon as I tried to grab them, they broke apart like the dust from a moth's wing.

"Wakey-wakey, sleepy head," Sarah's voice was scratchy as she tried to sing the words. "I know you're awake, Alice. You can't hide from me."

Opening my eyes, the lights overhead were blinding and I blinked against them. "Where am I?"

"Your new home," Sarah said. "I've been waiting to bring you home for such a long time."

I turned my head to the side and found myself face to face with something straight out of a nightmare. There was still a little blonde hair on the skull but no flesh. The thin strands arranged artfully around what should have been its face. It stared back at me, its eyeless sockets letting me see all the way into the back of the cranium.

The scream tore at the back of my throat and I bucked and thrashed on the bed. The restraints around my wrists and ankles cut painfully into my skin.

"Don't be afraid, Clara didn't mean to frighten you." Sarah's voice broke through the panic ripping me asunder. Her words bringing with them a kind of blissful insanity that I longed to sink into.

I was dreaming. This had to be nightmare. It had to be. It couldn't be real. This wasn't Clara on the dirty, stained mattress next to me. I wasn't staring at the skeletal remains of my dead sister. It wasn't possible.

Tears blurred my vision and I continued to scream until my voice broke hoarsely over the sound.

"I thought you'd be happy to see her," Sarah said. And even in the frantic panic taking over my mind, I could hear the hurt in her voice as she spoke. "I thought this was what you wanted. You're always harping on about wanting to find Clara and I've brought you both back together."

I turned my face away from the body on the bed next to me, twisting my neck as far as it would go, just so I could avoid looking at the skull.

"Don't be so rude," Sarah said, kneeling down next to me.

"How could you do this?" My voice was a twisted, unrecognisable wreckage but at least it worked.

"I'm doing it so we can all be together again. We were always meant to be a family."

"I'm not your family," I said. "Clara wasn't your family..."

"Clara was an entitled little bitch who always got her own way." The vehement violence of Sarah's words shocked me into silence.

"You know she actually regretted getting pregnant. I didn't. I loved every short second of it..." Sarah closed her eyes and ran her hands over the front of her flat stomach. "I found out two weeks before Clara that I was pregnant. I was going to have someone of my own to love. She was going to be mine..."

Shock kept me from speaking, forcing me to listen to Sarah as she rambled. The cuff over my right hand shifted a little. Was I imagining it?

"I did everything right. Everything." Sarah opened her eyes and stared down at me. "I tried to protect her but I was weak..."

The initial panic had worn away, leaving me

exhausted. If I was going to get out of this, then I needed to play along with Sarah.

"What happened to her?" I whispered.

"He did," she said. "He was so angry when he found out I was pregnant. Said I'd tried to trap him..."

"I'm sorry."

"It's not your fault." Sarah stood up abruptly, her weight disappearing from the edge of the bed.

Tracking her movements across the room wasn't easy and she disappeared from sight at the bottom of the bed. I tugged at the cuff on my wrist a little harder, feeling the restraint begin to loosen. It wasn't enough to slip my hand out but it was a start.

"I won't let him hurt you," she said, coming back into view. "He wants to you know. Ever since that night, he's wanted you. I protected you all these years, kept him from going after you."

"Why Clara?" Simply saying her name was painful, my throat felt like I'd swallowed a mouthful of razor blades.

"When I lost the baby, he panicked. Worried I was going to leave him. He thought if he took Clara's baby, it would make up for it. But when he saw you he panicked... Thought it would be too much." She leaned down over me, her expression one of exultation. "But when I saw you I knew it was fate. Who lets their child walk along the road late at night? I'd cared for you. Cared for you when your mother couldn't, wouldn't..." She twisted her face up in disgust.

"We came back for you."

"But you took Clara instead," I said.

Sarah nodded. "She was easy. Too clumsy and slow in the dark."

"How did she die?"

Sarah's expression shifted. "I don't want to talk about that."

"Sarah, please," I said, struggling to pull myself up on the bed. My movements jiggled the corpse next to me, the bones rattling against the plastic they were cocooned inside and I halted. "Please tell me what happened to her."

With her back to me, Sarah's shoulder's tightened.

"He was an animal, couldn't wait to get home..."

My stomach clenched painfully and I gritted my teeth against the ache in my chest.

"What did he do to her?"

"In the end, nothing..."

Sarah's words hit me like a slap.

"But you said?"

"She fought and went into labour..." Sarah's voice took on a dreamy note. "The baby lived for an hour. I held him the whole time."

"And Clara?"

"She bled out. Dick was so mad."

I swallowed back the bile that flooded up my throat. Turning my face back, I stared at what remained of my sister. She had fought. Fought to escape. And she'd died anyway...

"In case you were worried, I didn't let him near her once she died. I took care of her myself. Her and the baby. Wrapped them up nice and snug."

"You're a monster," I said, the words tripping off the tip of my tongue.

"What did you say?" Sarah's voice dropped sending alarm bells ringing in my head. But I was too far gone to care anymore. "You say he's an animal. You helped him. You helped him kill Clara and kill her child. You helped him murder all of those poor girls and for what? You think he's a monster but you're the fucking monster!"

The palm of her hand cracked against the side of my face. The sting of her blow brought the taste of blood to my mouth.

"Don't you ever tell me who I am," she hissed. "You don't know what I've had to do over the years to keep you safe. What I've had to sacrifice to protect you so we could all be here like this..."

The creak of a bolt sliding open made Sarah freeze. Her eyes were wide as she turned away from me and faced the other end of the room.

I strained to see what she was looking at but I couldn't see anything beyond the end of the bed. It was then I realised I wasn't wearing the clothes I'd dressed myself in that morning.

The pale pink dress was short, cutting off mid thigh, reminding me of the kinds of dresses my mother had made Clara and me wear when we were small. My toes were painted a pale pink that matched the dress and without having to look, I knew my fingernails would match.

"Help!" I screamed as the sound of heavy footsteps on a set of stairs met my ears.

"Shut up!" Sarah clamped her hand over my mouth and I bit down on her palm.

She squealed and snatched her hand back, her expression a mask of terror as she turned to the end of the room once more.

"If I knew we were going to have company, I'd have washed up." Dick said. The sound of his voice turned the blood in my veins to ice. "I've waited a long time for this..."

59

THE HOUSE WAS in darkness as Ronan parked outside.

"Do you think she's in?" he asked, scanning the overgrown garden.

"Well she's not answering the phone number she gave us and this is the only listed address we've got for her." I climbed out of the car and closed the door carefully.

"You try the front," I said. "I'm going to go around the back."

The phone in my pocket chose that moment to ring. Sliding it out of my pocket, I stared at the number and swore softly.

Brady was the last person I wanted to talk to but if I didn't answer and something went wrong...

"Siobhan here," I said, pressing the phone to my ear.

"Where are you, Geraghty?" He sounded more than a little pissed off.

"I'm out following up on a lead. We've got a pretty good suspect and—"

"Get your ass back to the station. Detective Carroll left you in the office going over the case files with strict instructions not to budge."

"Sir, I couldn't ignore this lead." I fought to keep my voice steady.

Silence greeted me over the line and my stomach churned.

"Where are you?"

"Out at the Coughlan house."

"I don't want you to do anything until I get there, do you hear me, Geraghty? You've screwed up enough things to do with this case. I'll have your ass if you go against me on this one."

"Yes sir," I said, my heart sinking. The line went dead and I caught Ronan watching me over the top of the car.

"What did the boss man say?"

"He said we're not to do anything until he gets here..."

"Are we just going to sit out here twiddling our thumbs then?"

"He said we couldn't go in, not that we shouldn't secure the perimeter."

Ronan grinned at me.

60

A HAND SLID up my leg and I tried to squirm away.

"Get your hands off her!" Sarah's voice was icy and the hand disappeared from my leg.

"Babe, you know I'm sorry about earlier."

I twisted my head and could just make out Dick standing in front of the bed. Sarah's body blocked my view as she stepped between us.

"You know how I get and—"

The sound of a crack echoed in the room. Dick's face reddened where Sarah had struck him and he grimaced.

"I've told you before about doing that," he said through gritted teeth.

"She's not for you. She's mine." Sarah said as Dick tried to push her out of the way.

"We always share," he said. "This one is no different. I let you have your fun when I've had mine."

He shoved her hard and I was only vaguely aware of the sound of Sarah hitting the ground. The cuff on my wrist was looser with every second that ticked by. Tugging and pulling at it, I fought to loosen it the rest of the way.

The sound of a zipper sliding down brought terror clutching its way up my throat. This was how Clara must have felt.

I fought harder.

The bed dipped and strong hands slid up over my ankles. "You're special," Dick said huskily. "Older than I usually like but I've waited so long for you I'm going to enjoy this." He jerked my legs apart, his knee pressing between them as he climbed over me.

He shoved Clara's plastic wrapped remains violently toward the edge of the bed, spilling her bones onto the grubby mattress next to me. Something sharp pressed against my side as Dick's weight bore down on me.

From the corner of my eye, I watched Sarah crawl to the bed. When she climbed unsteadily to her feet, blood trickled from the side of her mouth. In her hands, she clutched a hammer.

Dick's hands slid up over my sides as he moved over me, his mouth coming down on my neck. His damp breath was moist against my skin as he bit down hard enough to rip a scream from me. The scent of his sickly sweat invaded my senses. I couldn't escape it. Couldn't fight free of the hold he had on me.

"Scream for me." His breath beat against my skin, heavy with his excitement.

Don't think about it. Don't think about it.

"Scream for me, Alice."

His hand slid around my throat, grip tightening as he choked off my air supply and I still wouldn't give him what he wanted.

My hand was almost free.

The dull thud of the hammer striking the back of his skull registered in the back of my mind.

He jerked up, his movements uncoordinated as he swung away from me. Blood splattered onto my face and chest as Sarah struck him again, a glancing blow that caught him across the nose.

"Bitch," he said, his voice clogged with blood as he staggered from the bed.

I pulled my hand free of the leather restraint and went to work on freeing my other arm.

Sarah screamed and then there was a dull moan. The sound of a body hitting the floor and then other wet sounds. My gaze was focused on the restraint keeping my other hand in place. If I looked up, I would lose what precious advantage I had. Whatever my chances might be with Sarah, if he killed her I knew what would happen to me.

61

PEERING in through the back window, I scanned the dark tidy kitchen, searching for any sign that Sarah was in fact home.

"Anything?" Ronan asked, moving up beside me, a silent shadow in the darkness.

"Is she going somewhere?" I said, shining my torch-light back into the corner where I'd spotted the suitcase during my first sweep. I strained to read the tag on the bag.

"Looks like it," he said.

"It's already tagged. You said Alice McCarthy called in the domestic report this morning."

"Yeah, but why would she still be here?"

"I don't know, I—" I cut off, as a muffled sound drew my attention. "Did you hear that?"

The noise came again and in the distance, the sound of sirens started to cut through the night air.

I rattled the door handle and found it unlocked. As I pushed open the door, the muffled scream became louder and I darted into the house without waiting for Ronan.

62

I RIPPED AT THE CUFF, tearing my fingernails in my frenzy to get free.

I'd read the newspaper reports on the other victims and the torture they'd endured. I knew what would happen if Dick came for me.

The sound of a chair scraping the floor overhead brought me a renewed sense of urgency as I pulled the cuff off.

"I told you I'd protect you," Sarah said. Her hand caught my hair as she tried to jerk me back onto the bed. From the corner of my eye, I caught sight of the hammer, slick with blood, raised in her other hand.

"Gardaí!"

My hand closed over the sharp piece of bone that had dug into my side as Sarah brought the hammer down over me.

I rolled my body in against her, the blunt end of

her hammer striking my collarbone as my hand drove the bone shard into her.

Light exploded behind my eyes as the pain of her blow ricocheted through me. The hammer fell against my back.

The darkness claimed me.

63

THE FLASH of the emergency lights threw strange shadows up and over the trees, reflecting back shapes that weren't really there.

"Make sure you push the reporters back from—"

"Geraghty!" Brady's voice cut over me and I turned to see him ducking beneath the tape cordoning off the front of the house. His hair seemed greyer than I remembered and part of me wondered if maybe I'd caused it with my disobedience of a direct order.

"Sir," I said, bracing myself for his wrath.

"What did I tell you?" His voice was white-hot with fury.

"Not to go in," I said.

"And you went in anyway."

I nodded. "We heard screams, sir. I couldn't wait and risk anymore lives lost."

"You took a hell of a risk."

"I know."

"How many dead?"

"One," I said. "Dick Coughlan, also known as Keith Richard Reardon. It seems his wife took a hammer to his skull."

Brady's lips thinned. "And the other two?"

"Alice McCarthy is on her way to the hospital. She's badly shook up but her injuries don't appear to be life threatening. Sarah Coughlan suffered one stab wound to the abdomen. Paramedics have her stabilised and the hospital is prepping for surgery."

"Who stabbed her?"

"Best I can tell is that Alice McCarthy managed to get herself free and stabbed Ms Coughlan with a rib bone."

Brady's eyes widened and for the first time since I'd met him I watched him struggle for words.

"Whose rib bone?"

"That's up to forensics," I said. "But Alice McCarthy when she came around was babbling about her sister's bones so..."

"Jesus Christ," Brady swore violently and turned away. "When the press get a hold of this, they're going to have a field day."

I kept quiet, not wanting to draw his ire.

Finally, he turned back to me. "Under the circumstances, you did the best you could. I'd have done the same thing. Your dogged determination paid off. This time at least." For Brady to admit that, I really had done a good job. He wasn't the kind to hand out compliments, no matter how earned they might be.

"However." I felt my stomach drop as his tone changed. "Your blatant disregard for protocol and ignoring direct orders, not to mention not keeping your superior officer in the loop regarding the case..." He sighed. "I can't just ignore these things."

I nodded and bit down on the inside of my cheek to keep my emotions in check. No way was I going to tear up in front of him.

"When you've tidied this mess up and return to Dublin, there will be disciplinary action."

"You're putting me back in charge?" I couldn't keep the surprise from my voice.

"Don't screw this up. Any more mistakes and I'll be looking for your badge."

I shook my head. "Don't worry, Sir, I promise. No more mistakes."

"And for god's sake," he said, "learn to play nice with the local Gardaí. They can help you, you know."

I nodded and kept my mouth shut, watching as he turned to stalk away.

Rosie caught my eye as she ducked beneath the tape. She was already dressed in her white forensic jump suit and the blue and red lights bounced off her body.

"We're going to move the body in the basement," she said, sounding far too happy for someone who was about to get her hands on a dead body. "Dorian's found another room off the main space, he thinks it's the original burial spot for the other bodies. He's reasonably sure we'll pull a few other bodies up out of the ground before we're done in there."

"At least it'll bring some closure to the families."

She nodded, chewing her lip as she glanced up at the house. "I've put the female skeletal remains together as best I can. There's a rib bone missing."

"It's still embedded in one of the perpetrators on her way to the hospital."

"How did that happen?" Rosie asked, sounding genuinely intrigued.

"The McCarthy girl stabbed her with it when she was fighting her off."

"Well good for her," Rosie said. "Metal as hell. But I guess that's survival for you."

I nodded.

"There are some smaller bones mixed in with the female remains."

Despite knowing Clara's baby couldn't possibly have survived, my heart still sank.

"A baby?"

Rosie nodded. "Looks that way, yeah."

I caught sight of Ronan walking away from the house. "I've got to go," I said and Rosie let me go with a quick wave.

"Are you going with Sarah Coughlan?" I asked, falling into step next to him.

"Yeah, if only to make sure she comes through the

surgery. I can't believe that bastard in there got away with it all."

"He had his head caved in with a hammer," I said. "I'm not sure I would consider that getting away with anything."

Ronan's smile was a grim one. "I suppose not. Did you get your ass handed to you?"

"Surprisingly not as much as I thought I would."

His smile warmed up. "Good. I'd hate to tank my career by punching out your boss."

I couldn't stop the laughter that bubbled up inside me. Ronan inclined his head to someone behind me. "He's eager to chat with you."

Turning, I caught sight of Paul crossing the grass toward me. As he reached my side he hesitated.

"I'll leave you to it," Ronan said grudgingly.

"Are you all right?" Paul asked, his eyes travelling over me.

"I'm fine."

"When they said you'd been forced to breach..." he let his breath out in a whoosh.

"You told Brady I'd defied a direct order?"

He nodded. "If I'd known, I wouldn't—"

"You were doing your job," I said with a sigh, letting go the resentment I'd felt lance through me.

"I was an asshole," he said. "I shouldn't have volunteered to come down here. I should have known the position it would put you in."

It was my turn to nod. "Yeah, you should have."

"Brady told me the good news," he said with a small smile.

"When are you supposed to go back up?"

He shrugged. "The weekend is mine, so long as I'm back by Monday he'll be happy."

I smiled. "See, I told you I'd see you at the weekend."

"Detective Geraghty!"

"I've got to go."

Paul nodded, his fingers brushing mine gently. "I'll see you later."

"I look forward to it." I stalked away, leaving him to stare after me, the feel of his eyes on me sending darts of heat rushing up my spine.

64

As I LISTENED to the sound of the priest's voice drone over the graveside prayer, I kept my gaze trained on the coffin.

I'd waited so long to get Clara back and now that she'd been found, I found myself at a loss as to what I should be feeling.

There was an empty feeling in the pit of my stomach.

As the priest finished up, the first notes of Key to My Life by Boyzone began to play and the white coffin holding Clara and her baby's remains began to lower into the ground.

Hot tears burned the back of my throat and blurred my vision as I watched the ground swallow her up. It was over...

Or at least as over as something like this could ever be.

People moved toward us, a sea of faces and hands that needed shaking. Their words melded together into one continuous drone of sympathy and sorrow.

"I'm so sorry for your loss..."

A strong hand grasped mine and I jerked back, feeling Declan's hand against my back as he steadied me. Him coming to see me in the hospital had been the only thing to get me through the ordeal that had followed. It had been easy to fall into a comfortable relationship with him, his constant presence lending me the strength I needed to face the stares and whispers.

The headlines had certainly been gruesome enough.

"Are you all right?" He whispered against my ear.

Nodding, I swallowed around the lump in my throat and plastered a smile on my face. My mother caught my eye and gave me a tentative smile. Things would never be the same between us but we were both trying and that alone was progress.

"How are you?" Detective Geraghty's voice snapped me out of my reverie and I found her standing in front of me.

The other mourners knew her and gave us a wide berth, making me all the more grateful for her sudden appearance.

"Honestly," I said, "I don't know."

"I get that. This isn't the kind of thing you just put behind you."

I shook my head and dropped my gaze to my hands. The same hands that had used my own sister's rib bone to stab Sarah with.

"Has she said anything?" I couldn't bring myself to use her name aloud.

"We've got a full confession from her," Siobhan said. "The moment she came round after the surgery we couldn't get her to stop talking. They haven't decided whether she's fit to stand trial though."

The knot of tension that had gathered in the pit of my stomach suddenly doubled in size.

"You don't mean she'll get out!"

Siobhan shook her head. "There's no fear of that happening. She's going away for this. Life really will mean life in this case. It's really just deciding whether she belongs in a secure psychiatric facility or if prison is the answer."

"Oh..." I knotted my fingers into the black sleeve of my jacket. "Well at least there'll be justice for Clara and the baby..."

Siobhan smiled sympathetically. "And you."

When I didn't answer her, she touched her fingers to my arm, drawing my eyes back up to her face.

"You did the right thing, Alice. Clara would have been proud."

Swallowing past the sudden dryness of my throat I gave her a tentative smile in return.

"I'll let you get back to your family." She gave my

arm one last squeeze before disappearing into the crowd.

It didn't take long for the cemetery to empty of people. Once the coffin was in the ground, everyone else only seemed interested in heading to the pub.

"You go on ahead," I said. "I just want a few minutes here."

Declan's expression spoke of his reluctance but he let me go and I watched as he moved quickly through the headstones.

Picking up the two white roses I'd brought with me, I paused at the edge of the grave and stared down into the hole. They'd tried to cover it up with a little greenery and while it was a nice touch, it didn't change the truth. Clara and her baby were both in the cold ground.

"I'm sorry, I couldn't save you."

It felt wrong to stand at the edge of her grave. She should have been here. They both should have been.

It wasn't fair.

Raising my face, I studied the other new graves in the cemetery. Some many lives stolen. And those were just the ones who belonged here. There were others in the ground in other graves in other towns. Taken before their time.

But there was a terrible relief in knowing where Clara was. At least she'd come home.

There were others who never would.

In a way we were the lucky ones.

Tossing the roses into the grave, I watched as the earth swallowed them.

"I love you."

I blinked back the tears and lifted my face as the first of the fat raindrops began to fall from the sky.

Catching sight of Declan, I felt my heart lift.

Whether I liked it or not, life would go on. And Siobhan was right; we would have justice for Clara and all the other lost girls.

WANT TO KNOW WHEN THE NEXT BOOK IS COMING?

Sign-up to the mailing list to receive an email every
time I launch a new book.
Mailing List

Or Join me on Facebook
https://www.facebook.com/BilindaPSheehan/

Alternatively send me an email.
bilindasheehan@gmail.com

My website is bilindasheehan.com

OTHER BOOKS BY THE AUTHOR

Watch out for the next book coming soon from Bilinda P. Sheehan by joining her mailing list.

Bilinda P. Sheehan also writes Urban Fantasy under the name Bilinda Sheehan

Jenna Faith Series

Cast in Stone

Stakes and Stones

Heart of Stone

The Shadow Sorceress Series

A Grave Magic

Blood Craft

Grim Rites

Wild Hunt

Touch of Shadow

Embrace of Darkness

A Wicked Power

Bones and Bounties

Banshee Blues

Huntress Moon

Kiss of the Banshee

Roll the Bones

Book 5 - Coming Soon

Printed in Great Britain
by Amazon